Criminy™

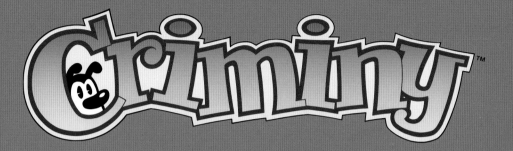

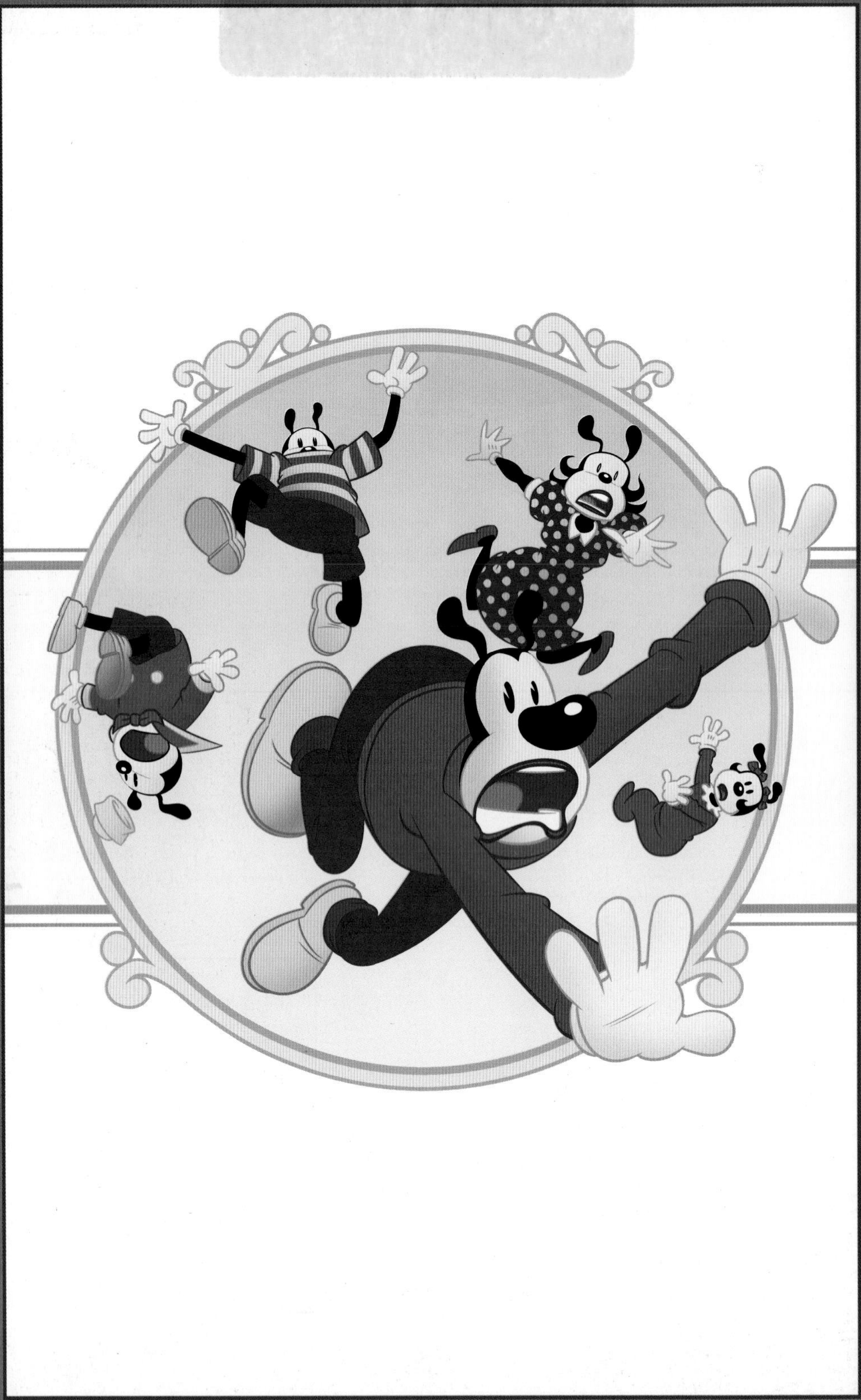

ROGER LANGRIDGE

artist

RYAN FERRIER

writer

DARK HORSE BOOKS

president and publisher
MIKE RICHARDSON

editor
DANIEL CHABON

assistant editor
BRETT ISRAEL

designer
BRENNAN THOME

digital art technicians
CHRISTIANNE GILLENARDO-GOUDREAU
SAMANTHA HUMMER

Published by Dark Horse Books
A division of Dark Horse Comics, Inc.
10956 SE Main Street
Milwaukie, OR 97222

DarkHorse.com

To find a comic shop in your area, check out the
Comic Shop Locator Service: comicshoplocator.com

First edition: September 2018
ISBN 978-1-50670-744-0

10 9 8 7 6 5 4 3 2 1
Printed in China

Library of Congress Cataloging-in-Publication Data

Names: Langridge, Roger, writer, artist. I Ferrier, Ryan, writer.
Title: Criminy / Roger Langridge, writer and artist ; Ryan Ferrier, writer.
Description: First edition. I Milwaukie, OR : Dark Horse Books, September
   2018. I Summary: "Daggum Criminy's peaceful life is suddenly interrupted
   as pirates invade his island, casting Criminy's family out as refugees
   into the wild unknown in search of a new home. Soon, the Criminys find
   themselves hopping from one strange locale to another, each with their own
   bizarre environment, people, and challenges."-- Provided by publisher.
Identifiers: LCCN 2018014379 I ISBN 9781506707440 (paperback)
Subjects: LCSH: Graphic novels. I CYAC: Graphic novels. I Families--Fiction.
   I Refugees--Fiction. I Adventure and adventurers--Fiction. I BISAC:
   JUVENILE FICTION / Comics & Graphic Novels / General.
Classification: LCC PZ7.7.L362 Cr 2018 I DDC 741.5/973--dc23
LC record available at https://lccn.loc.gov/2018014379

NEIL HANKERSON Executive Vice President TOM WEDDLE Chief Financial Officer RANDY
STRADLEY Vice President of Publishing NICK McWHORTER Chief Business Development Officer
MATT PARKINSON Vice President of Marketing DALE LaFOUNTAIN Vice President of Information
Technology CARA NIECE Vice President of Production and Scheduling MARK BERNARDI Vice
President of Book Trade and Digital Sales KEN LIZZI General Counsel DAVE MARSHALL Editor in
Chief DAVEY ESTRADA Editorial Director CHRIS WARNER Senior Books Editor CARY GRAZZINI
Director of Specialty Projects LIA RIBACCHI Art Director VANESSA TODD Director of Print Purchasing
MATT DRYER Director of Digital Art and Prepress MICHAEL GOMBOS Director of International
Publishing and Licensing KARI YADRO Director of Custom Programs

CHAPTER ONE

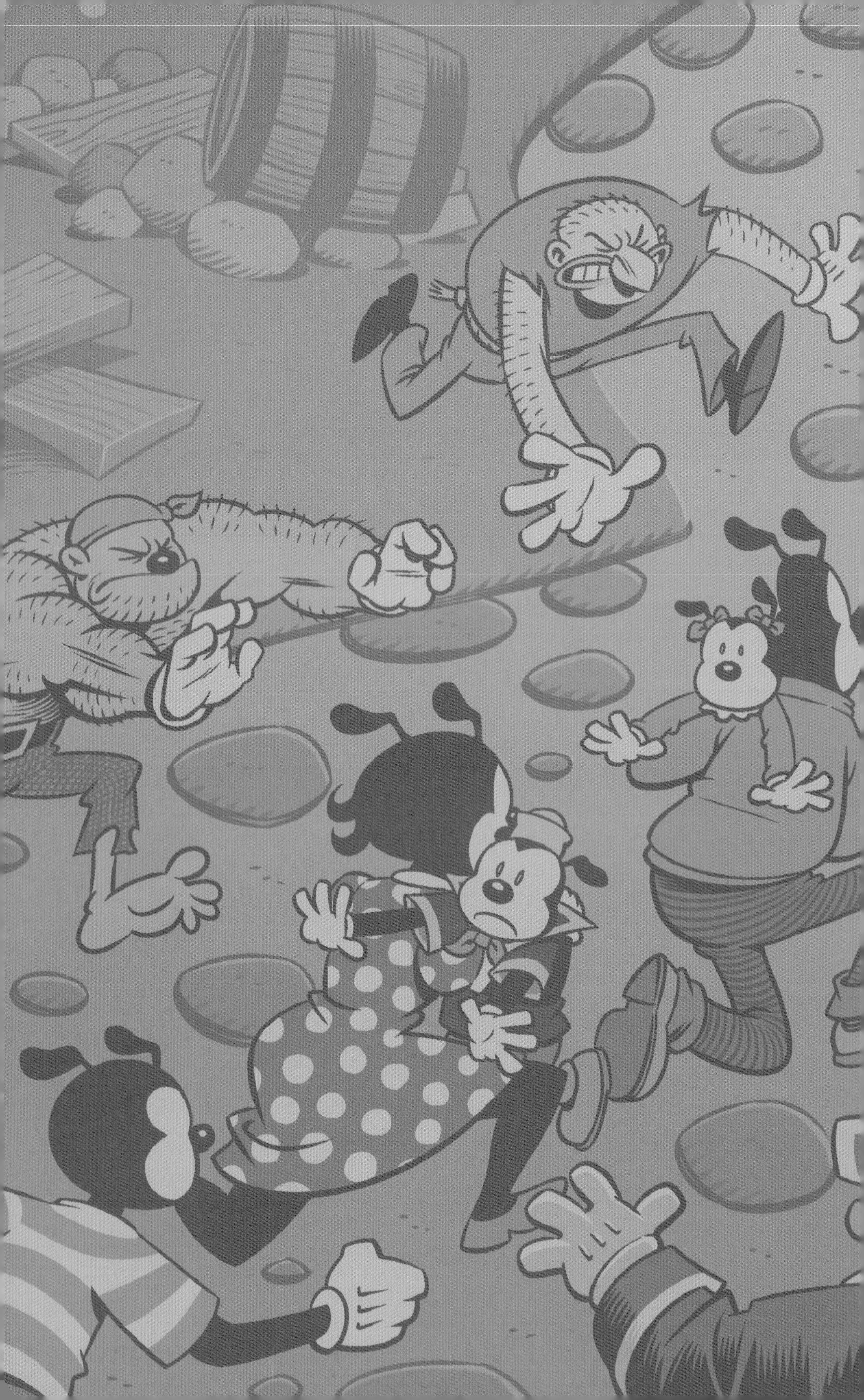

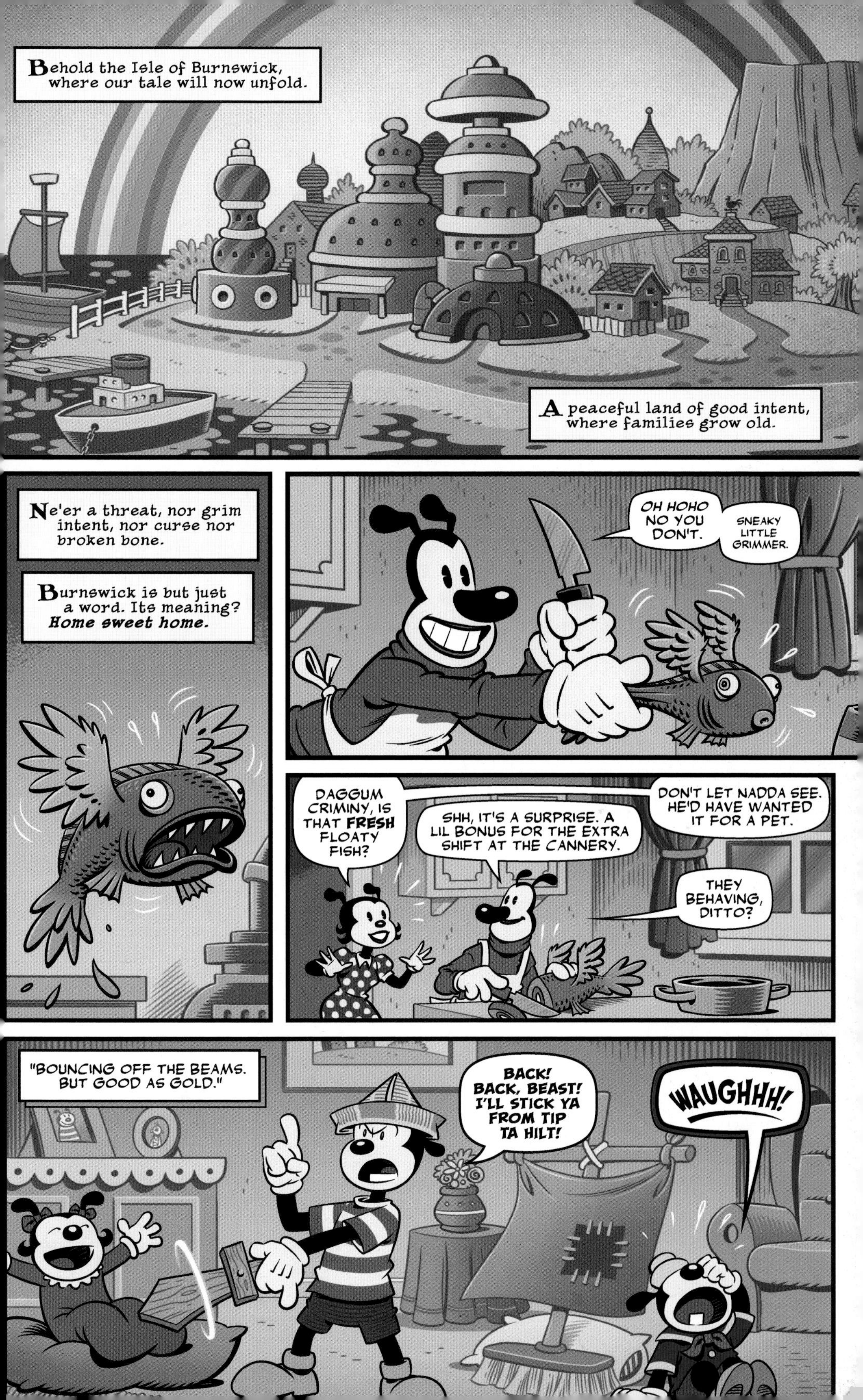
Behold the Isle of Burnswick, where our tale will now unfold.
A peaceful land of good intent, where families grow old.
Ne'er a threat, nor grim intent, nor curse nor broken bone.
Burnswick is but just a word. Its meaning? *Home sweet home.*
OH HOHO NO YOU DON'T.
SNEAKY LITTLE GRIMMER.
DAGGUM CRIMINY, IS THAT **FRESH** FLOATY FISH?
SHH, IT'S A SURPRISE. A LIL BONUS FOR THE EXTRA SHIFT AT THE CANNERY.
DON'T LET NADDA SEE. HE'D HAVE WANTED IT FOR A PET.
THEY BEHAVING, DITTO?
"BOUNCING OFF THE BEAMS. BUT GOOD AS GOLD."
BACK! BACK, BEAST! I'LL STICK YA FROM TIP TA HILT!
WAUGHHH!

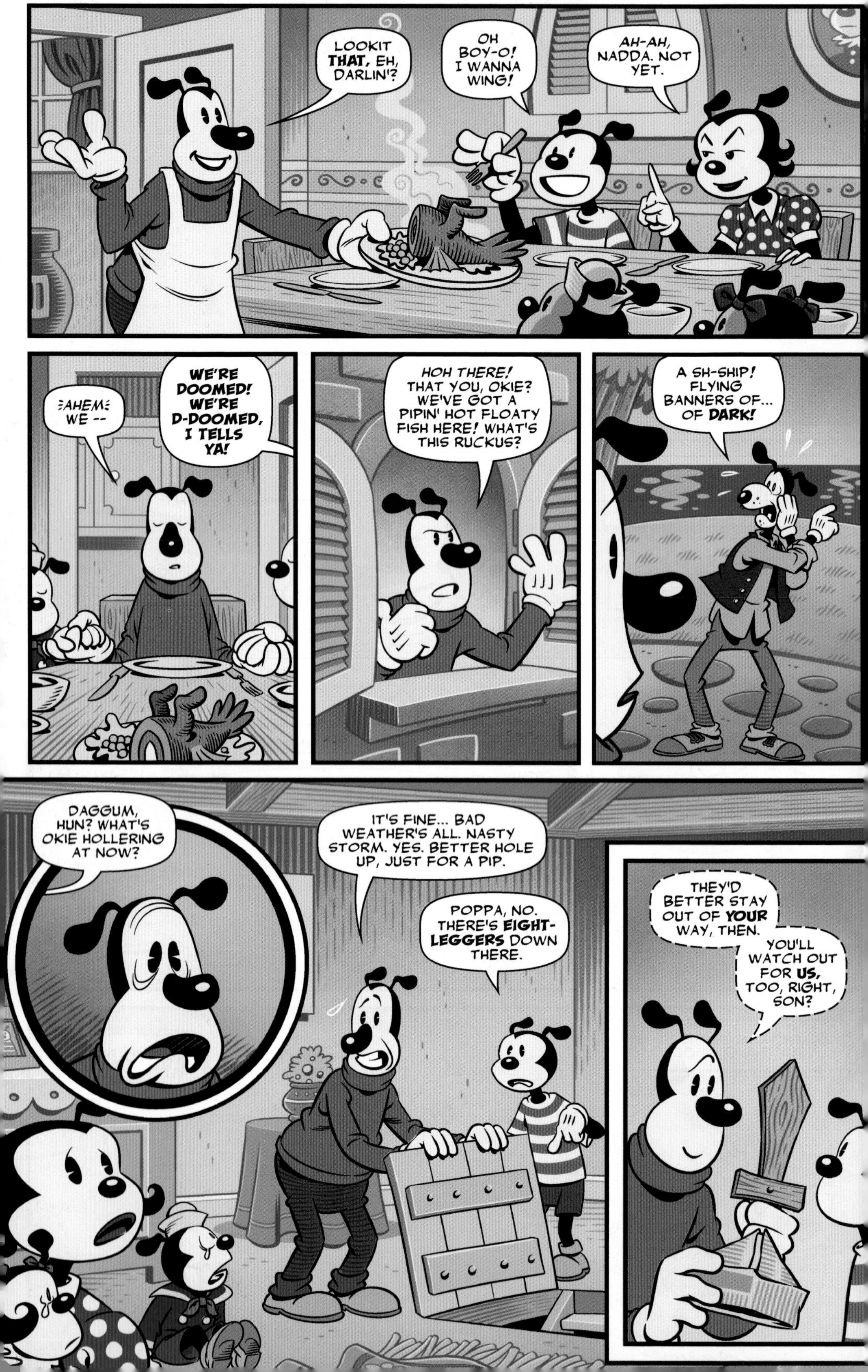
LOOKIT THAT, EH, DARLIN'?
OH BOY-O! I WANNA WING!
AH-AH, NADDA. NOT YET.
AHEM WE --
WE'RE DOOMED! WE'RE D-DOOMED, I TELLS YA!
HOH THERE! THAT YOU, OKIE? WE'VE GOT A PIPIN' HOT FLOATY FISH HERE! WHAT'S THIS RUCKUS?
A SH-SHIP! FLYING BANNERS OF... OF DARK!
DAGGUM, HUN? WHAT'S OKIE HOLLERING AT NOW?
IT'S FINE... BAD WEATHER'S ALL. NASTY STORM. YES. BETTER HOLE UP, JUST FOR A PIP.
POPPA, NO. THERE'S EIGHT-LEGGERS DOWN THERE.
THEY'D BETTER STAY OUT OF YOUR WAY, THEN.
YOU'LL WATCH OUT FOR US, TOO, RIGHT, SON?

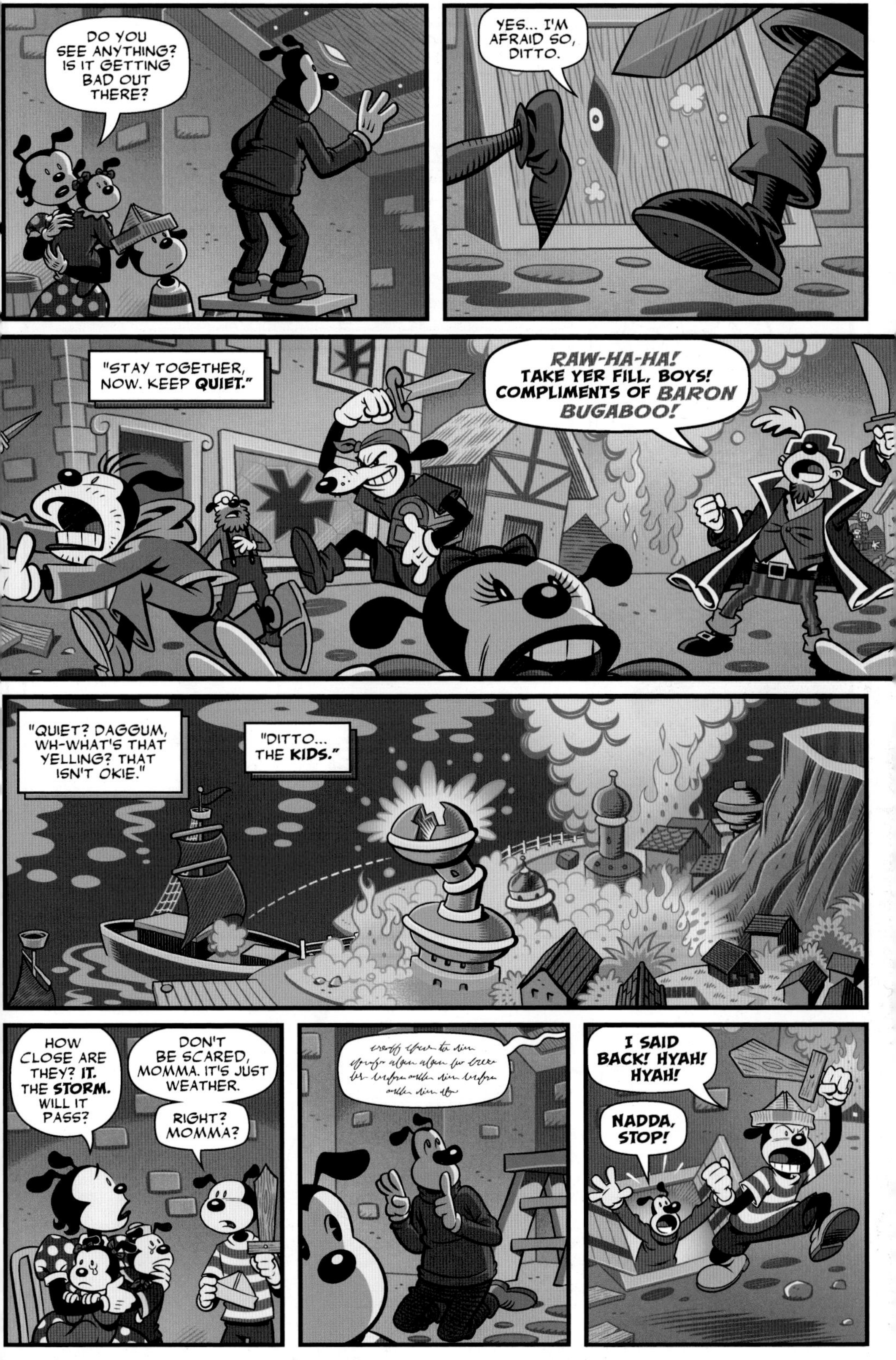
DO YOU SEE ANYTHING? IS IT GETTING BAD OUT THERE?
YES... I'M AFRAID SO, DITTO.
"STAY TOGETHER, NOW. KEEP QUIET."
RAW-HA-HA! TAKE YER FILL, BOYS! COMPLIMENTS OF BARON BUGABOO!
"QUIET? DAGGUM, WH-WHAT'S THAT YELLING? THAT ISN'T OKIE."
"DITTO... THE KIDS."
HOW CLOSE ARE THEY? IT. THE STORM. WILL IT PASS?
DON'T BE SCARED, MOMMA. IT'S JUST WEATHER.
RIGHT? MOMMA?
I SAID BACK! HYAH! HYAH!
NADDA, STOP!

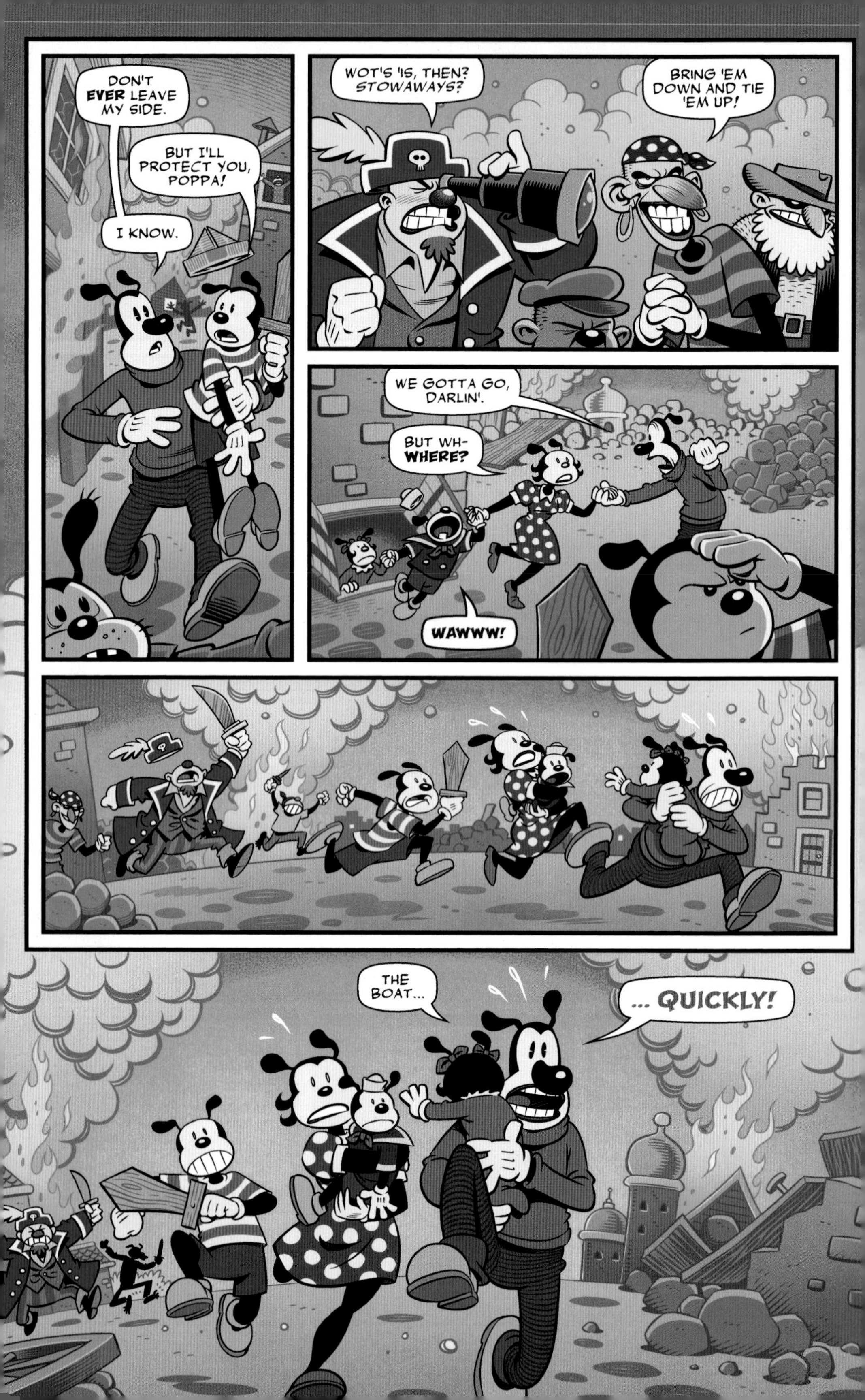
DON'T **EVER** LEAVE MY SIDE.
BUT I'LL PROTECT YOU, POPPA!
I KNOW.
WOT'S 'IS, THEN? STOWAWAYS?
BRING 'EM DOWN AND TIE 'EM UP!
WE GOTTA GO, DARLIN'.
BUT WH- **WHERE?**
WAWWW!
THE BOAT...
... QUICKLY!

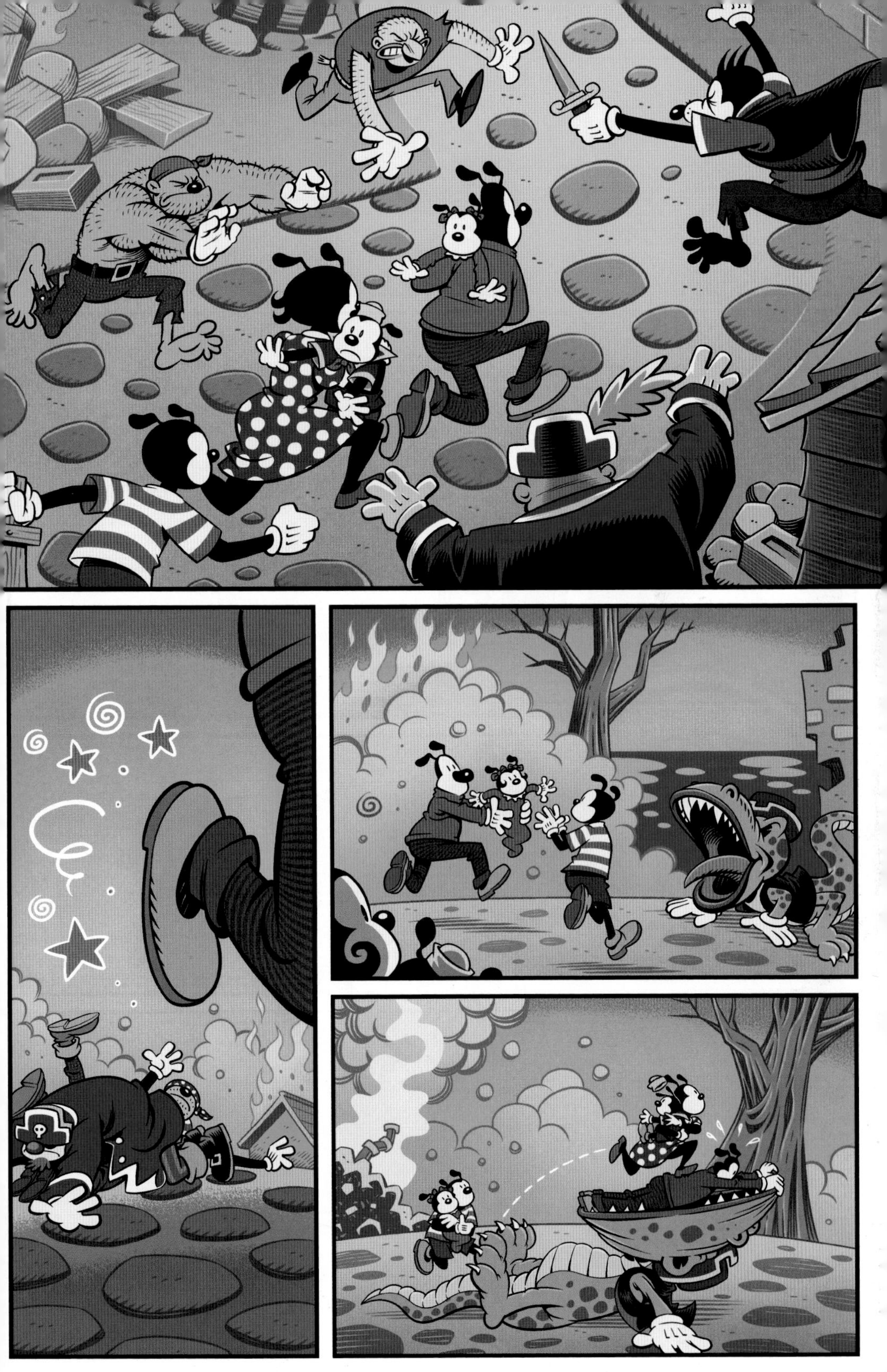

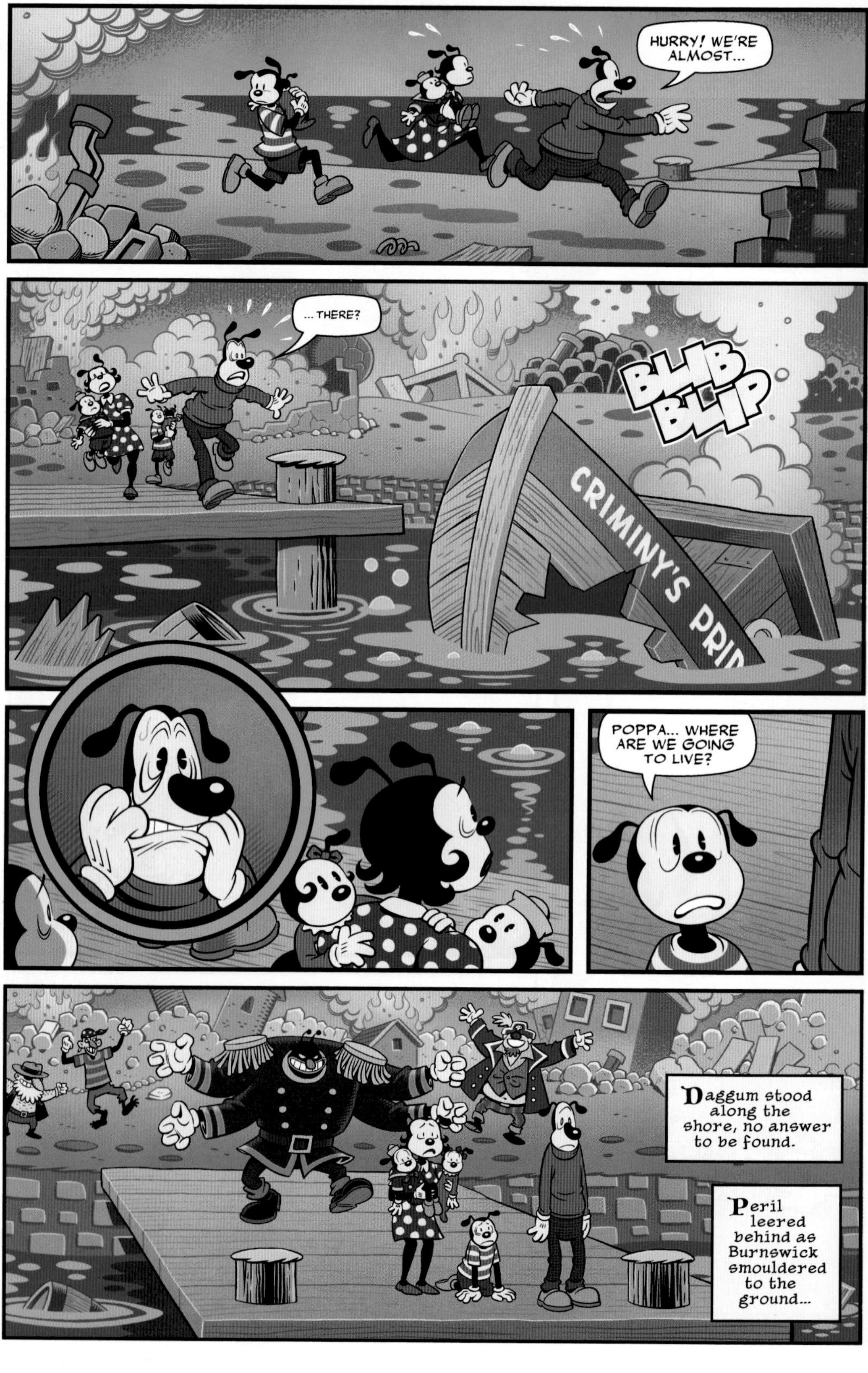
HURRY! WE'RE ALMOST...
... THERE?
BLUB BLUP
CRIMINY'S PRID
POPPA... WHERE ARE WE GOING TO LIVE?
Daggum stood along the shore, no answer to be found.
Peril leered behind as Burnswick smouldered to the ground...

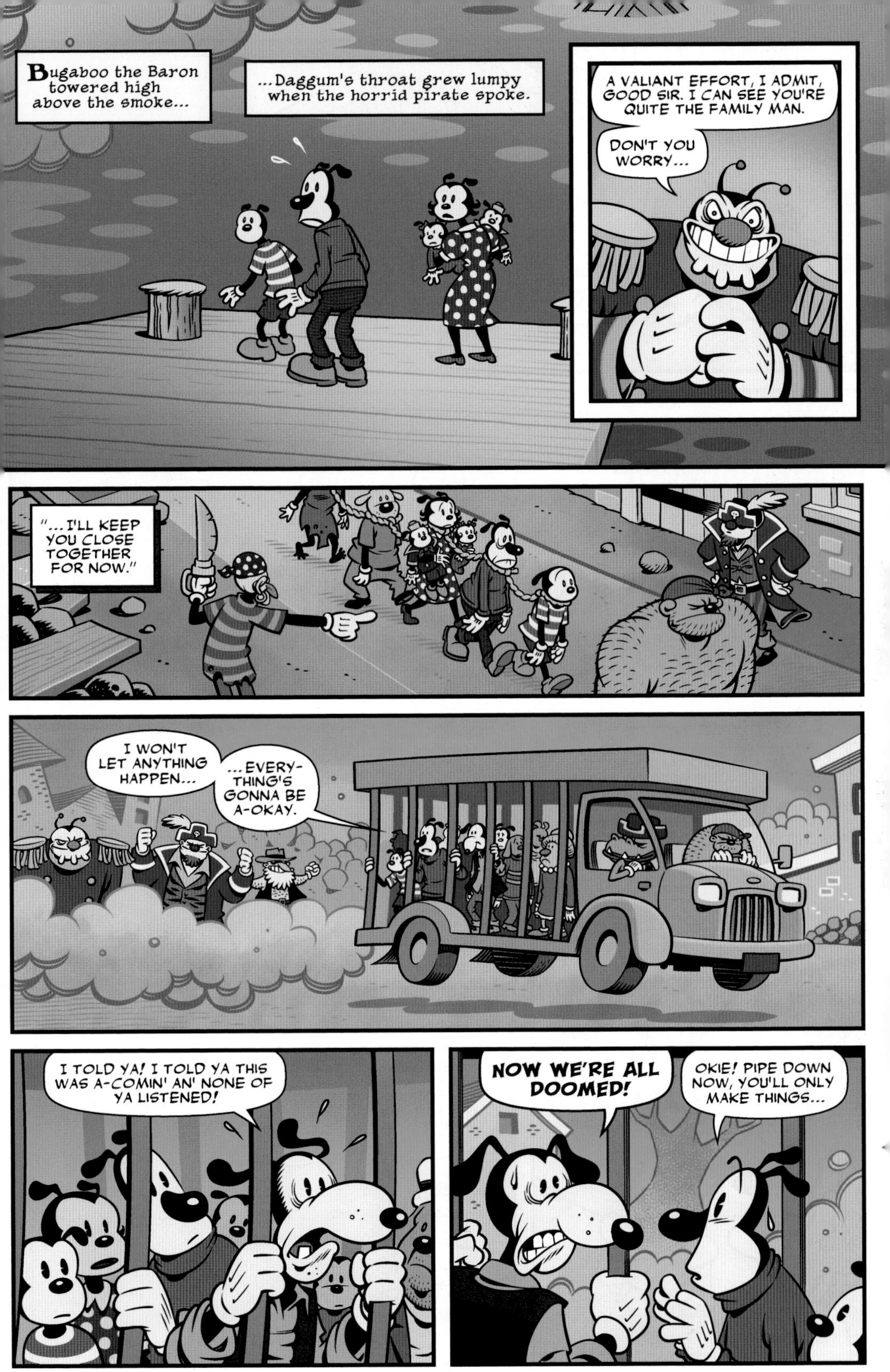
Bugaboo the Baron towered high above the smoke...
...Daggum's throat grew lumpy when the horrid pirate spoke.
A VALIANT EFFORT, I ADMIT, GOOD SIR. I CAN SEE YOU'RE QUITE THE FAMILY MAN.
DON'T YOU WORRY...
"...I'LL KEEP YOU CLOSE TOGETHER FOR NOW."
I WON'T LET ANYTHING HAPPEN...
...EVERY-THING'S GONNA BE A-OKAY.
I TOLD YA! I TOLD YA THIS WAS A-COMIN' AN' NONE OF YA LISTENED!
NOW WE'RE ALL DOOMED!
OKIE! PIPE DOWN NOW, YOU'LL ONLY MAKE THINGS...

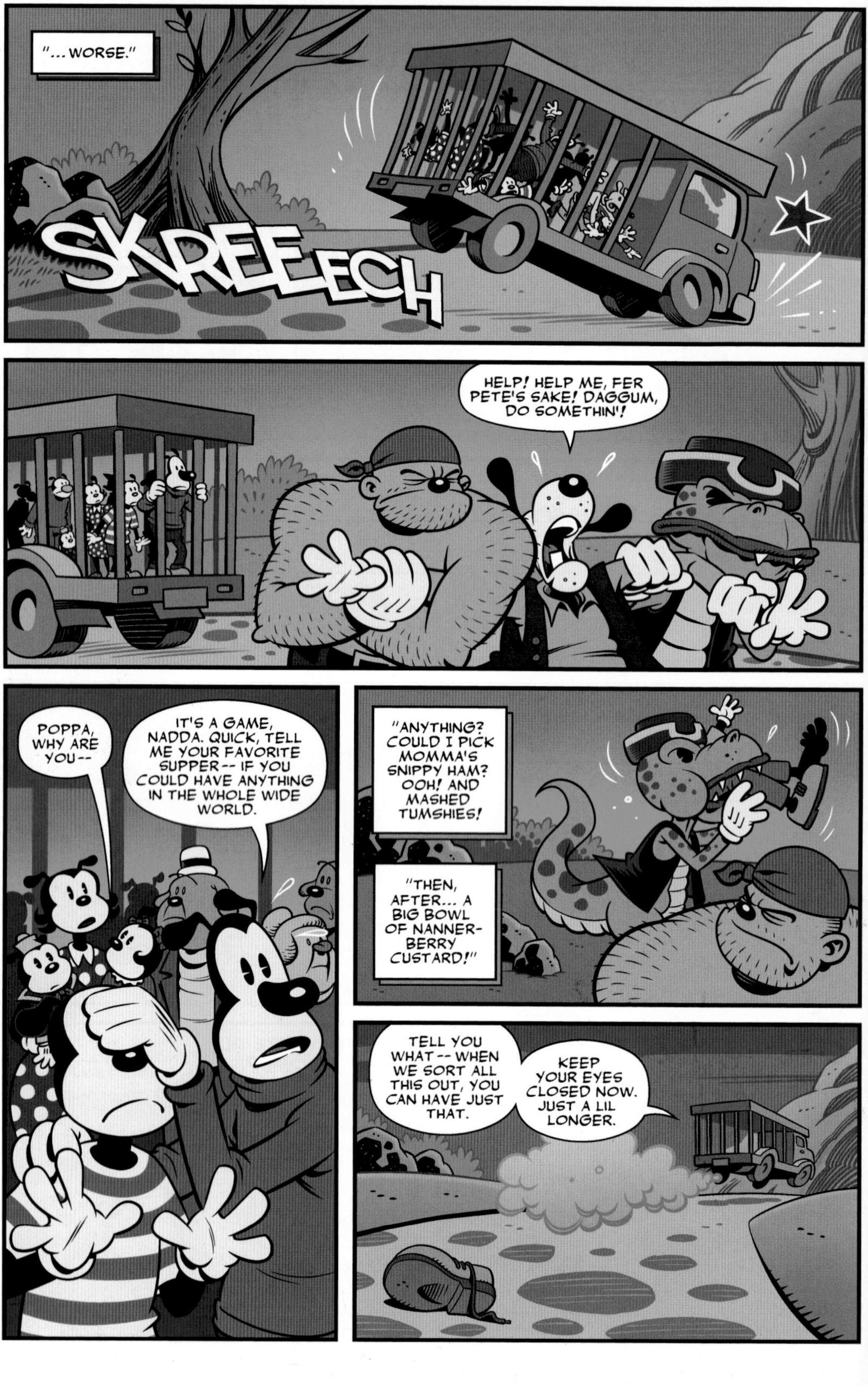
"...WORSE."
SKREEECH
HELP! HELP ME, FER PETE'S SAKE! DAGGUM, DO SOMETHIN'!
POPPA, WHY ARE YOU--
IT'S A GAME, NADDA. QUICK, TELL ME YOUR FAVORITE SUPPER-- IF YOU COULD HAVE ANYTHING IN THE WHOLE WIDE WORLD.
"ANYTHING? COULD I PICK MOMMA'S SNIPPY HAM? OOH! AND MASHED TUMSHIES!
"THEN, AFTER... A BIG BOWL OF NANNER-BERRY CUSTARD!"
TELL YOU WHAT-- WHEN WE SORT ALL THIS OUT, YOU CAN HAVE JUST THAT.
KEEP YOUR EYES CLOSED NOW. JUST A LIL LONGER.

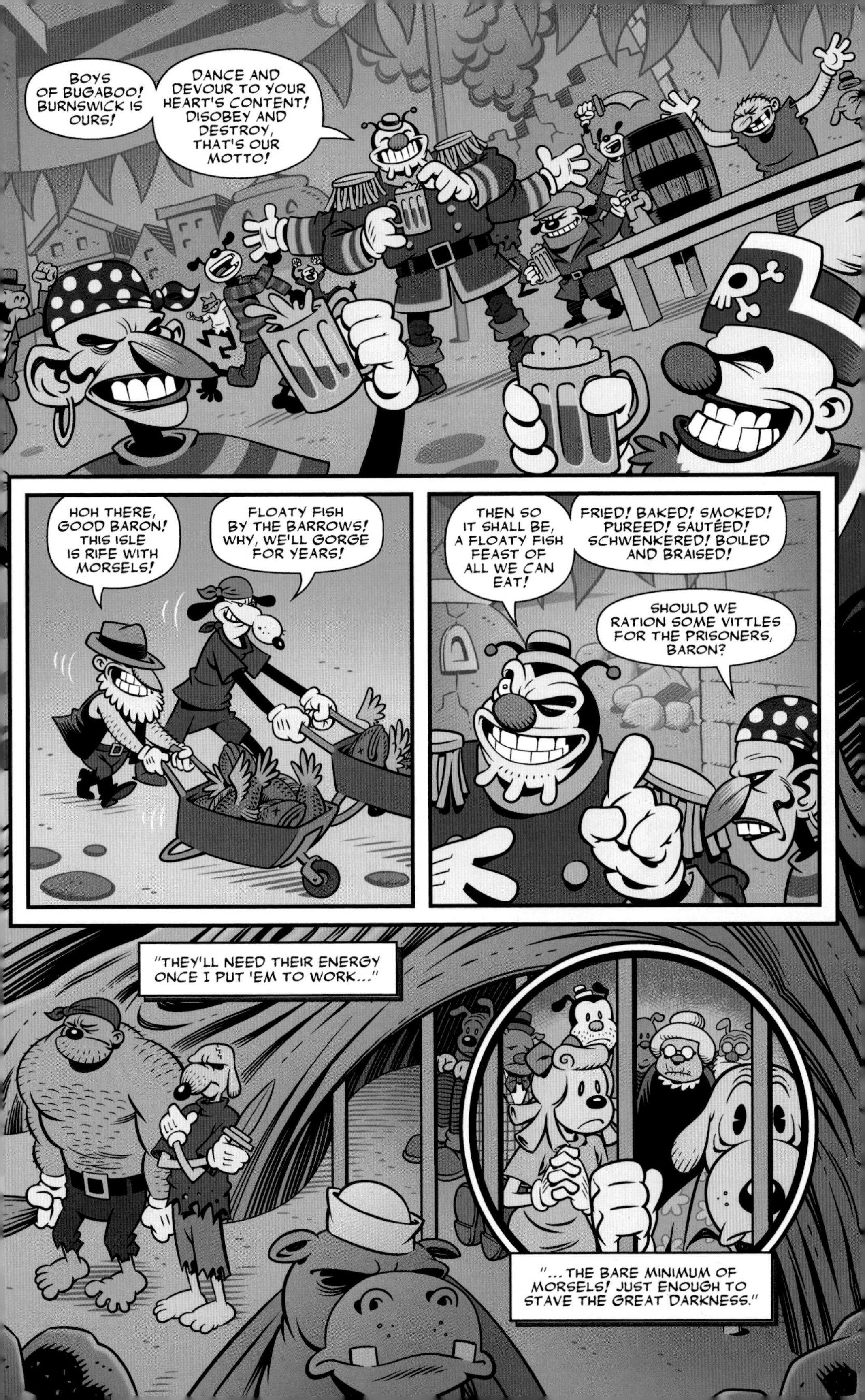
BOYS OF BUGABOO! BURNSWICK IS OURS!
DANCE AND DEVOUR TO YOUR HEART'S CONTENT! DISOBEY AND DESTROY, THAT'S OUR MOTTO!
HOH THERE, GOOD BARON! THIS ISLE IS RIFE WITH MORSELS!
FLOATY FISH BY THE BARROWS! WHY, WE'LL GORGE FOR YEARS!
THEN SO IT SHALL BE, A FLOATY FISH FEAST OF ALL WE CAN EAT!
FRIED! BAKED! SMOKED! PUREED! SAUTÉED! SCHWENKERED! BOILED AND BRAISED!
SHOULD WE RATION SOME VITTLES FOR THE PRISONERS, BARON?
"THEY'LL NEED THEIR ENERGY ONCE I PUT 'EM TO WORK..."
"...THE BARE MINIMUM OF MORSELS! JUST ENOUGH TO STAVE THE GREAT DARKNESS."

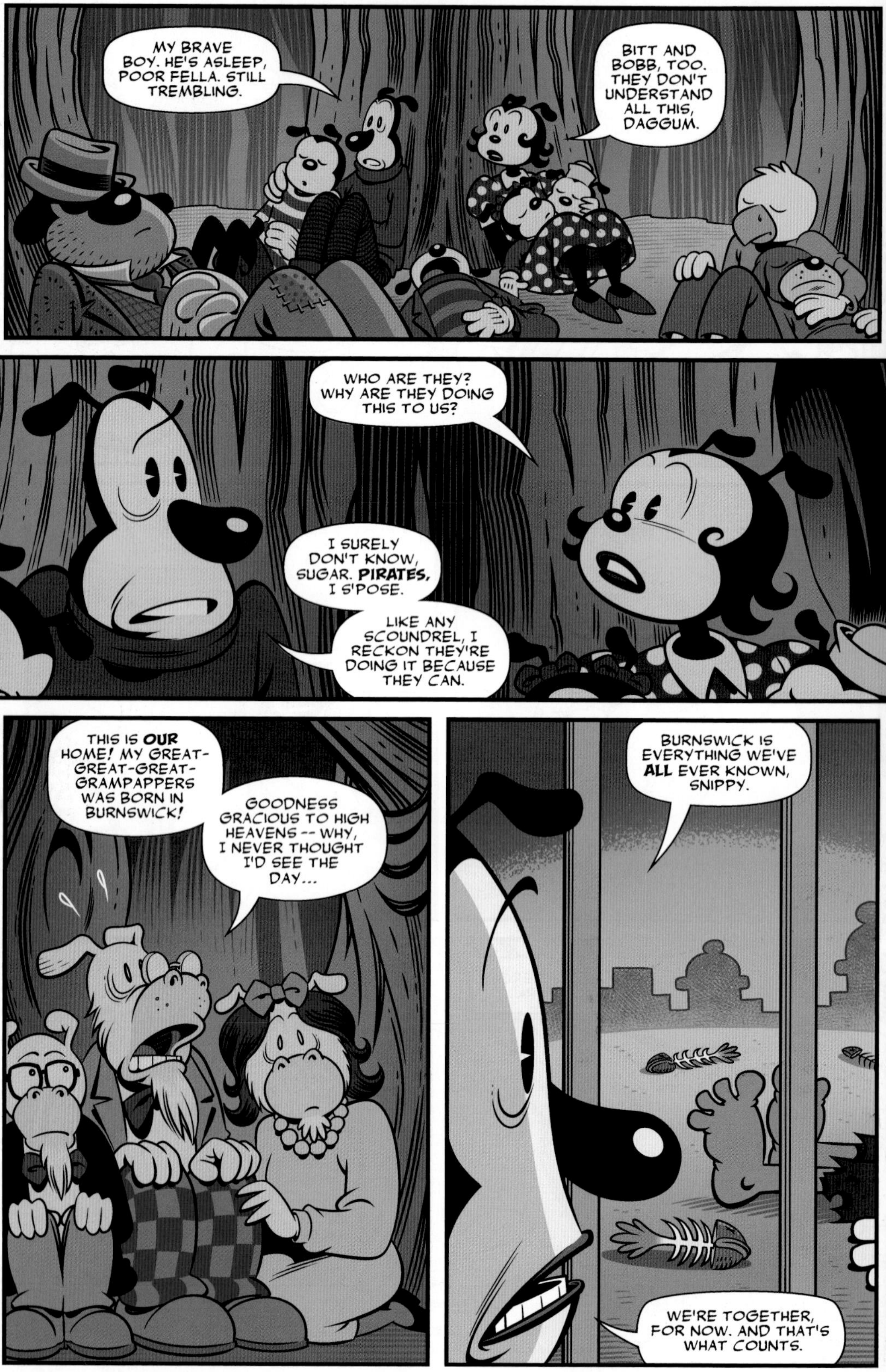
MY BRAVE BOY. HE'S ASLEEP, POOR FELLA. STILL TREMBLING.
BITT AND BOBB, TOO. THEY DON'T UNDERSTAND ALL THIS, DAGGUM.
WHO ARE THEY? WHY ARE THEY DOING THIS TO US?
I SURELY DON'T KNOW, SUGAR. **PIRATES,** I S'POSE.
LIKE ANY SCOUNDREL, I RECKON THEY'RE DOING IT BECAUSE THEY CAN.
THIS IS **OUR** HOME! MY GREAT-GREAT-GREAT-GRAMPAPPERS WAS BORN IN BURNSWICK!
GOODNESS GRACIOUS TO HIGH HEAVENS -- WHY, I NEVER THOUGHT I'D SEE THE DAY...
BURNSWICK IS EVERYTHING WE'VE **ALL** EVER KNOWN, SNIPPY.
WE'RE TOGETHER, FOR NOW. AND THAT'S WHAT COUNTS.

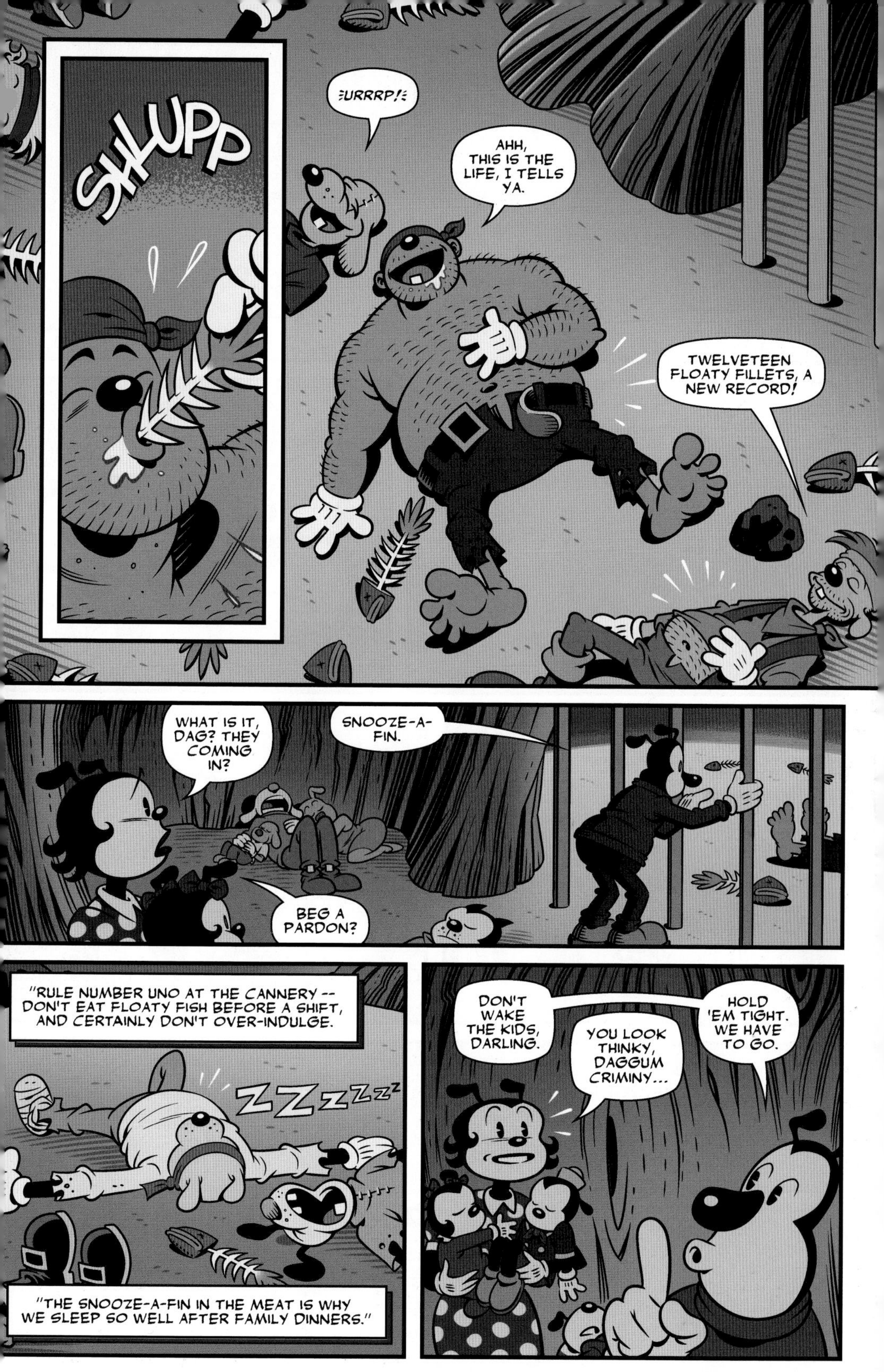
SHLUPP
URRRP!
AHH, THIS IS THE LIFE, I TELLS YA.
TWELVETEEN FLOATY FILLETS, A NEW RECORD!
WHAT IS IT, DAG? THEY COMING IN?
SNOOZE-A-FIN.
BEG A PARDON?
"RULE NUMBER UNO AT THE CANNERY -- DON'T EAT FLOATY FISH BEFORE A SHIFT, AND CERTAINLY DON'T OVER-INDULGE.
ZZZzzz
"THE SNOOZE-A-FIN IN THE MEAT IS WHY WE SLEEP SO WELL AFTER FAMILY DINNERS."
DON'T WAKE THE KIDS, DARLING.
HOLD 'EM TIGHT. WE HAVE TO GO.
YOU LOOK THINKY, DAGGUM CRIMINY...

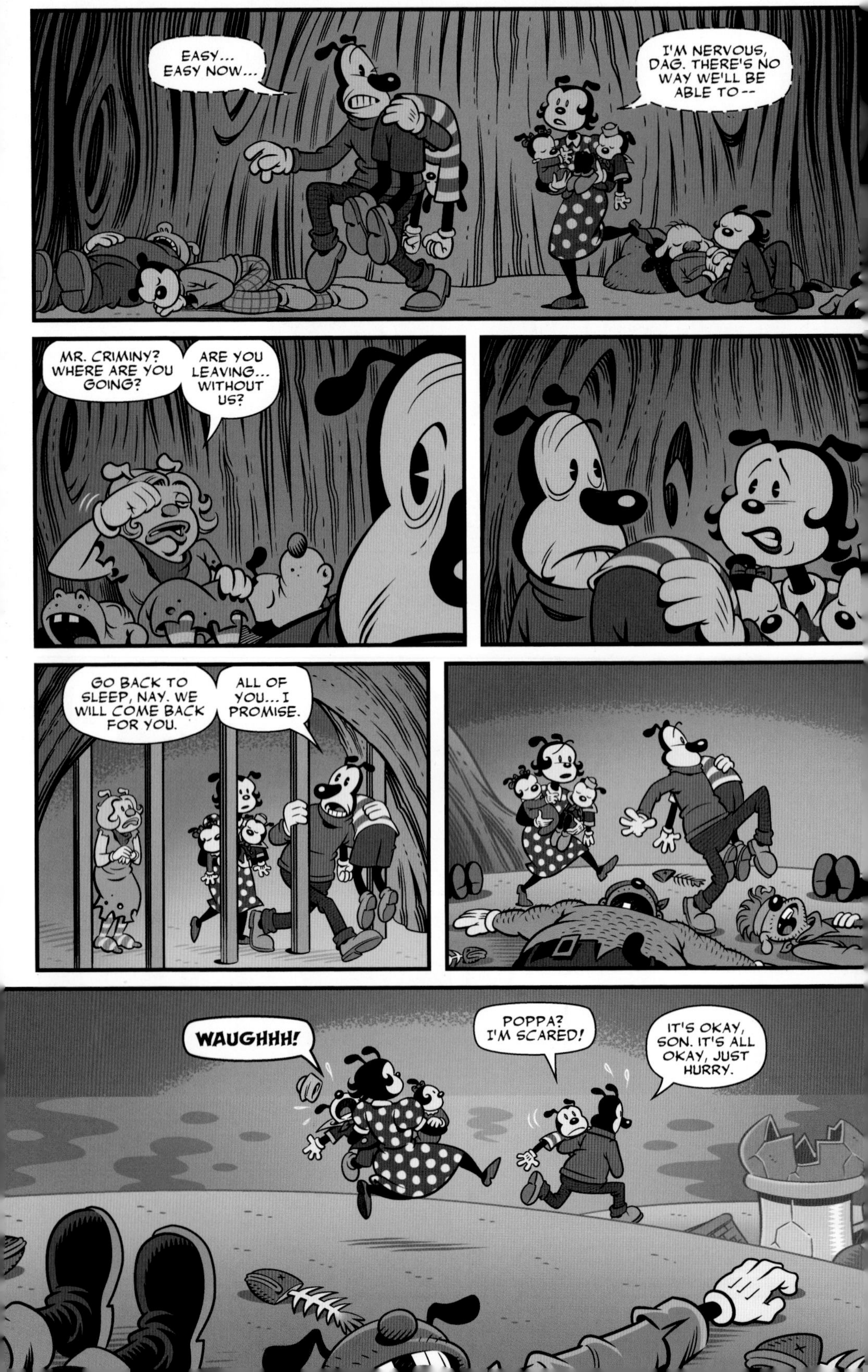
EASY... EASY NOW...
I'M NERVOUS, DAG. THERE'S NO WAY WE'LL BE ABLE TO--
MR. CRIMINY? WHERE ARE YOU GOING?
ARE YOU LEAVING... WITHOUT US?
GO BACK TO SLEEP, NAY. WE WILL COME BACK FOR YOU.
ALL OF YOU... I PROMISE.
WAUGHHH!
POPPA? I'M SCARED!
IT'S OKAY, SON. IT'S ALL OKAY, JUST HURRY.

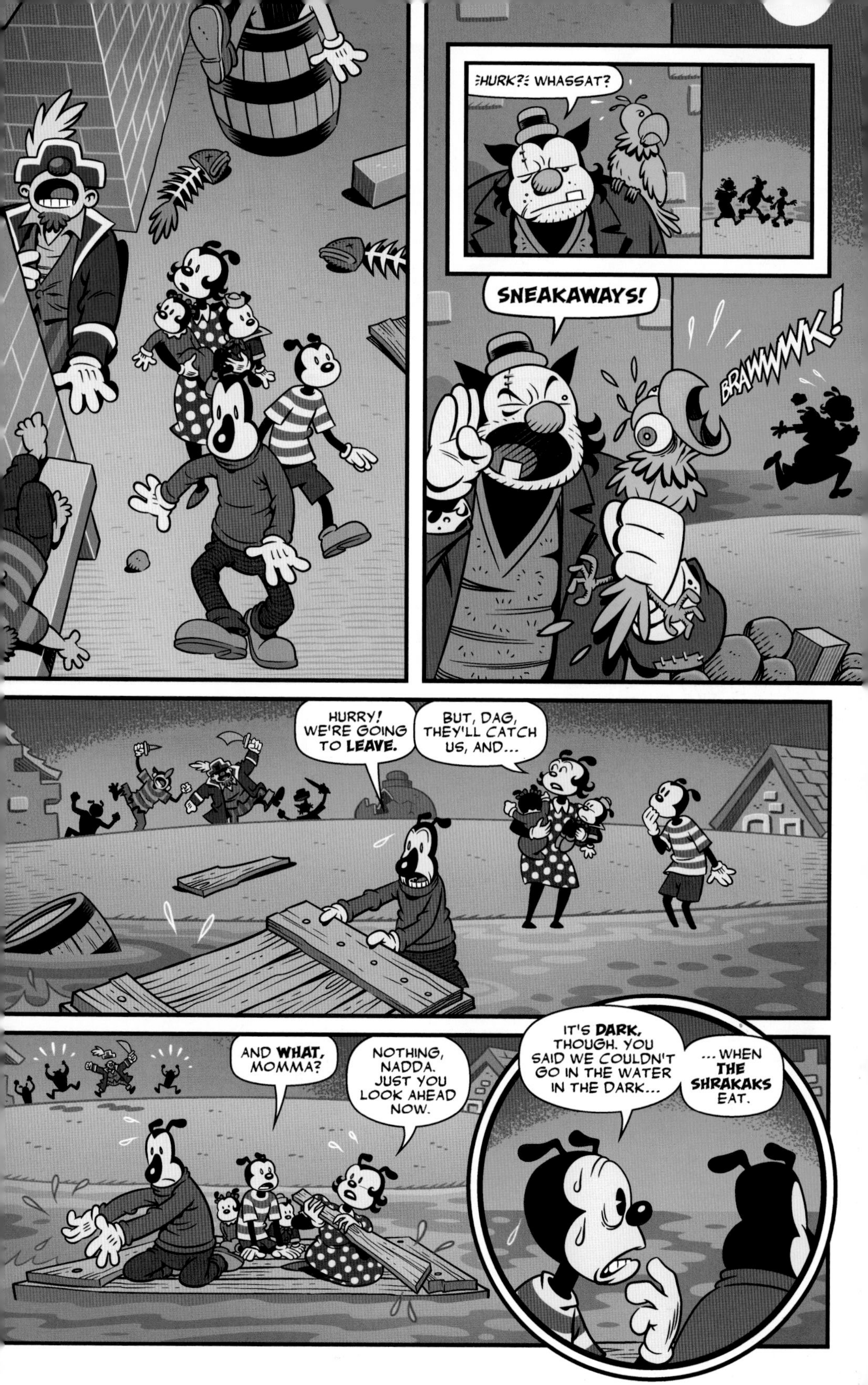

HURK? WHASSAT?
SNEAKAWAYS!
BRAWWWK!
HURRY! WE'RE GOING TO LEAVE.
BUT, DAG, THEY'LL CATCH US, AND...
AND WHAT, MOMMA?
NOTHING, NADDA. JUST YOU LOOK AHEAD NOW.
IT'S DARK, THOUGH. YOU SAID WE COULDN'T GO IN THE WATER IN THE DARK...
...WHEN THE SHRAKAKS EAT.

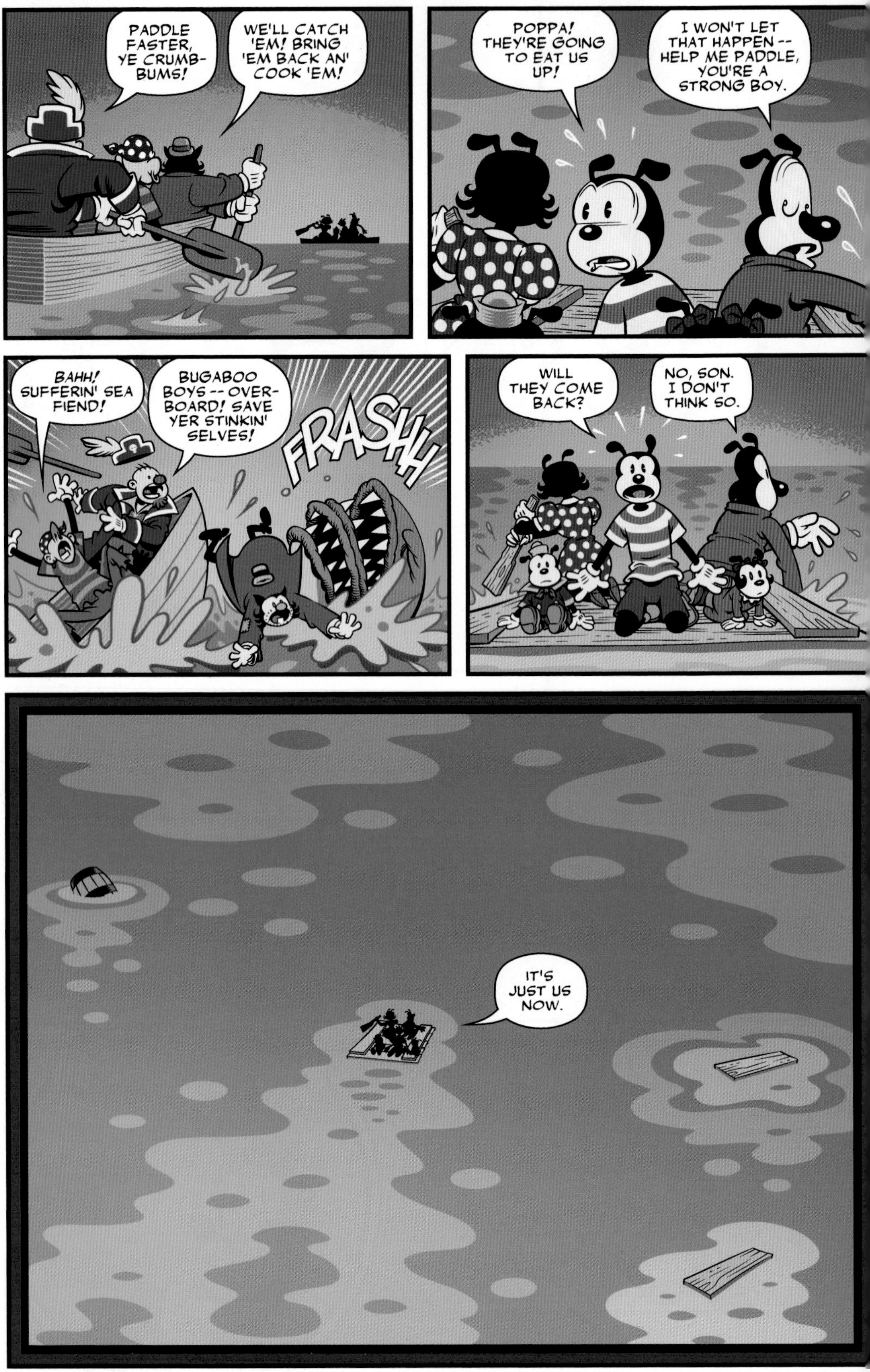
PADDLE FASTER, YE CRUMB-BUMS!
WE'LL CATCH 'EM! BRING 'EM BACK AN' COOK 'EM!
POPPA! THEY'RE GOING TO EAT US UP!
I WON'T LET THAT HAPPEN -- HELP ME PADDLE, YOU'RE A STRONG BOY.
BAHH! SUFFERIN' SEA FIEND!
BUGABOO BOYS -- OVER-BOARD! SAVE YER STINKIN' SELVES!
FRASHH
WILL THEY COME BACK?
NO, SON. I DON'T THINK SO.
IT'S JUST US NOW.

CHAPTER TWO

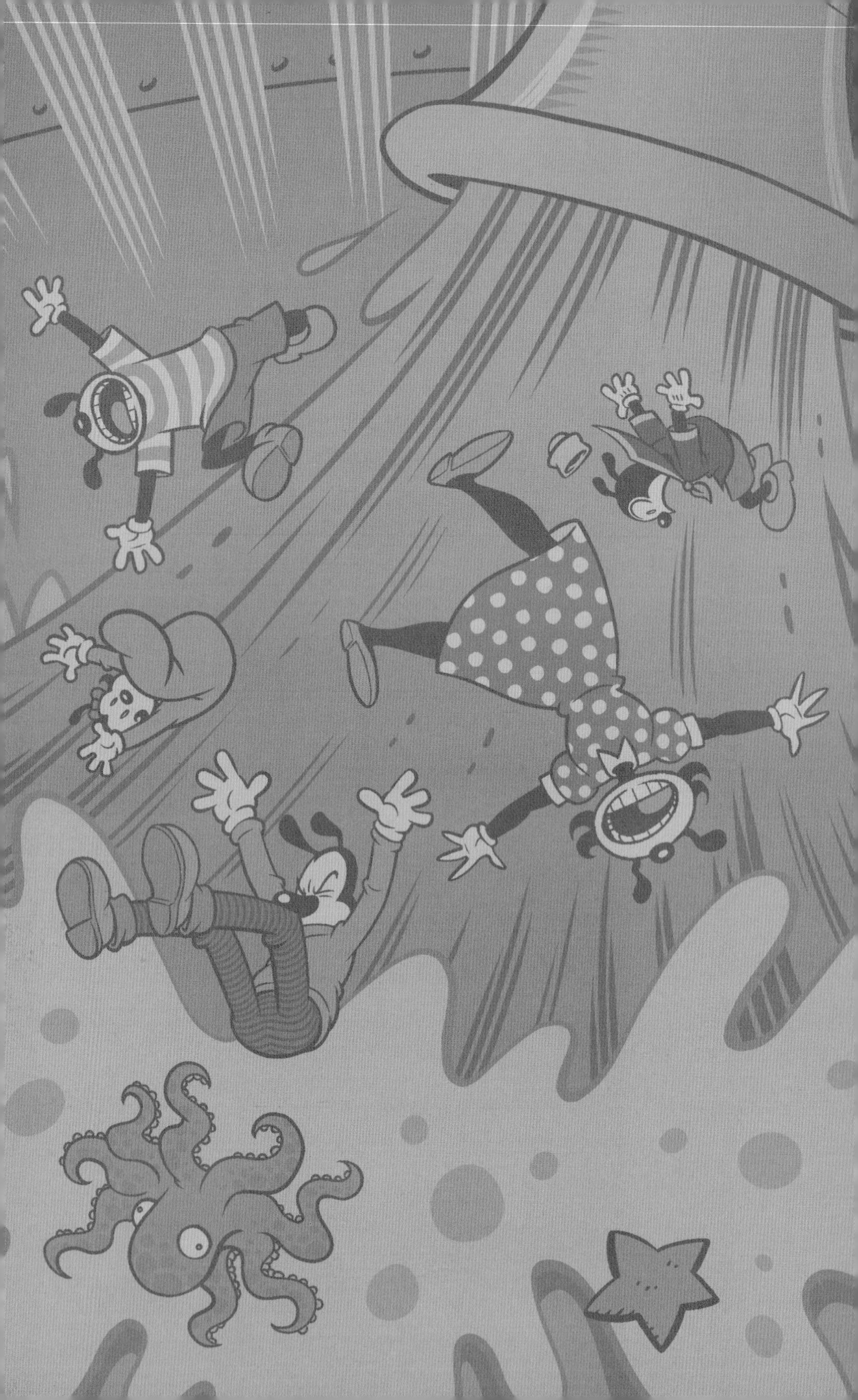

A family now lost at sea,
no end nor means in sight.

An endless drift awaits
before uncertainty of night.

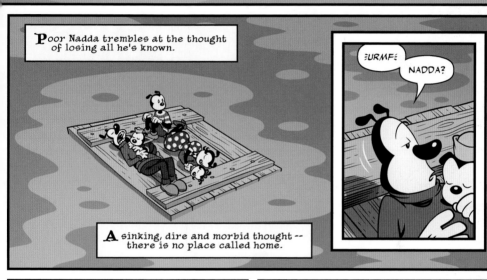

Poor Nadda trembles at the thought
of losing all he's known.

URMF

NADDA?

A sinking, dire and morbid thought --
there is no place called home.

SON, HOW LONG HAVE YOU BEEN AWAKE? DID YOU NOT SNOOZLE?

I WANTED TO STAY UP AND KEEP WATCH. FOR THE SHRAKAKS AGAIN.

YOU'RE A GOOD BOY, NADDA. MAYBE WE CAN CATCH A FEW BAGGY MINNIES OR SEA-BEANS FOR SUN SUPPER.

THERE'S NOTHING HERE, POPPA.

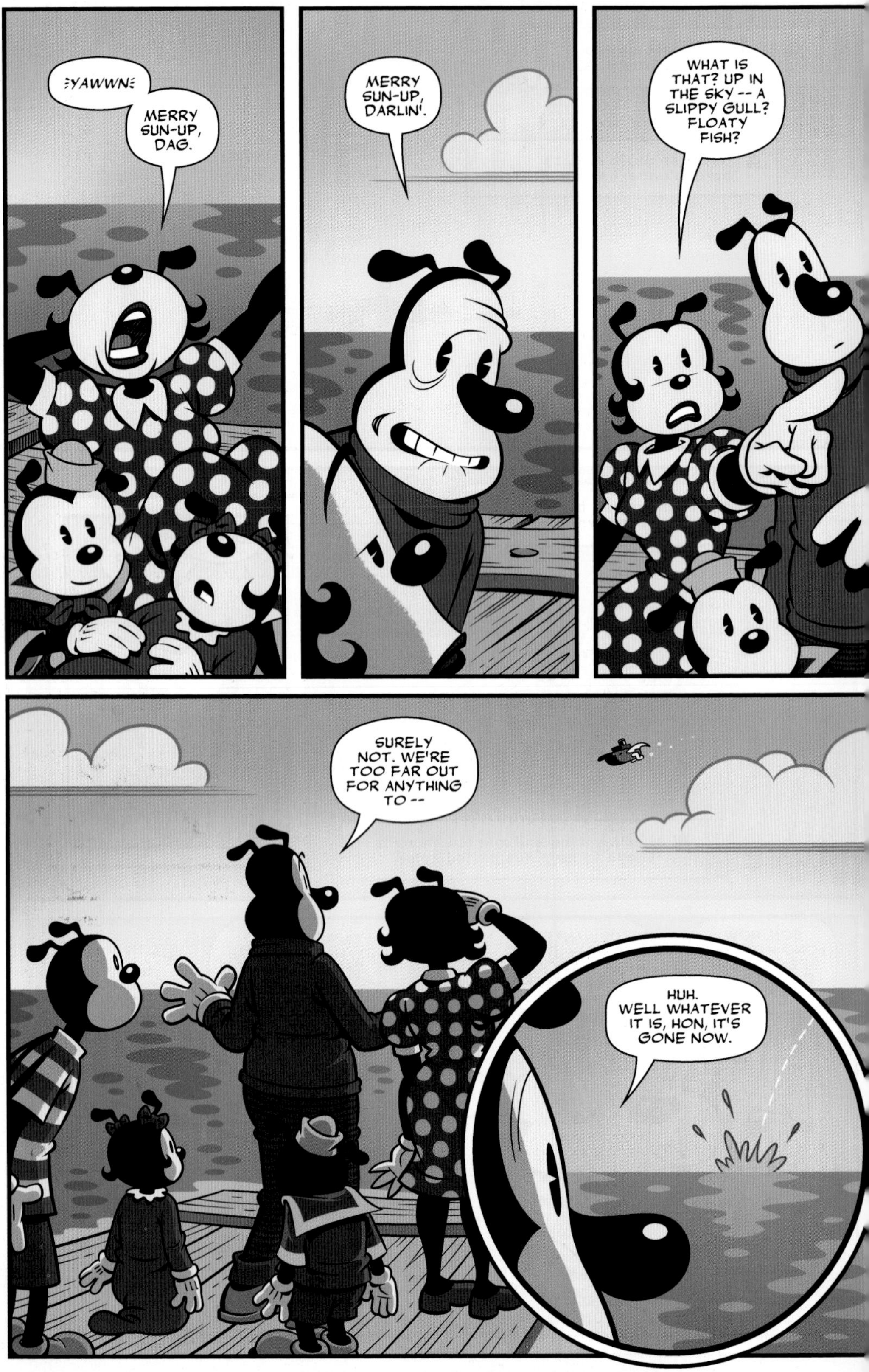

=YAWWN=
MERRY SUN-UP, DAG.
MERRY SUN-UP, DARLIN'.
WHAT IS THAT? UP IN THE SKY -- A SLIPPY GULL? FLOATY FISH?
SURELY NOT. WE'RE TOO FAR OUT FOR ANYTHING TO --
HUH. WELL WHATEVER IT IS, HON, IT'S GONE NOW.

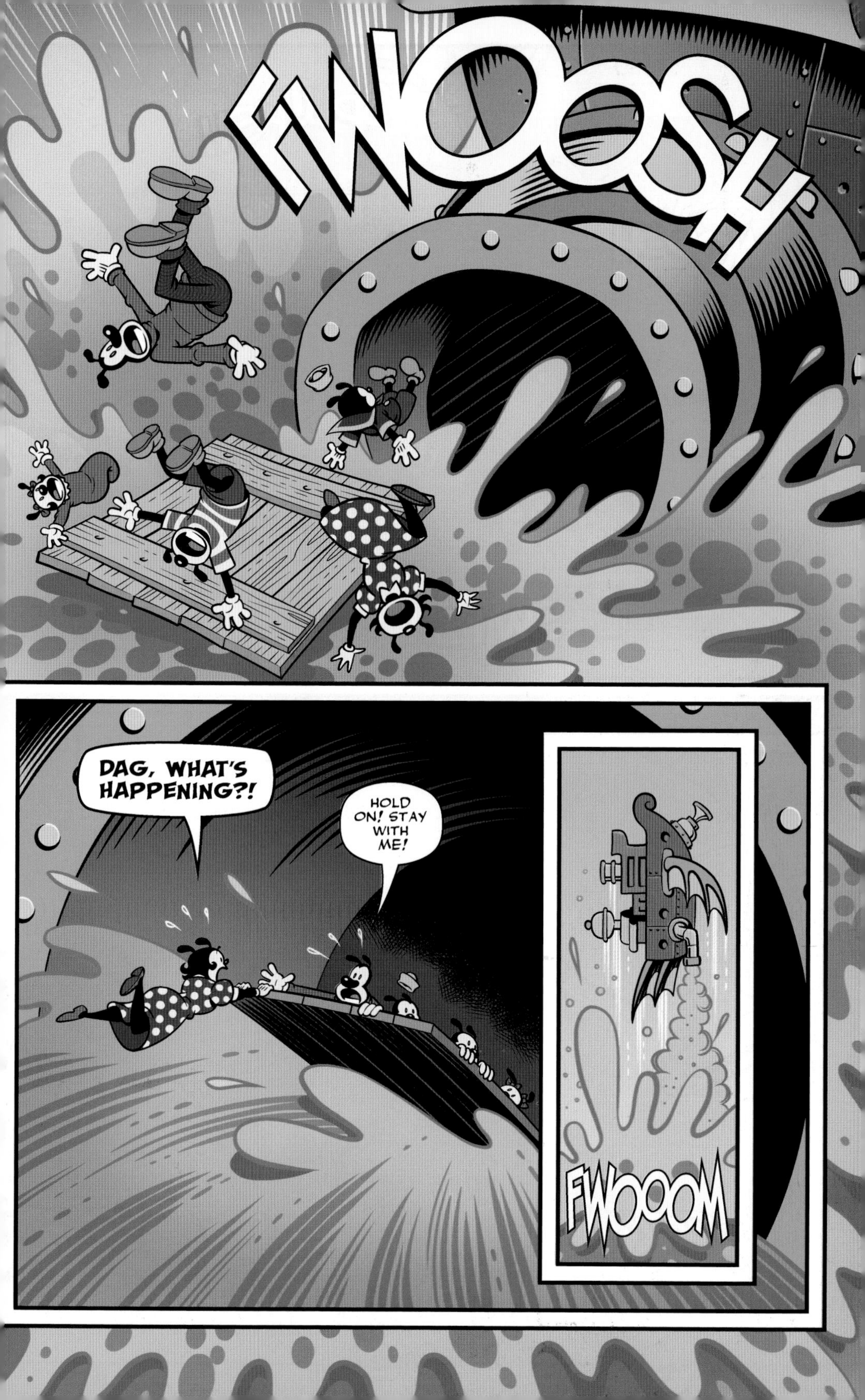
FWOOSH
DAG, WHAT'S HAPPENING?!
HOLD ON! STAY WITH ME!
FWOOOM

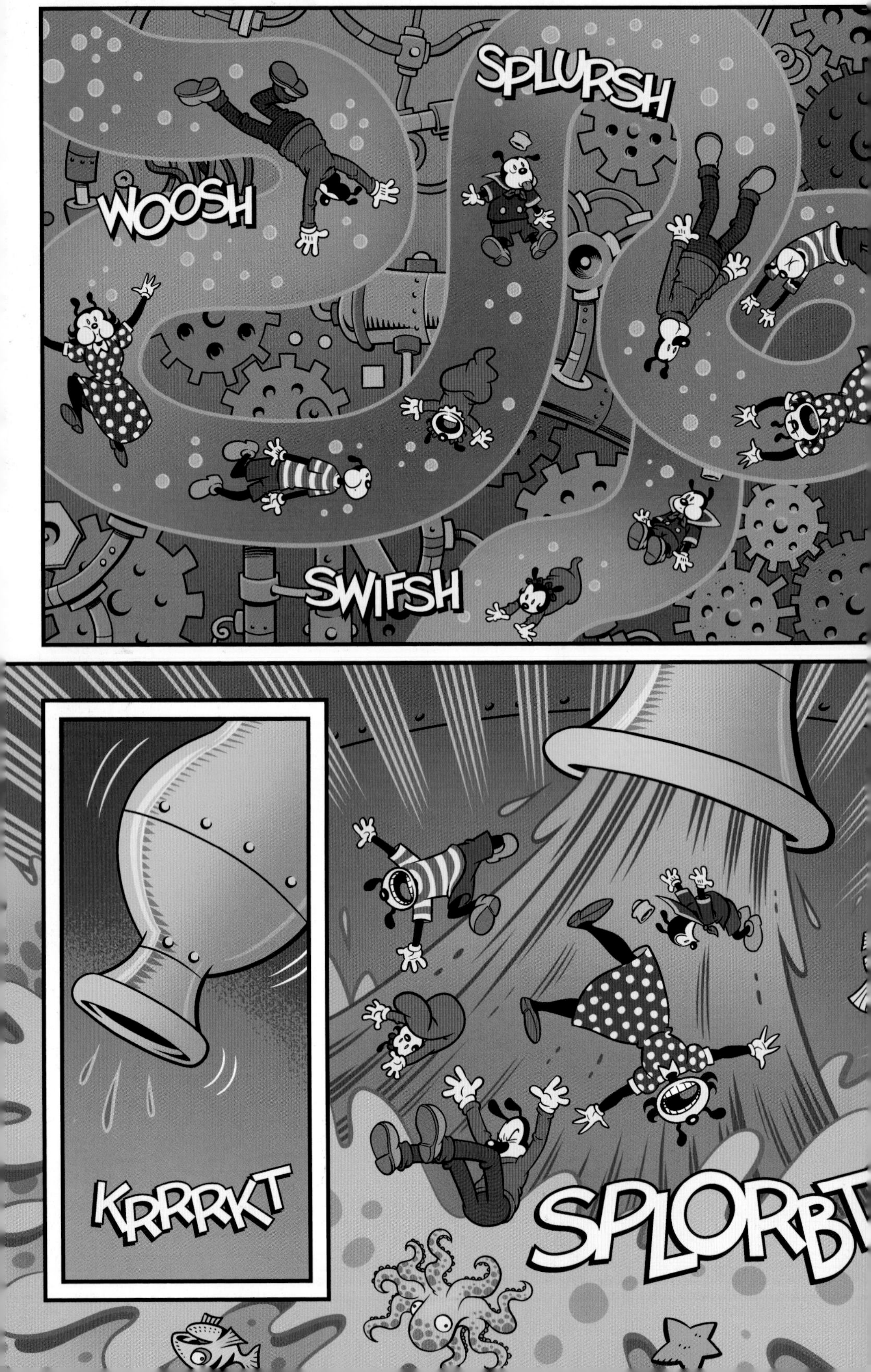
SPLURSH
WOOSH
SWIFSH
KRRRKT
SPLORBT

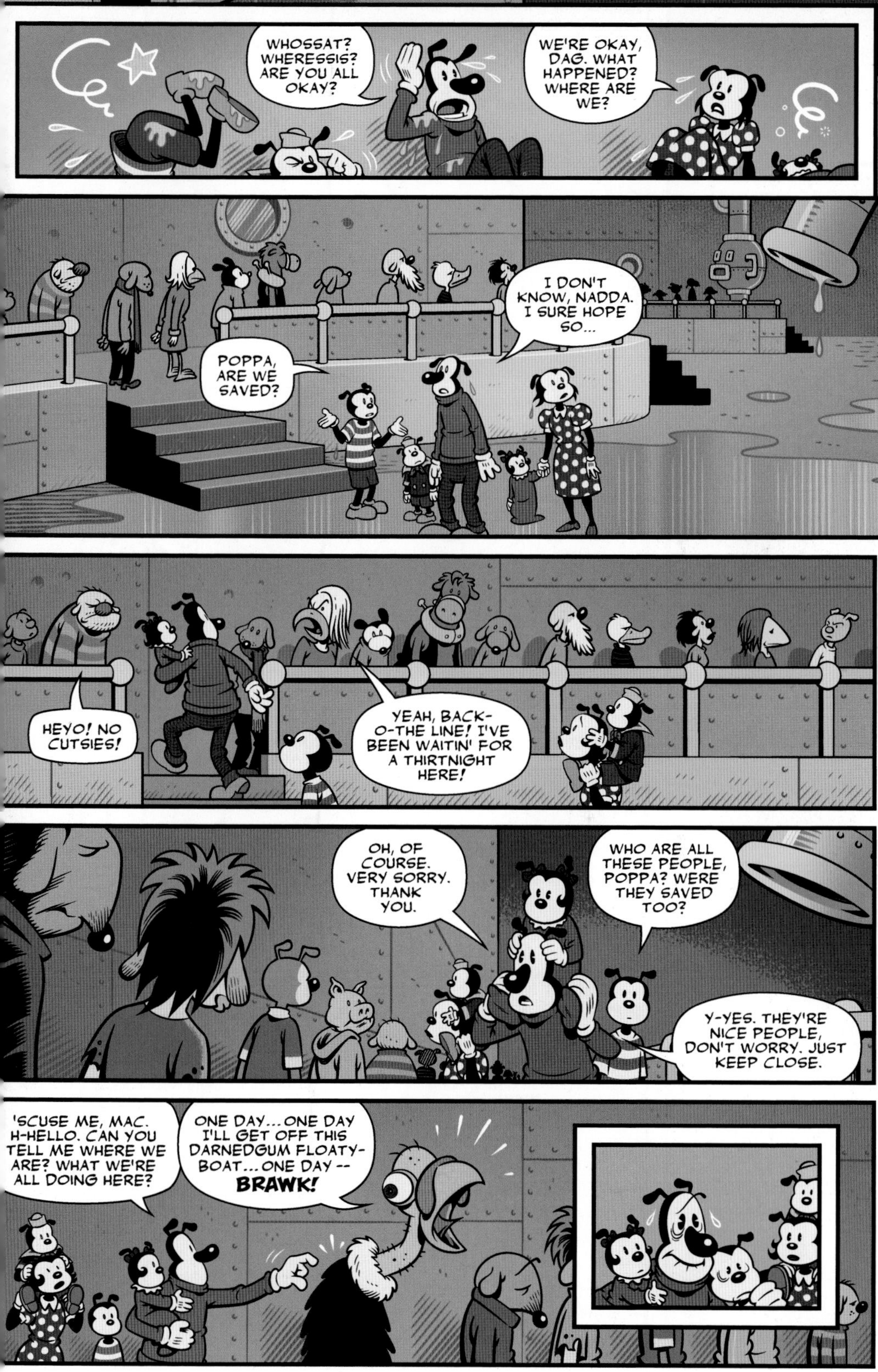
WHOSSAT? WHERESSIS? ARE YOU ALL OKAY?
WE'RE OKAY, DAG. WHAT HAPPENED? WHERE ARE WE?
POPPA, ARE WE SAVED?
I DON'T KNOW, NADDA. I SURE HOPE SO...
HEYO! NO CUTSIES!
YEAH, BACK-O-THE LINE! I'VE BEEN WAITIN' FOR A THIRTNIGHT HERE!
OH, OF COURSE. VERY SORRY. THANK YOU.
WHO ARE ALL THESE PEOPLE, POPPA? WERE THEY SAVED TOO?
Y-YES. THEY'RE NICE PEOPLE, DON'T WORRY. JUST KEEP CLOSE.
'SCUSE ME, MAC. H-HELLO. CAN YOU TELL ME WHERE WE ARE? WHAT WE'RE ALL DOING HERE?
ONE DAY... ONE DAY I'LL GET OFF THIS DARNEDGUM FLOATY-BOAT... ONE DAY -- BRAWK!

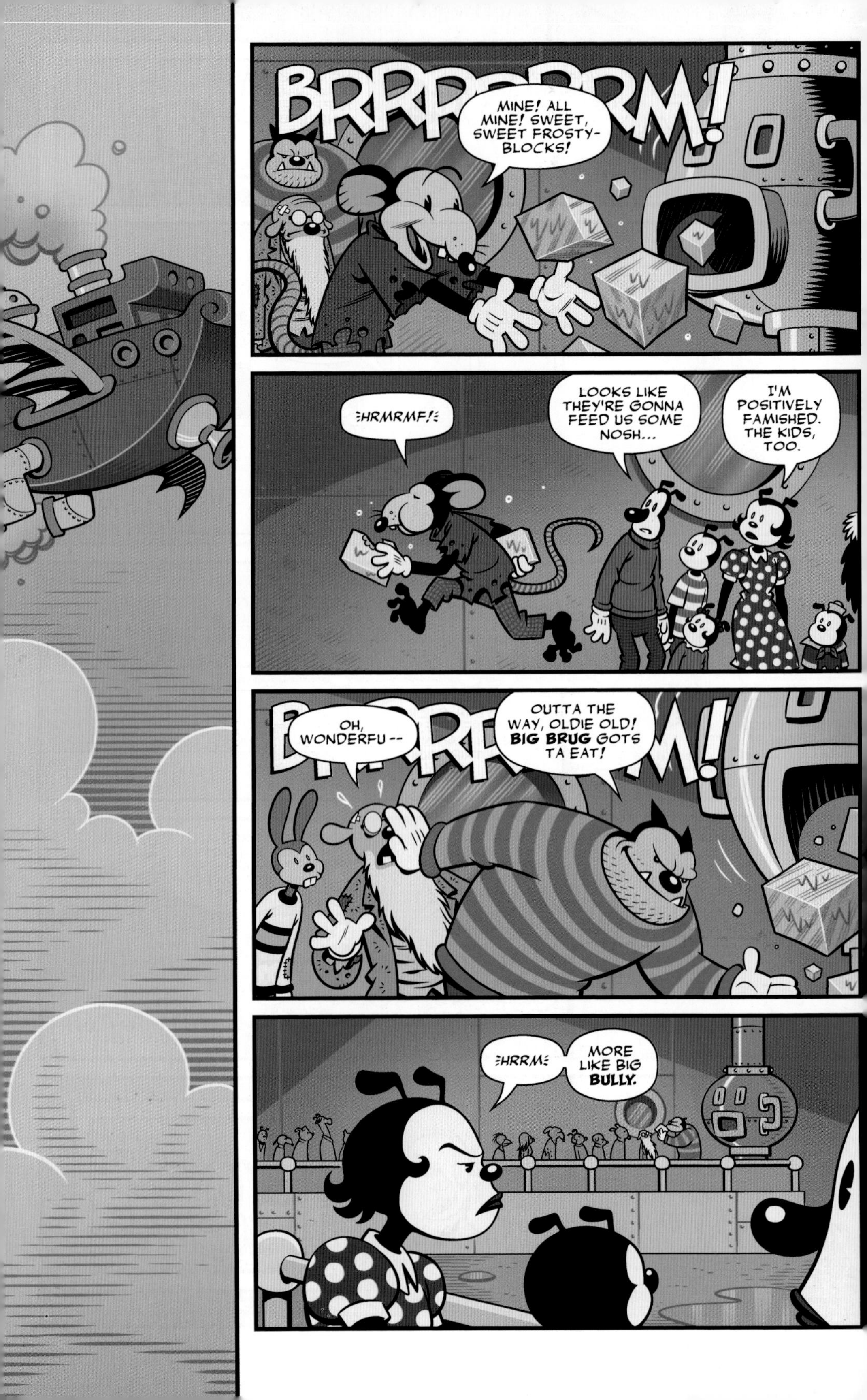
MINE! ALL MINE! SWEET, SWEET FROSTY-BLOCKS!
HRMRMF!
LOOKS LIKE THEY'RE GONNA FEED US SOME NOSH...
I'M POSITIVELY FAMISHED. THE KIDS, TOO.
OH, WONDERFU--
OUTTA THE WAY, OLDIE OLD! BIG BRUG GOTS TA EAT!
HRRM
MORE LIKE BIG BULLY.

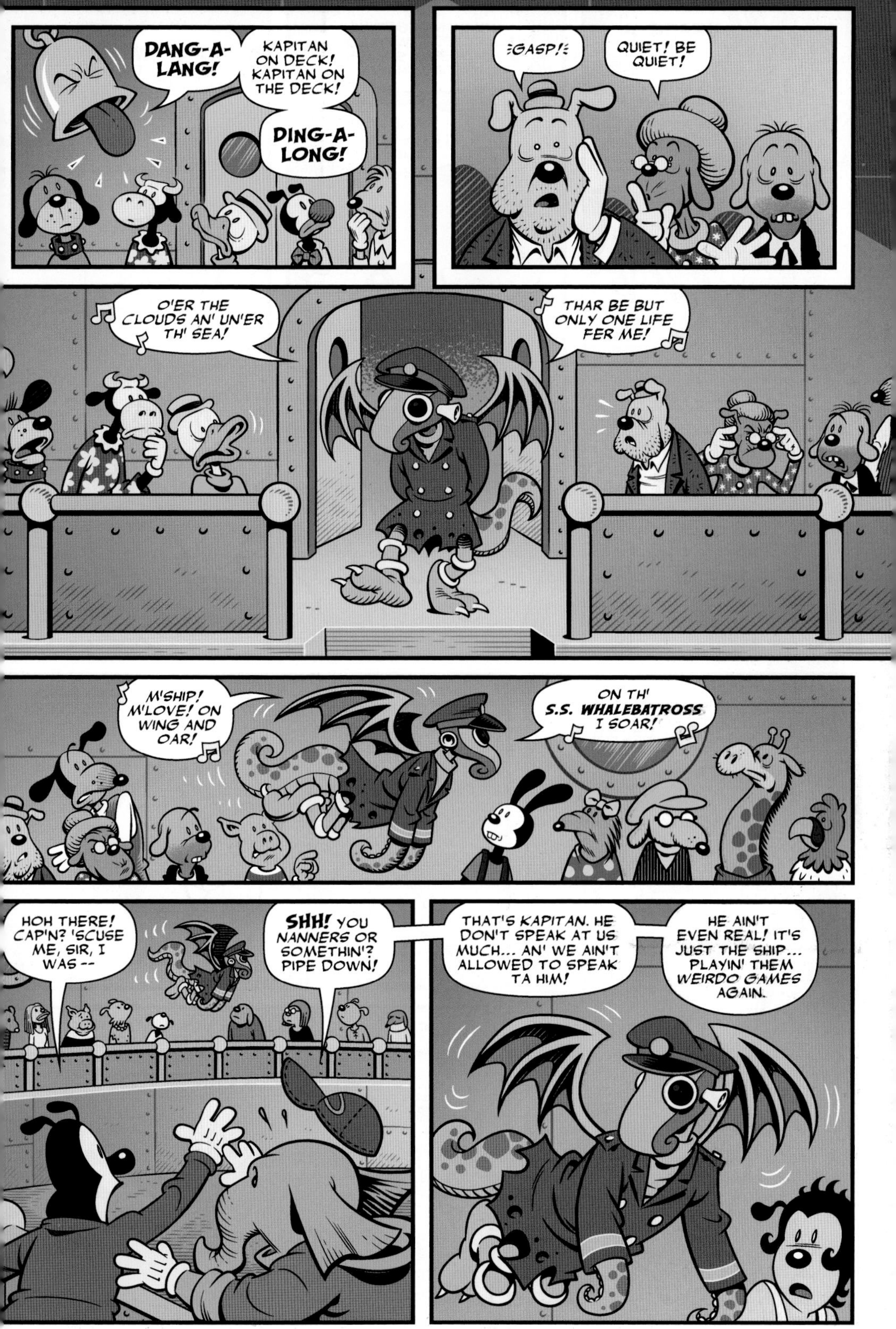
DANG-A-LANG!
KAPITAN ON DECK! KAPITAN ON THE DECK!
DING-A-LONG!
:GASP!:
QUIET! BE QUIET!
O'ER THE CLOUDS AN' UN'ER TH' SEA!
THAR BE BUT ONLY ONE LIFE FER ME!
M'SHIP! M'LOVE! ON WING AND OAR!
ON TH' S.S. WHALEBATROSS I SOAR!
HOH THERE! CAP'N? 'SCUSE ME, SIR, I WAS --
SHH! YOU NANNERS OR SOMETHIN'? PIPE DOWN!
THAT'S KAPITAN. HE DON'T SPEAK AT US MUCH... AN' WE AIN'T ALLOWED TO SPEAK TA HIM!
HE AIN'T EVEN REAL! IT'S JUST THE SHIP... PLAYIN' THEM WEIRDO GAMES AGAIN.

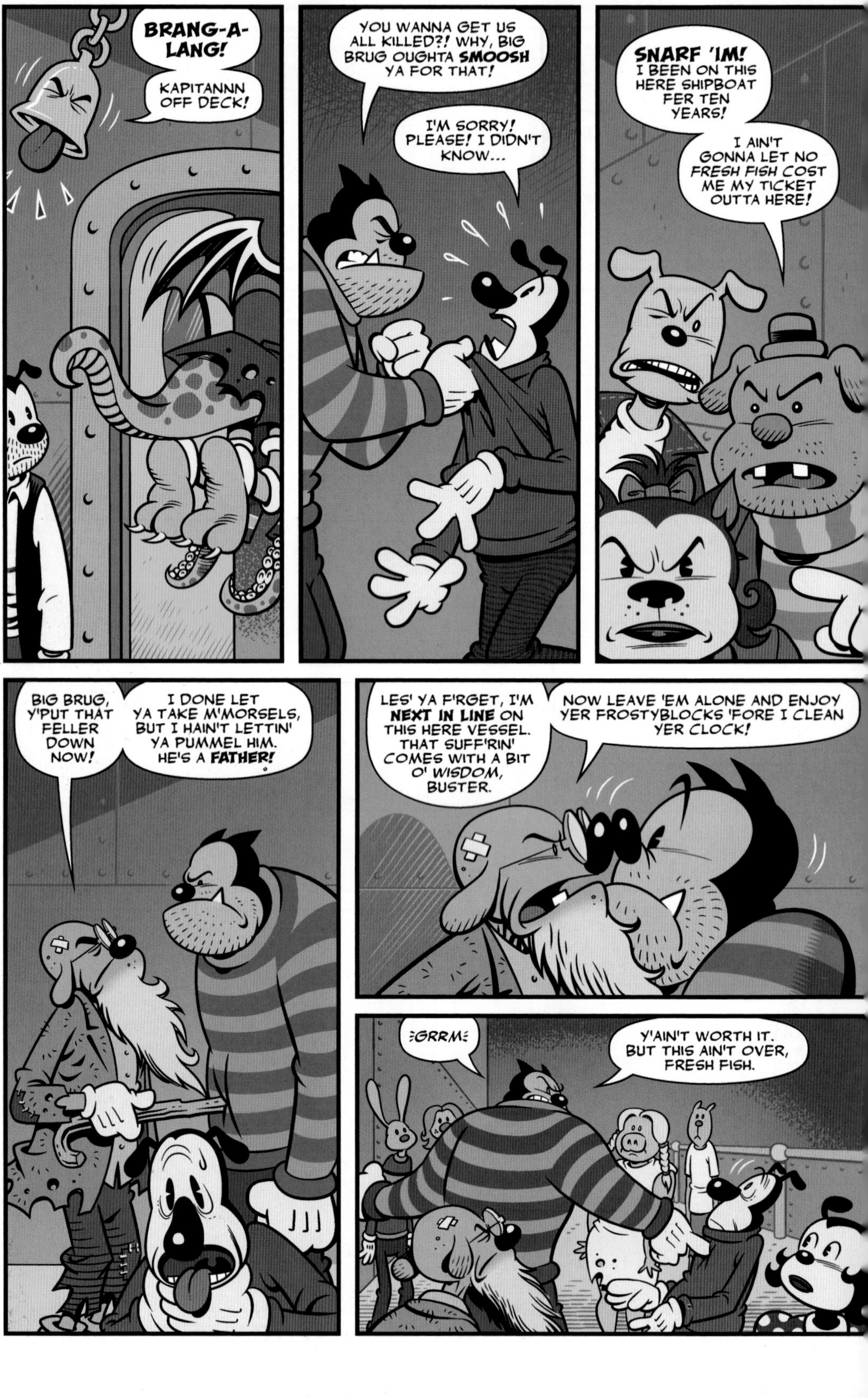
BRANG-A-LANG!
KAPITANNN OFF DECK!
YOU WANNA GET US ALL KILLED?! WHY, BIG BRUG OUGHTA SMOOSH YA FOR THAT!
I'M SORRY! PLEASE! I DIDN'T KNOW...
SNARF 'IM! I BEEN ON THIS HERE SHIPBOAT FER TEN YEARS!
I AIN'T GONNA LET NO FRESH FISH COST ME MY TICKET OUTTA HERE!
BIG BRUG, Y'PUT THAT FELLER DOWN NOW!
I DONE LET YA TAKE M'MORSELS, BUT I HAIN'T LETTIN' YA PUMMEL HIM. HE'S A FATHER!
LES' YA F'RGET, I'M NEXT IN LINE ON THIS HERE VESSEL. THAT SUFF'RIN' COMES WITH A BIT O' WISDOM, BUSTER.
NOW LEAVE 'EM ALONE AND ENJOY YER FROSTYBLOCKS 'FORE I CLEAN YER CLOCK!
GRRM
Y'AIN'T WORTH IT. BUT THIS AIN'T OVER, FRESH FISH.

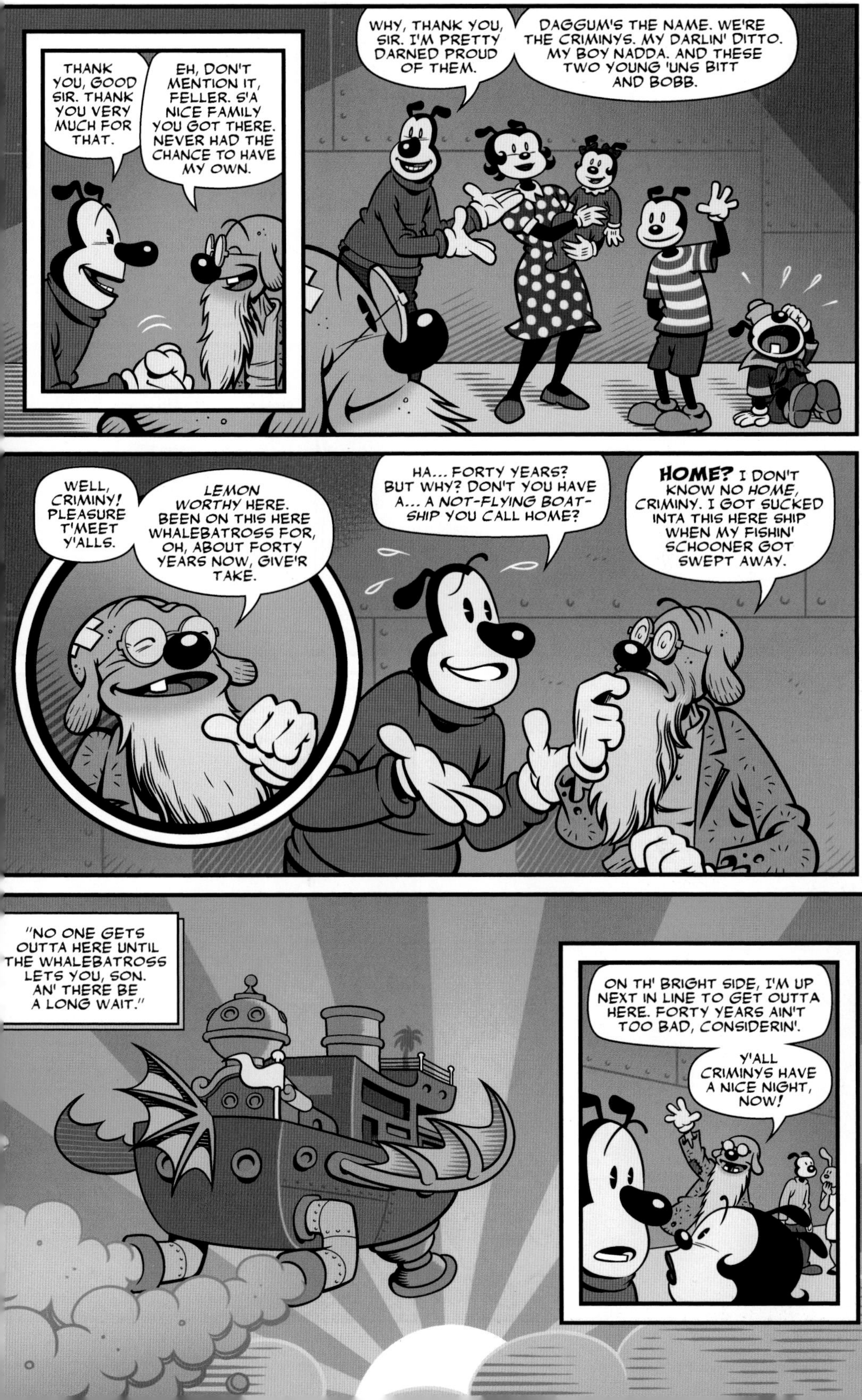
THANK YOU, GOOD SIR. THANK YOU VERY MUCH FOR THAT.
EH, DON'T MENTION IT, FELLER. S'A NICE FAMILY YOU GOT THERE. NEVER HAD THE CHANCE TO HAVE MY OWN.
WHY, THANK YOU, SIR. I'M PRETTY DARNED PROUD OF THEM.
DAGGUM'S THE NAME. WE'RE THE CRIMINYS. MY DARLIN' DITTO. MY BOY NADDA. AND THESE TWO YOUNG 'UNS BITT AND BOBB.
WELL, CRIMINY! PLEASURE T'MEET Y'ALLS.
LEMON WORTHY HERE. BEEN ON THIS HERE WHALEBATROSS FOR, OH, ABOUT FORTY YEARS NOW, GIVE'R TAKE.
HA... FORTY YEARS? BUT WHY? DON'T YOU HAVE A... A NOT-FLYING BOAT-SHIP YOU CALL HOME?
HOME? I DON'T KNOW NO HOME, CRIMINY. I GOT SUCKED INTA THIS HERE SHIP WHEN MY FISHIN' SCHOONER GOT SWEPT AWAY.
"NO ONE GETS OUTTA HERE UNTIL THE WHALEBATROSS LETS YOU, SON. AN' THERE BE A LONG WAIT."
ON TH' BRIGHT SIDE, I'M UP NEXT IN LINE TO GET OUTTA HERE. FORTY YEARS AIN'T TOO BAD, CONSIDERIN'.
Y'ALL CRIMINYS HAVE A NICE NIGHT, NOW!

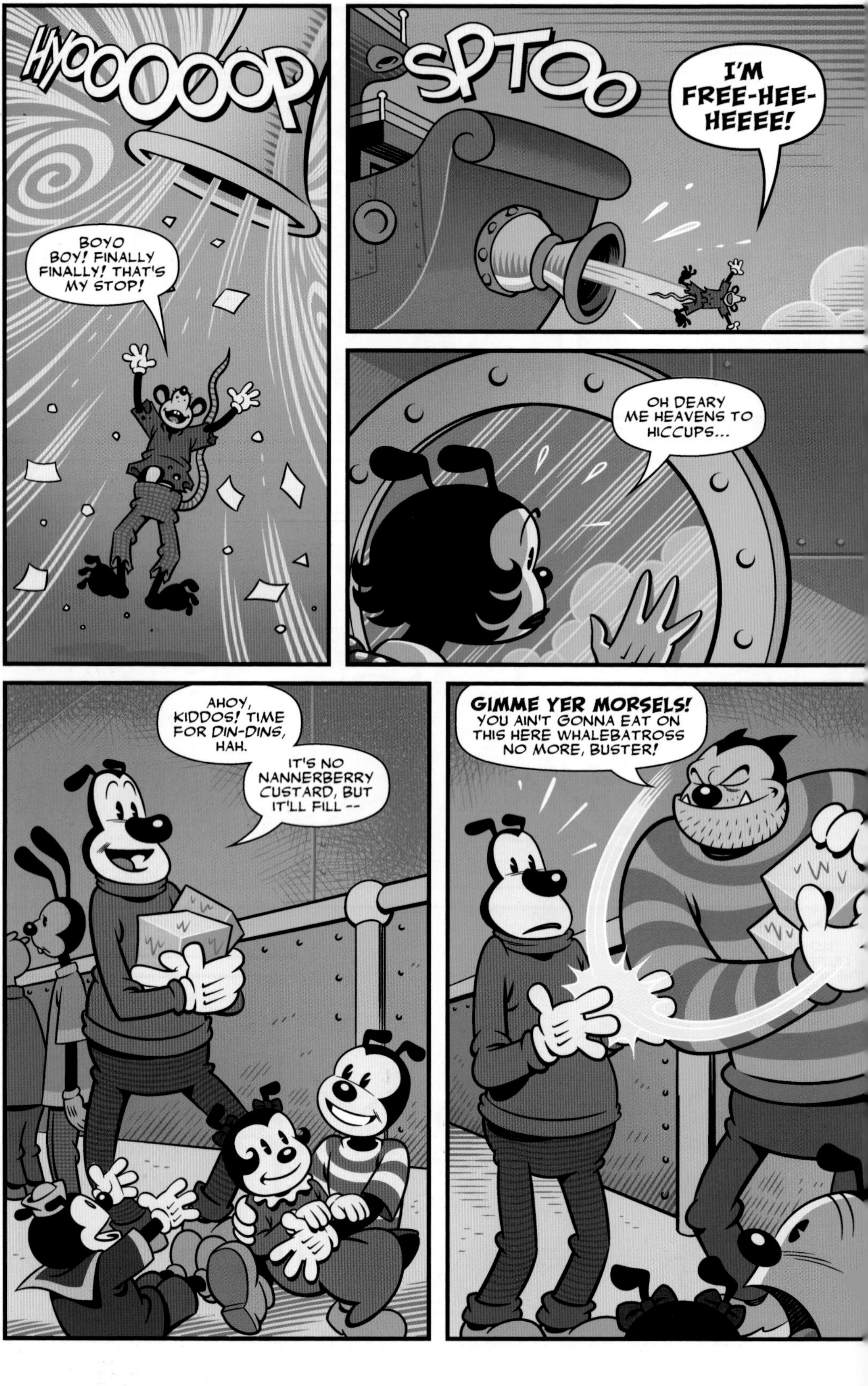
HYOOOOOOP
BOYO BOY! FINALLY FINALLY! THAT'S MY STOP!
SPTOO
I'M FREE-HEE-HEEEE!
OH DEARY ME HEAVENS TO HICCUPS...
AHOY, KIDDOS! TIME FOR DIN-DINS, HAH.
IT'S NO NANNERBERRY CUSTARD, BUT IT'LL FILL --
GIMME YER MORSELS! YOU AIN'T GONNA EAT ON THIS HERE WHALEBATROSS NO MORE, BUSTER!

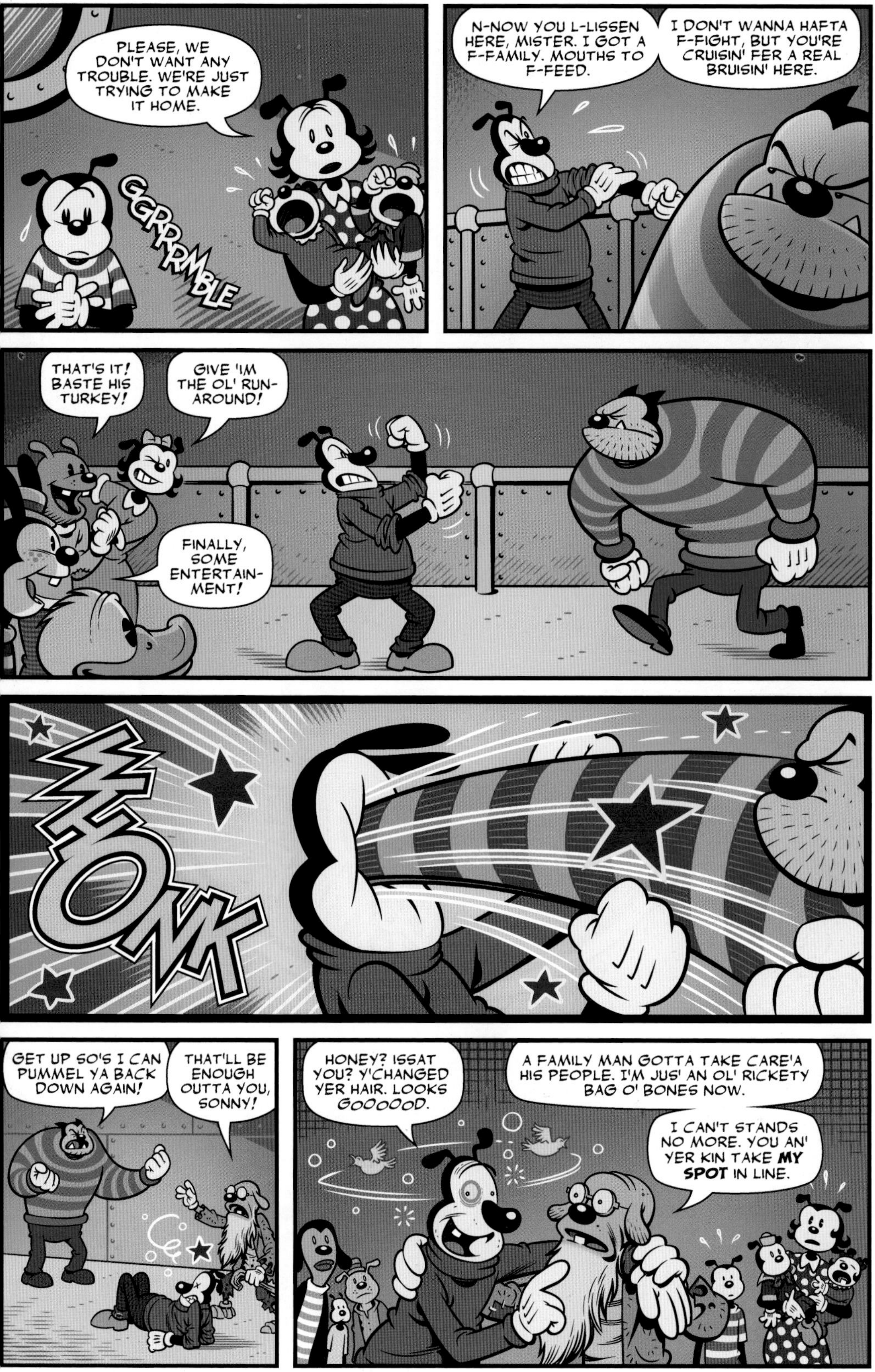
PLEASE, WE DON'T WANT ANY TROUBLE. WE'RE JUST TRYING TO MAKE IT HOME.
GGRRRMBLE
N-NOW YOU L-LISSEN HERE, MISTER. I GOT A F-FAMILY. MOUTHS TO F-FEED.
I DON'T WANNA HAFTA F-FIGHT, BUT YOU'RE CRUISIN' FER A REAL BRUISIN' HERE.
THAT'S IT! BASTE HIS TURKEY!
GIVE 'IM THE OL' RUN-AROUND!
FINALLY, SOME ENTERTAIN-MENT!
WHONK
GET UP SO'S I CAN PUMMEL YA BACK DOWN AGAIN!
THAT'LL BE ENOUGH OUTTA YOU, SONNY!
HONEY? ISSAT YOU? Y'CHANGED YER HAIR. LOOKS GOOOOOD.
A FAMILY MAN GOTTA TAKE CARE'A HIS PEOPLE. I'M JUS' AN OL' RICKETY BAG O' BONES NOW.
I CAN'T STANDS NO MORE. YOU AN' YER KIN TAKE **MY SPOT** IN LINE.

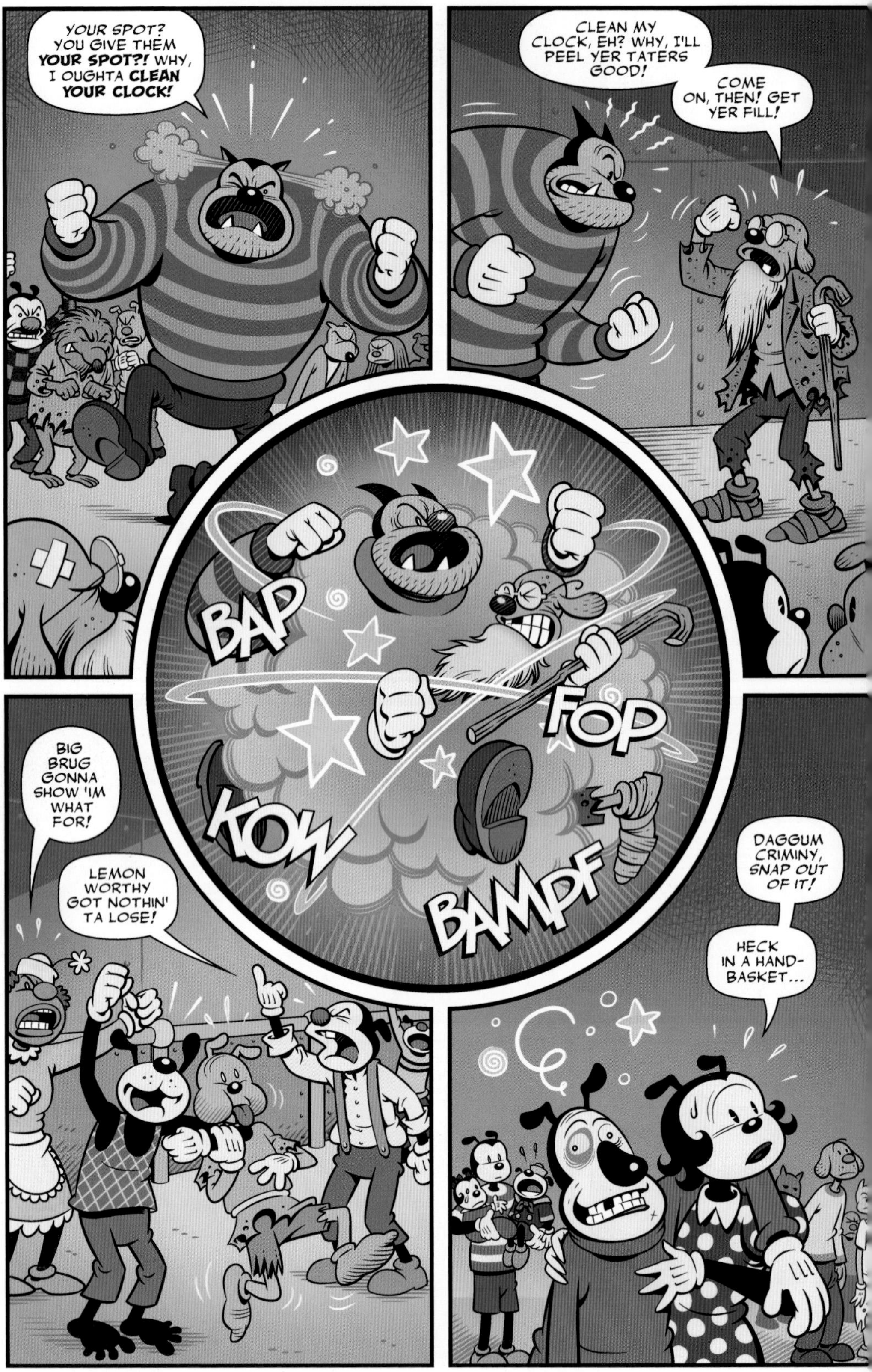
YOUR SPOT? YOU GIVE THEM **YOUR SPOT?!** WHY, I OUGHTA **CLEAN YOUR CLOCK!**
CLEAN MY CLOCK, EH? WHY, I'LL PEEL YER TATERS GOOD!
COME ON, THEN! GET YER FILL!
BAP
FOP
KOW
BAMPF
BIG BRUG GONNA SHOW 'IM WHAT FOR!
LEMON WORTHY GOT NOTHIN' TA LOSE!
DAGGUM CRIMINY, SNAP OUT OF IT!
HECK IN A HAND-BASKET...

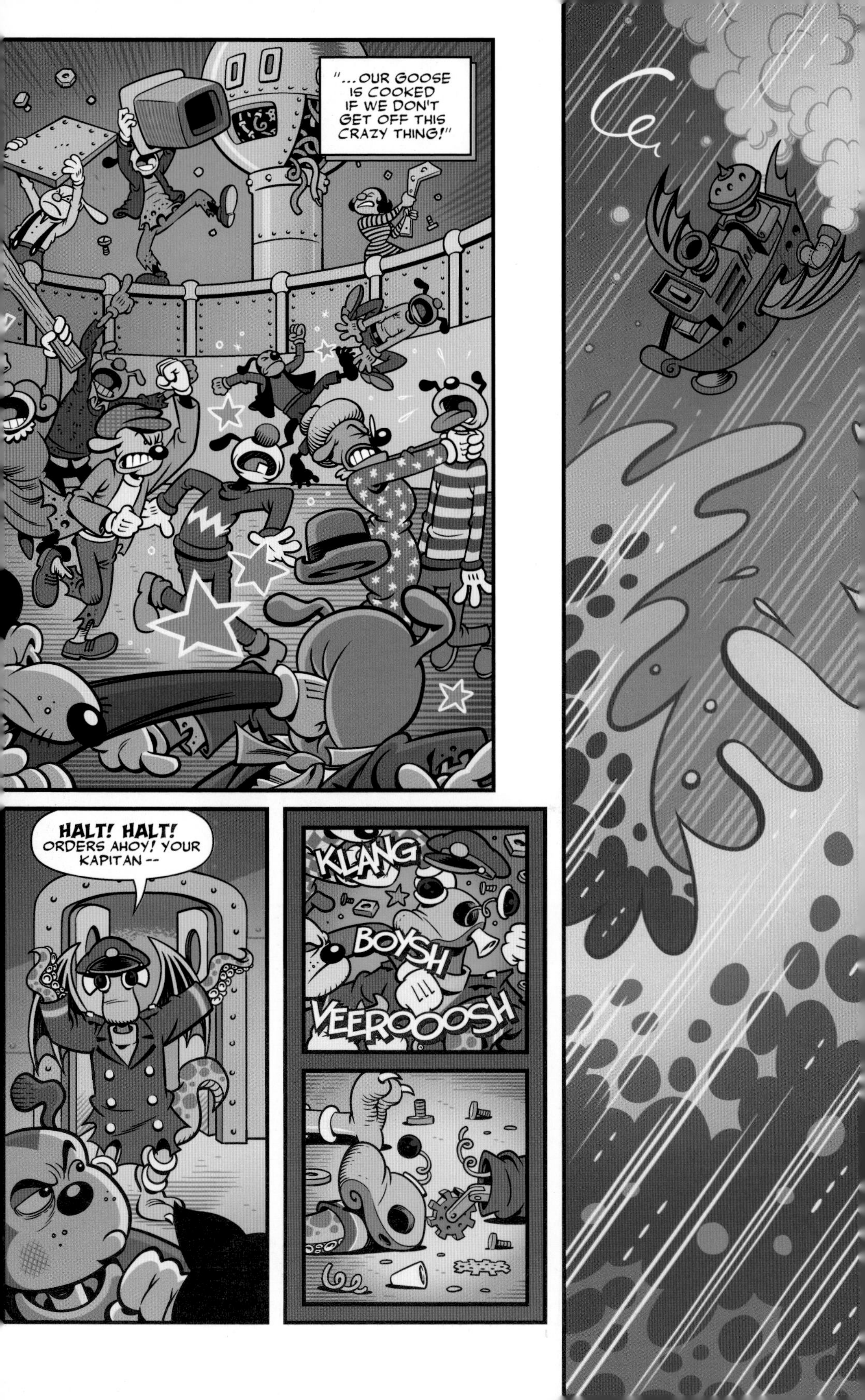
"...OUR GOOSE IS COOKED IF WE DON'T GET OFF THIS CRAZY THING!"
HALT! HALT! ORDERS AHOY! YOUR KAPITAN --
KLANG
BOYSH
VEEROOOSH

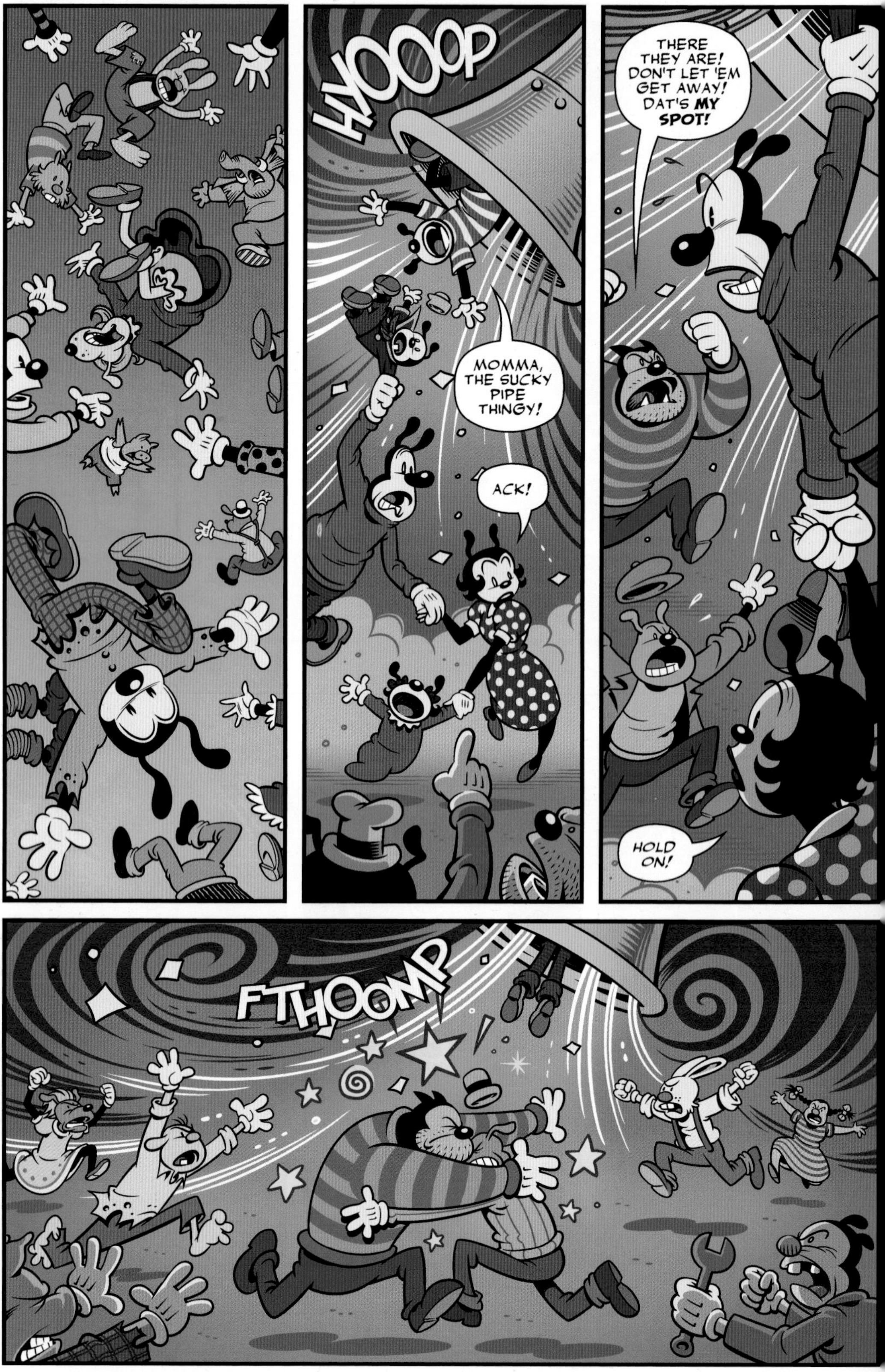

HYOOOP
MOMMA, THE SUCKY PIPE THINGY!
ACK!
THERE THEY ARE! DON'T LET 'EM GET AWAY! DAT'S **MY SPOT!**
HOLD ON!
FTHOOMP

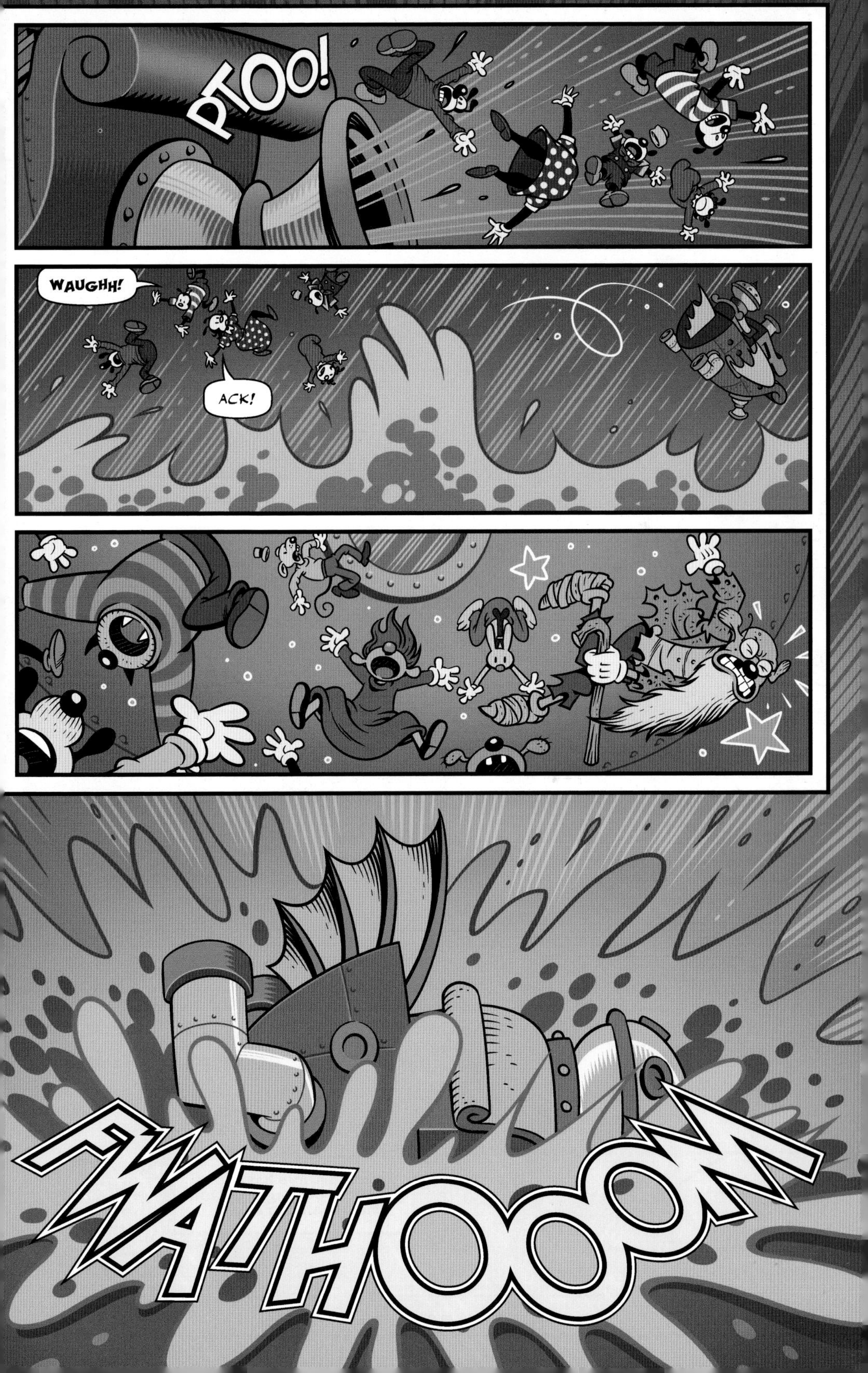
PTOO!
WAUGHH!
ACK!
FWATHOOOOM

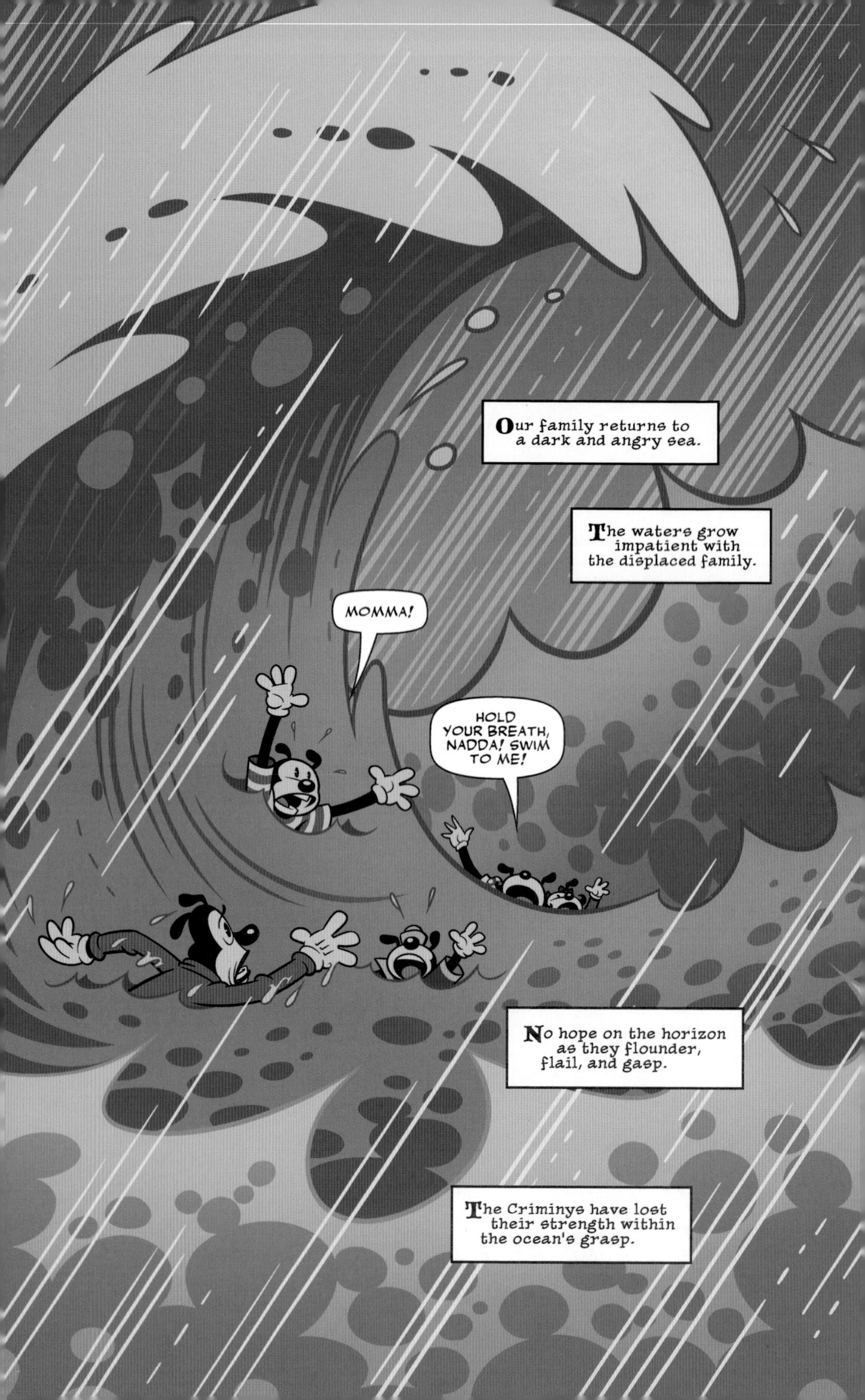
Our family returns to a dark and angry sea.
The waters grow impatient with the displaced family.
MOMMA!
HOLD YOUR BREATH, NADDA! SWIM TO ME!
No hope on the horizon as they flounder, flail, and gasp.
The Criminys have lost their strength within the ocean's grasp.

CHAPTER THREE

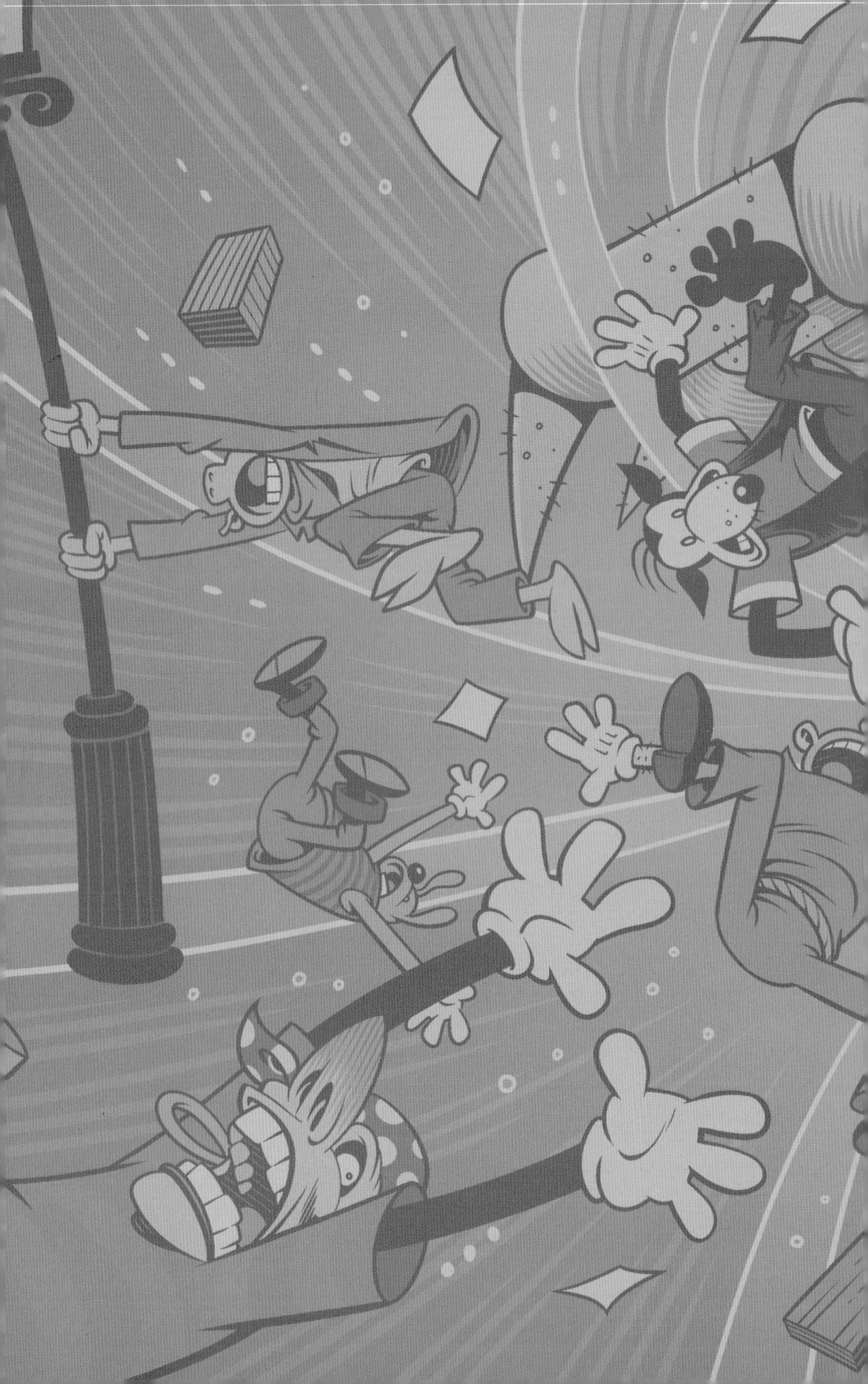

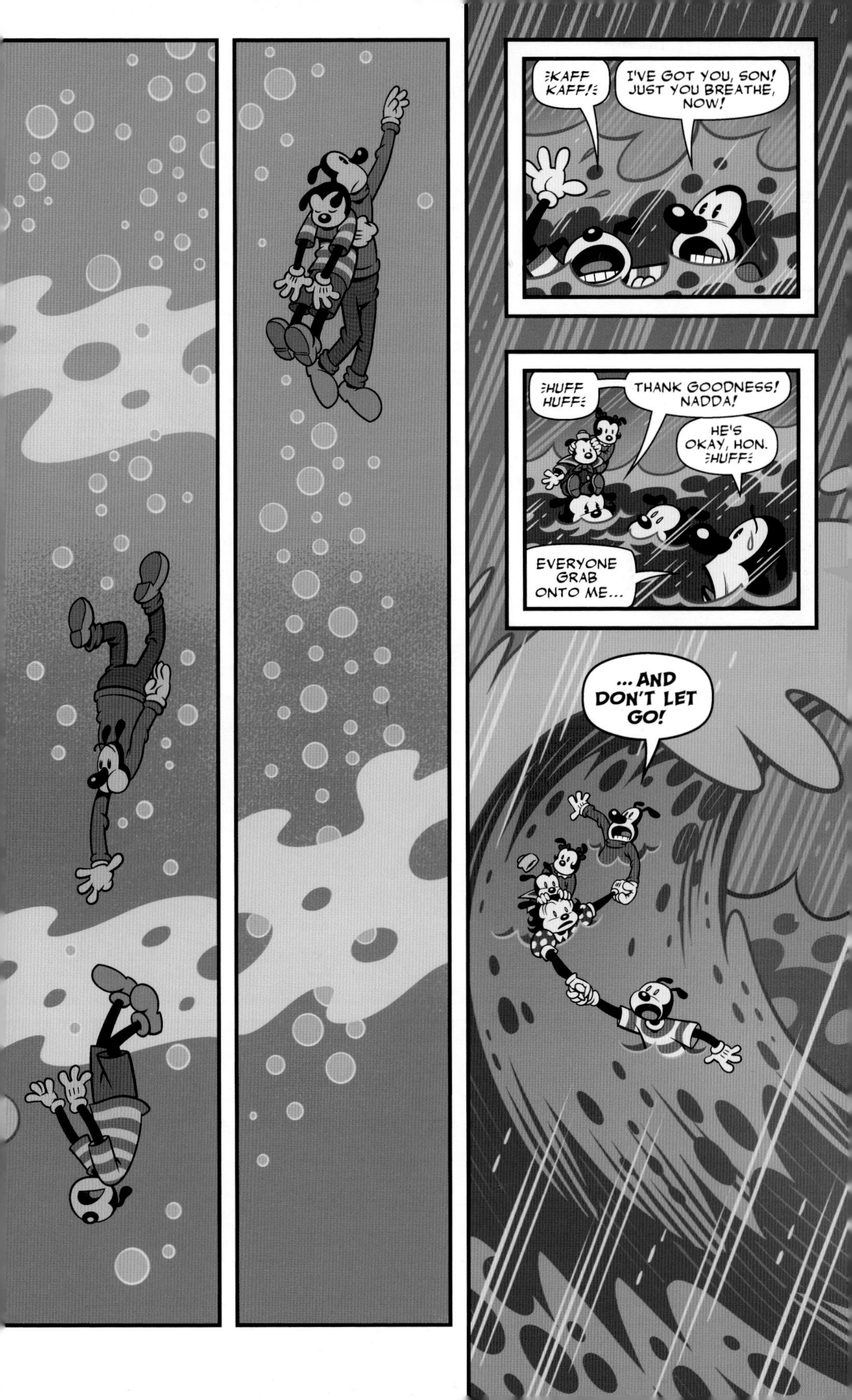

KAFF KAFF!
I'VE GOT YOU, SON! JUST YOU BREATHE, NOW!
HUFF HUFF
THANK GOODNESS! NADDA!
HE'S OKAY, HON. HUFF
EVERYONE GRAB ONTO ME...
...AND DON'T LET GO!

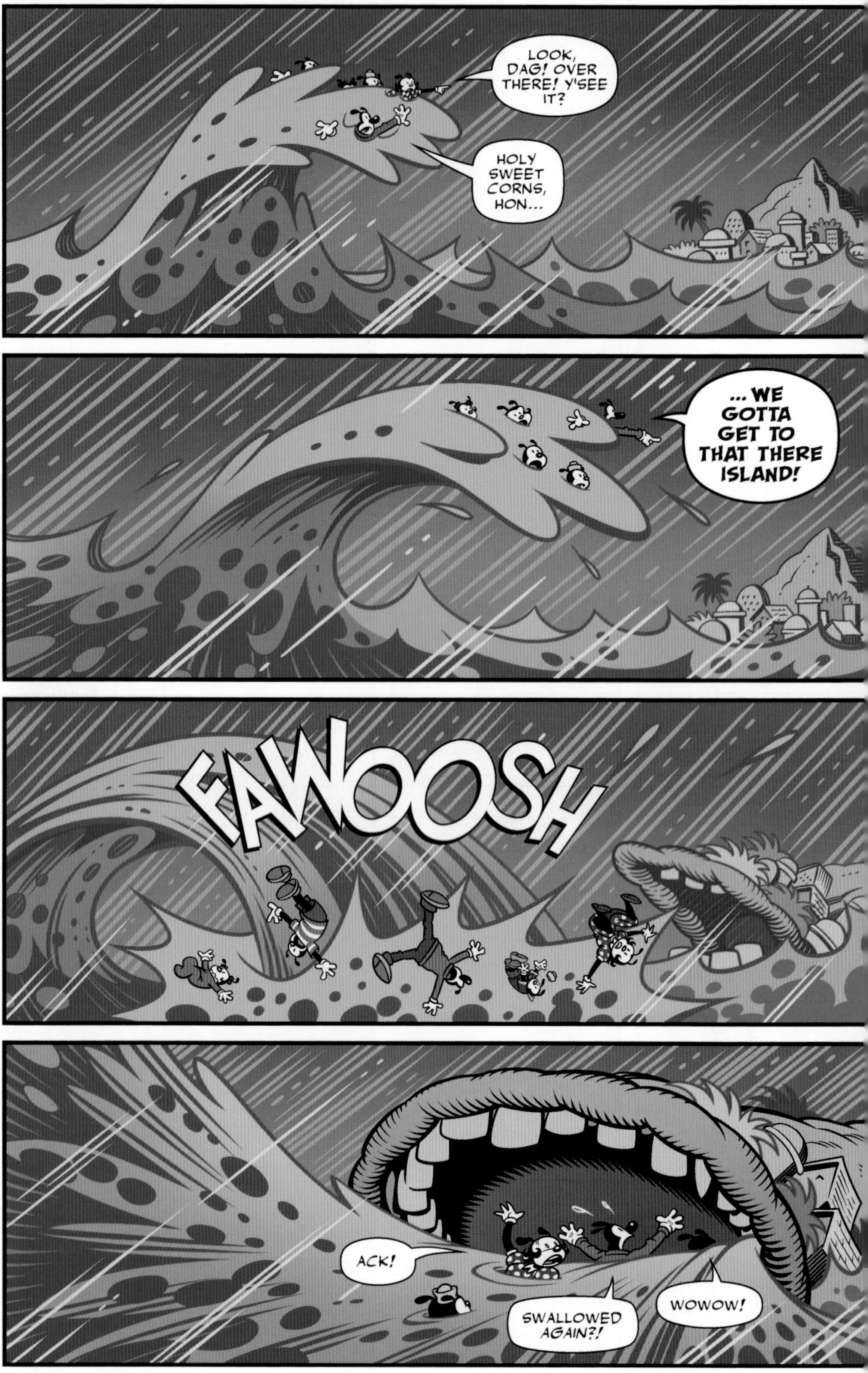
LOOK, DAG! OVER THERE! Y'SEE IT?
HOLY SWEET CORNS, HON...
...WE GOTTA GET TO THAT THERE ISLAND!
FAWOOSH
ACK!
SWALLOWED AGAIN?!
WOWOW!

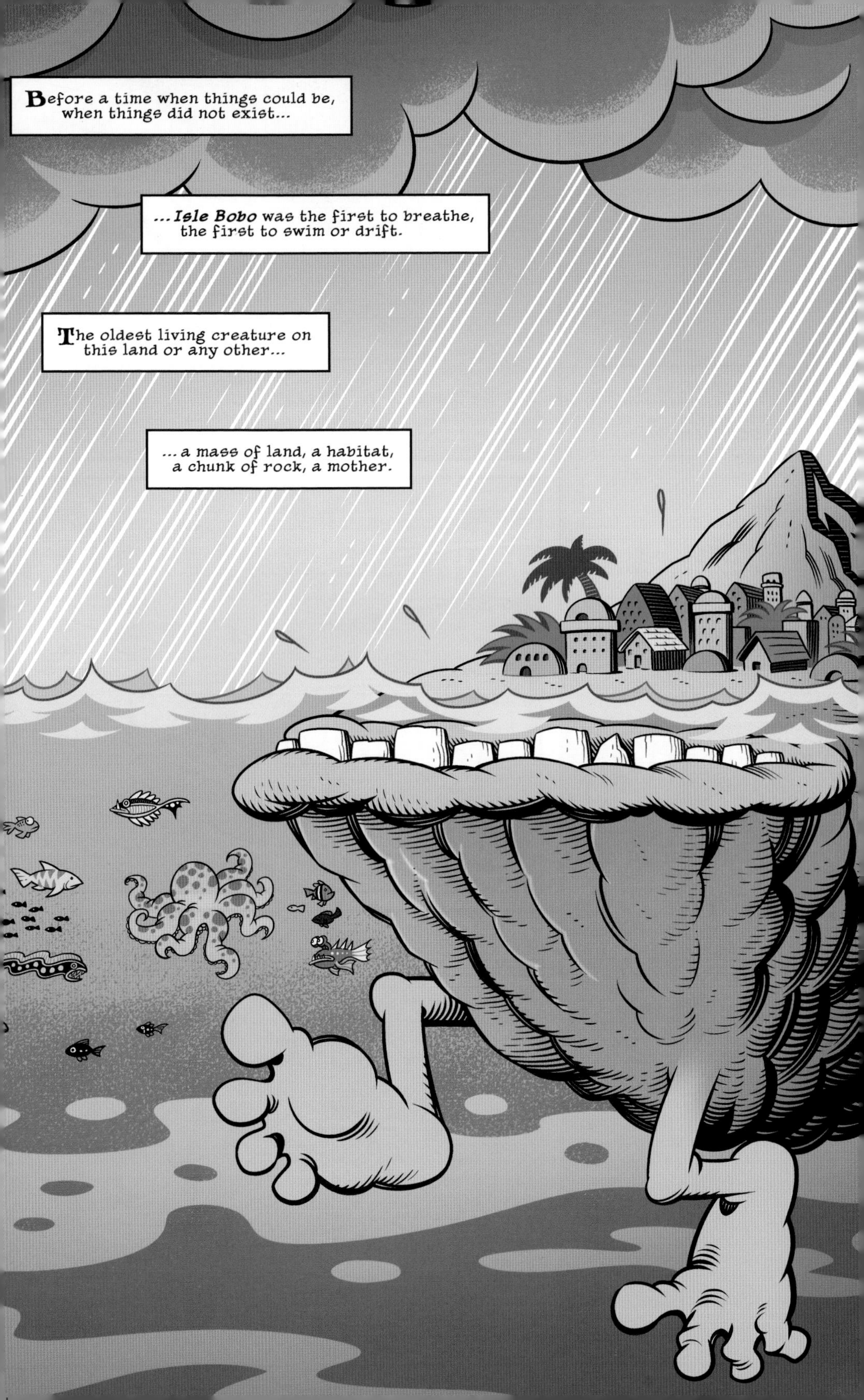
Before a time when things could be, when things did not exist...
...Isle Bobo was the first to breathe, the first to swim or drift.
The oldest living creature on this land or any other...
...a mass of land, a habitat, a chunk of rock, a mother.

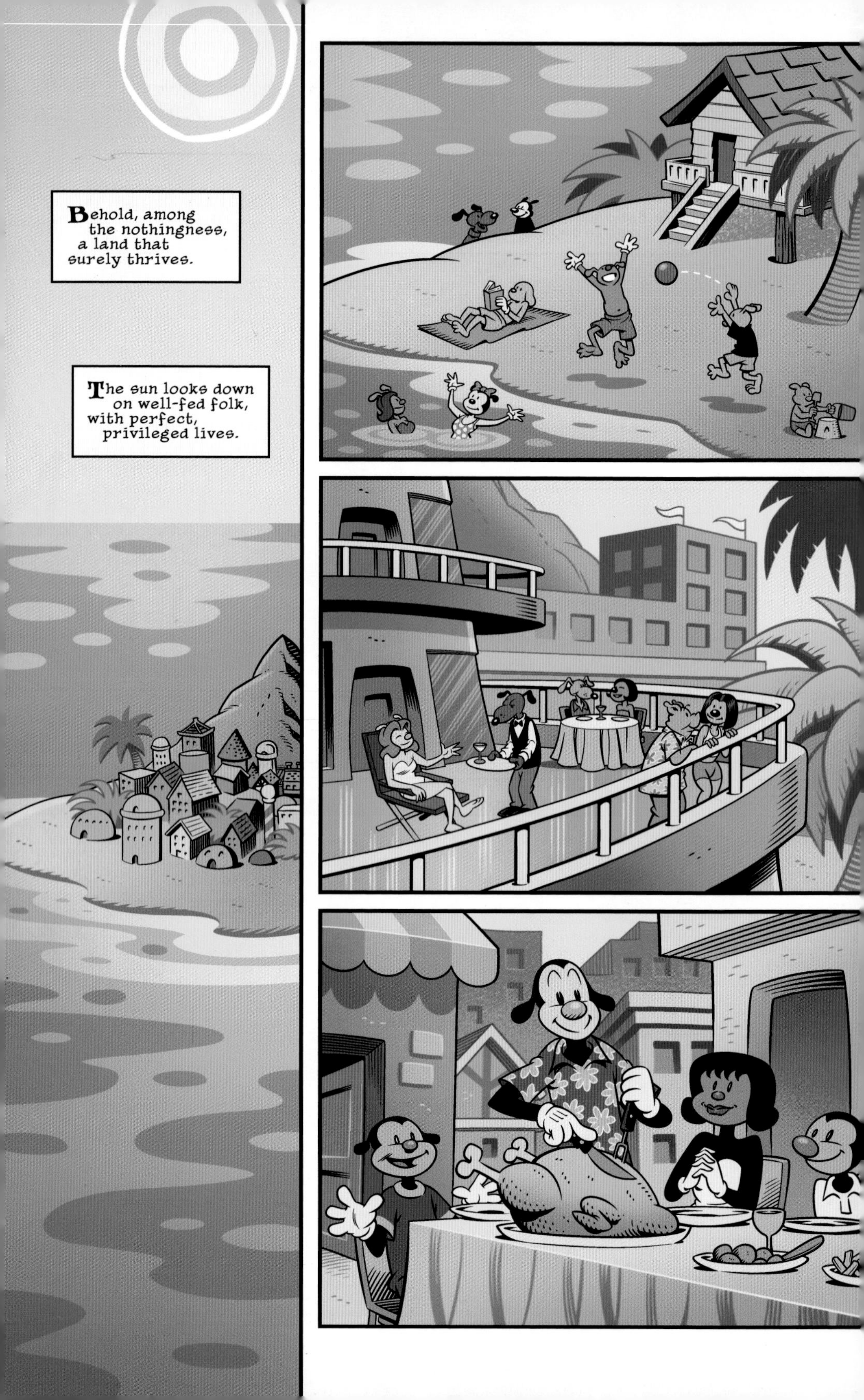
Behold, among the nothingness, a land that surely thrives.
The sun looks down on well-fed folk, with perfect, privileged lives.

Isle Bobo's belly's not so nice --
from pain there's no reprieve.

Down here you work...

...at whiptail's crack...

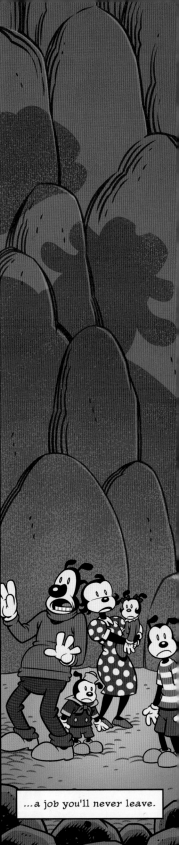

...a job you'll never leave.

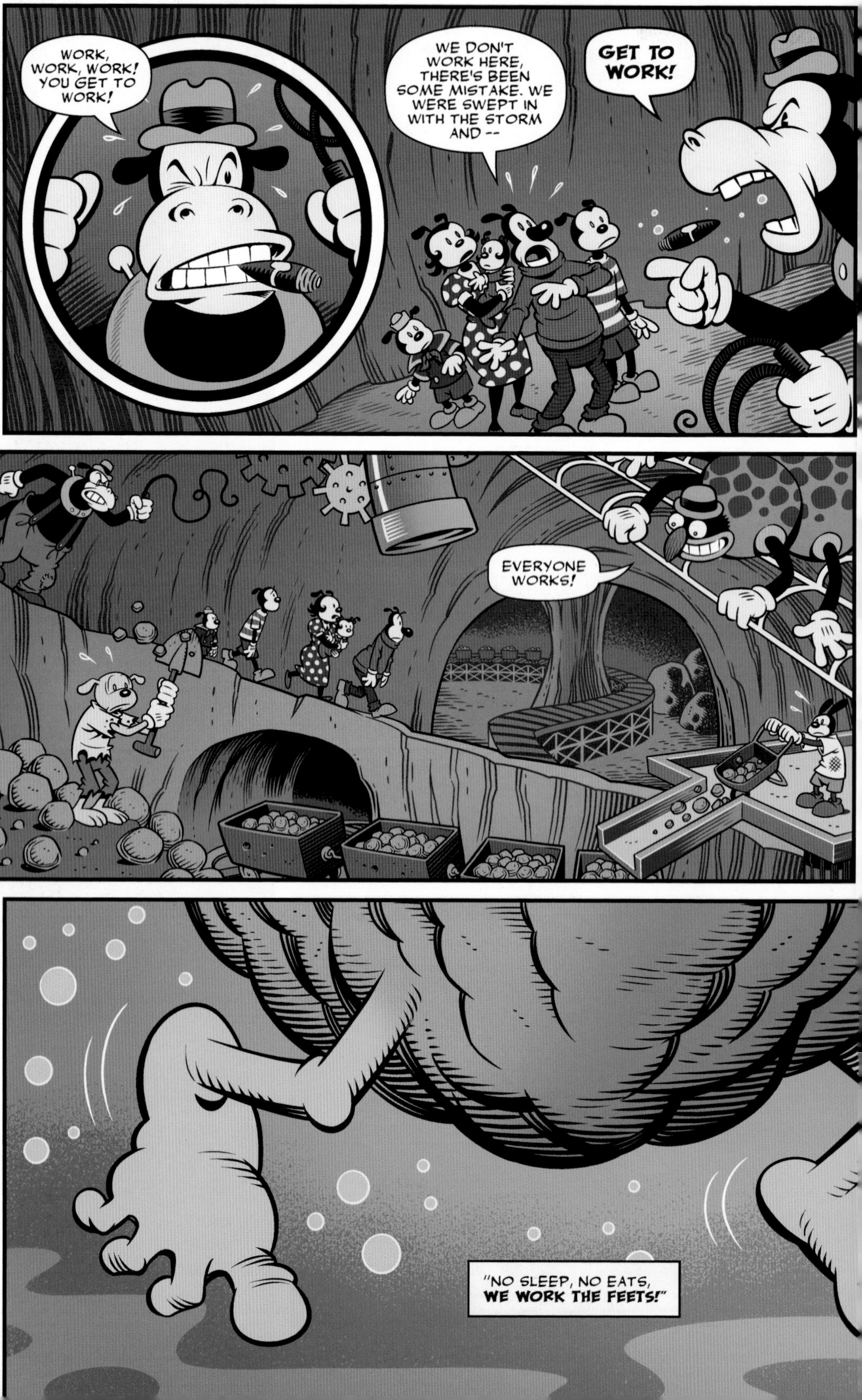
WORK, WORK, WORK! YOU GET TO WORK!
WE DON'T WORK HERE, THERE'S BEEN SOME MISTAKE. WE WERE SWEPT IN WITH THE STORM AND --
GET TO WORK!
EVERYONE WORKS!
"NO SLEEP, NO EATS, WE WORK THE FEETS!"

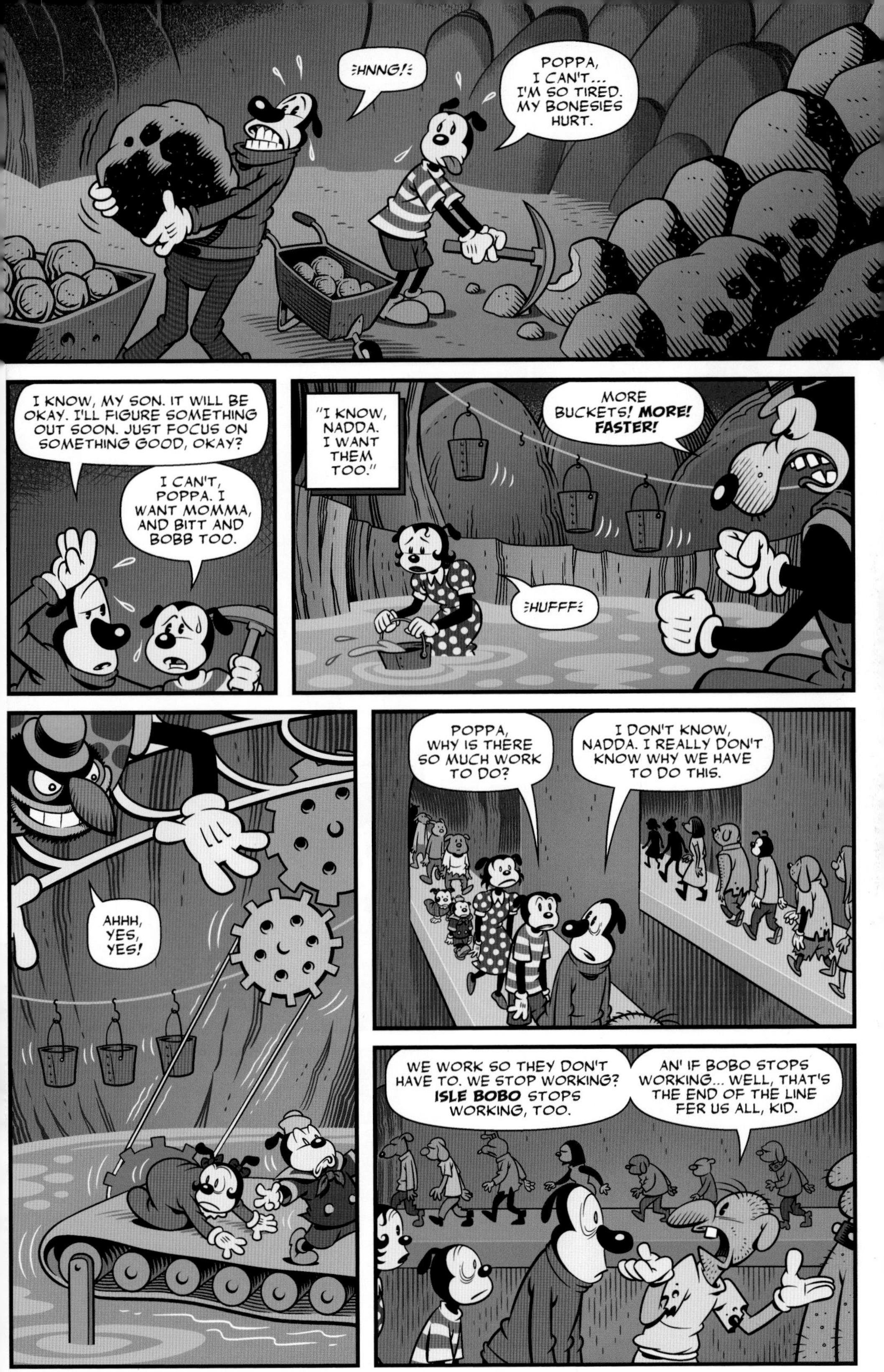

HNNG!
POPPA, I CAN'T... I'M SO TIRED. MY BONESIES HURT.
I KNOW, MY SON. IT WILL BE OKAY. I'LL FIGURE SOMETHING OUT SOON. JUST FOCUS ON SOMETHING GOOD, OKAY?
I CAN'T, POPPA. I WANT MOMMA, AND BITT AND BOBB TOO.
"I KNOW, NADDA. I WANT THEM TOO."
MORE BUCKETS! MORE! FASTER!
HUFFF
AHHH, YES, YES!
POPPA, WHY IS THERE SO MUCH WORK TO DO?
I DON'T KNOW, NADDA. I REALLY DON'T KNOW WHY WE HAVE TO DO THIS.
WE WORK SO THEY DON'T HAVE TO. WE STOP WORKING? ISLE BOBO STOPS WORKING, TOO.
AN' IF BOBO STOPS WORKING... WELL, THAT'S THE END OF THE LINE FER US ALL, KID.

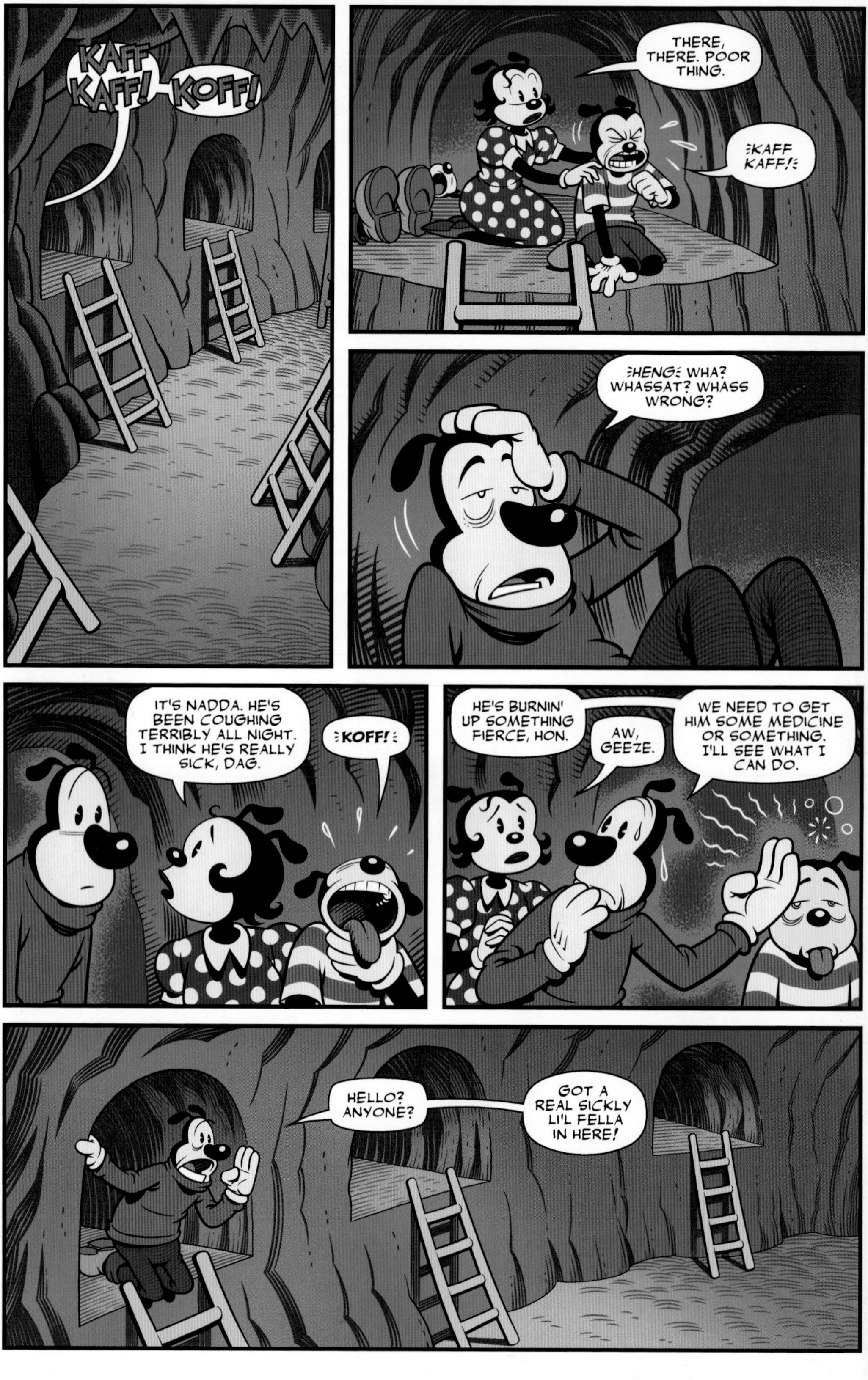
KAFF KAFF! KOFF!
THERE, THERE. POOR THING.
KAFF KAFF!
HENG WHA? WHASSAT? WHASS WRONG?
IT'S NADDA. HE'S BEEN COUGHING TERRIBLY ALL NIGHT. I THINK HE'S REALLY SICK, DAG.
KOFF!
HE'S BURNIN' UP SOMETHING FIERCE, HON.
AW, GEEZE.
WE NEED TO GET HIM SOME MEDICINE OR SOMETHING. I'LL SEE WHAT I CAN DO.
HELLO? ANYONE?
GOT A REAL SICKLY LI'L FELLA IN HERE!

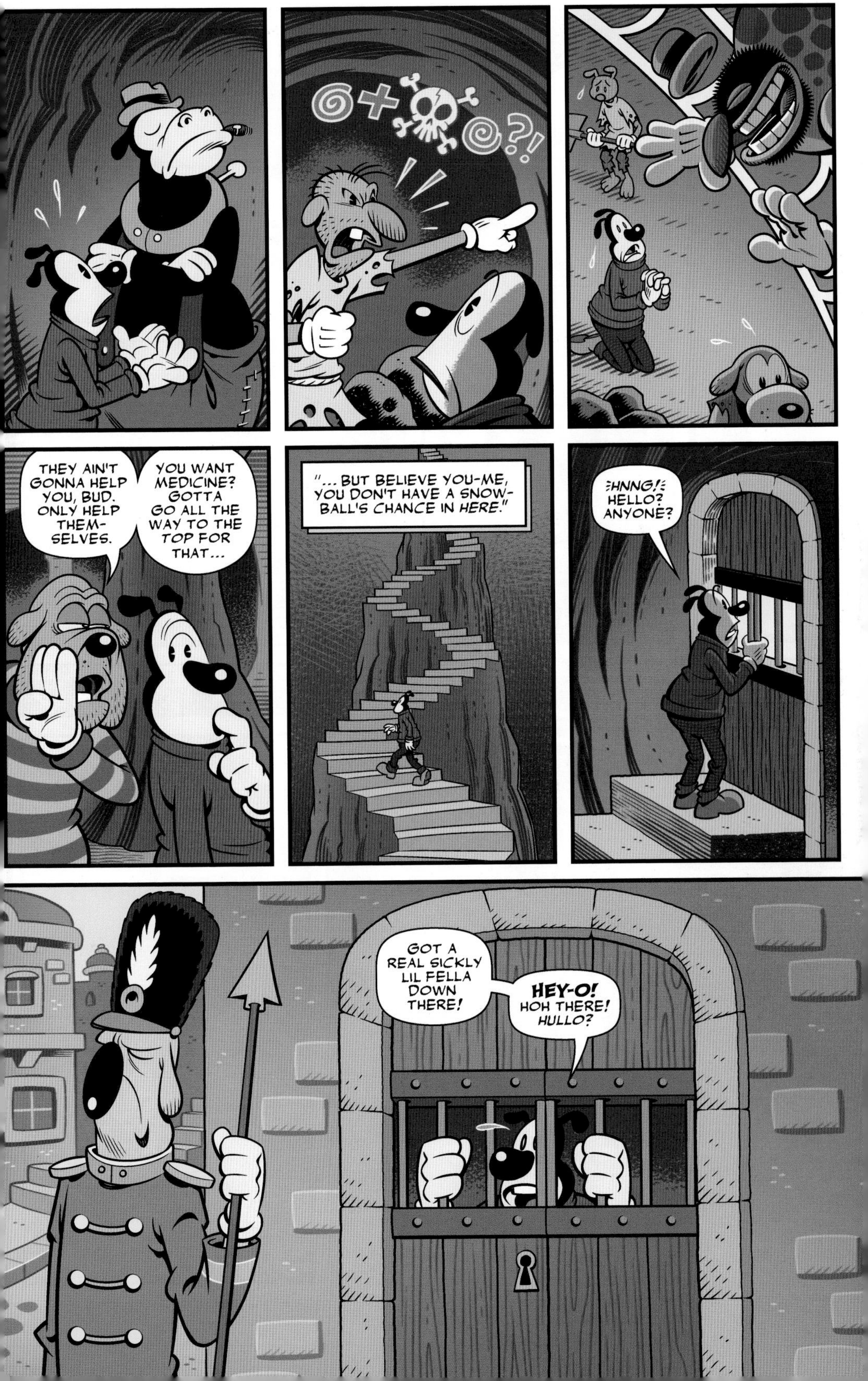

THEY AIN'T GONNA HELP YOU, BUD. ONLY HELP THEM-SELVES.
YOU WANT MEDICINE? GOTTA GO ALL THE WAY TO THE TOP FOR THAT...
"...BUT BELIEVE YOU-ME, YOU DON'T HAVE A SNOW-BALL'S CHANCE IN HERE."
HNNG! HELLO? ANYONE?
GOT A REAL SICKLY LIL FELLA DOWN THERE!
HEY-O! HOH THERE! HULLO?

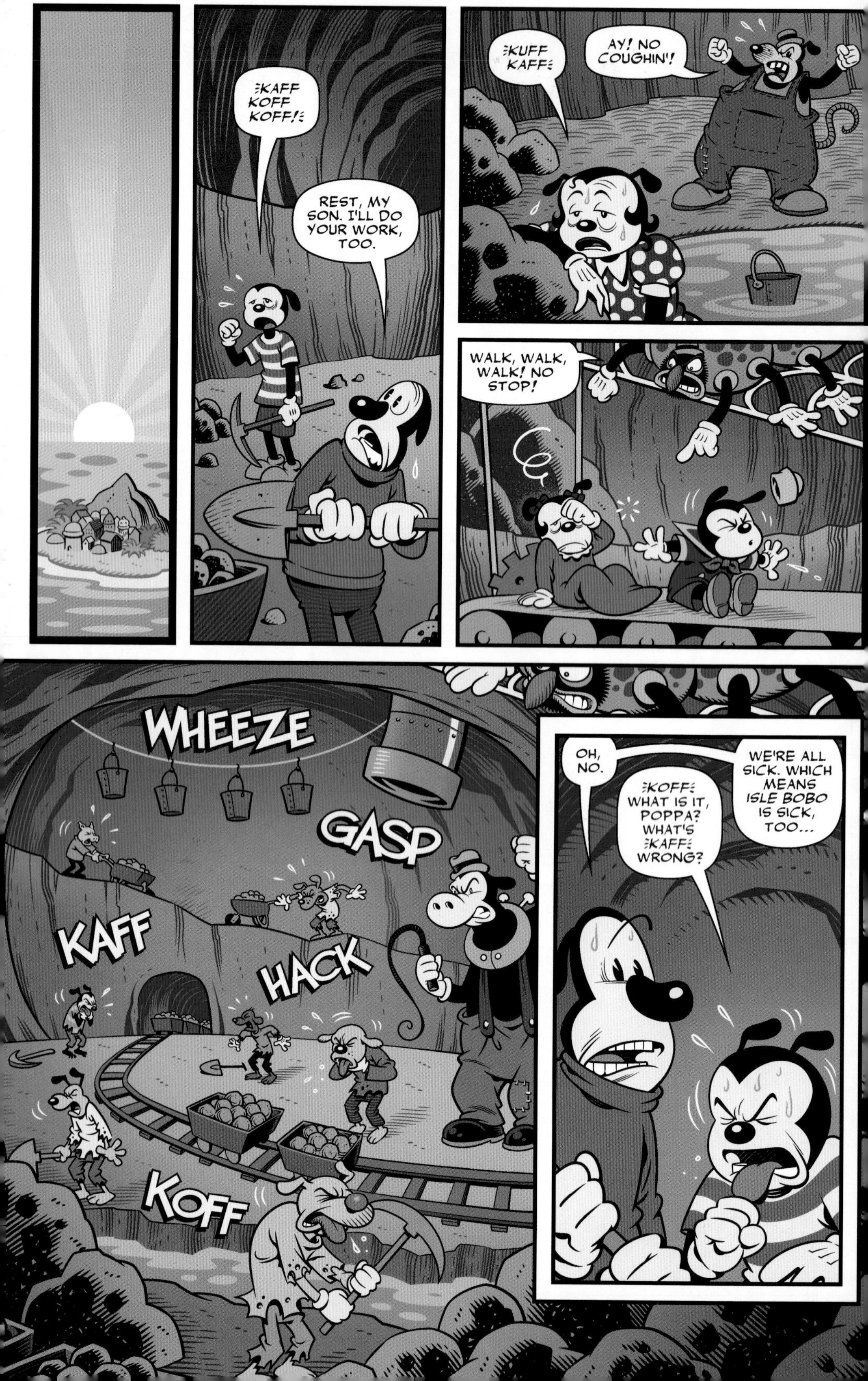

⁝KAFF KOFF KOFF!⁝
REST, MY SON. I'LL DO YOUR WORK, TOO.
⁝KUFF KAFF⁝
AY! NO COUGHIN'!
WALK, WALK, WALK! NO STOP!
WHEEZE
GASP
KAFF
HACK
KOFF
OH, NO.
⁝KOFF⁝ WHAT IS IT, POPPA? WHAT'S ⁝KAFF⁝ WRONG?
WE'RE ALL SICK. WHICH MEANS ISLE BOBO IS SICK, TOO...

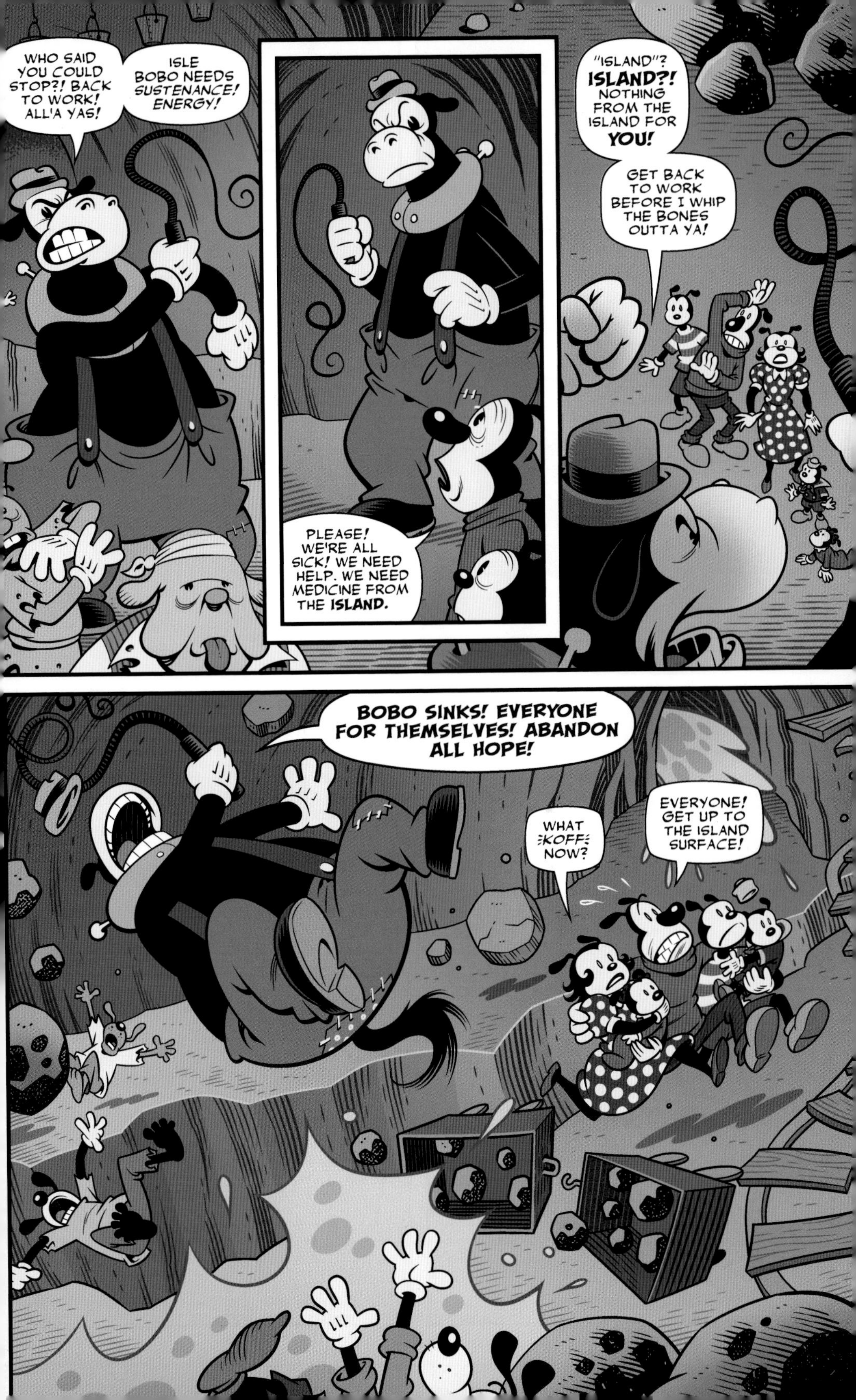
WHO SAID YOU COULD STOP?! BACK TO WORK! ALL'A YAS!
ISLE BOBO NEEDS SUSTENANCE! ENERGY!
PLEASE! WE'RE ALL SICK! WE NEED HELP. WE NEED MEDICINE FROM THE ISLAND.
"ISLAND"? ISLAND?! NOTHING FROM THE ISLAND FOR YOU!
GET BACK TO WORK BEFORE I WHIP THE BONES OUTTA YA!
BOBO SINKS! EVERYONE FOR THEMSELVES! ABANDON ALL HOPE!
WHAT KOFF NOW?
EVERYONE! GET UP TO THE ISLAND SURFACE!

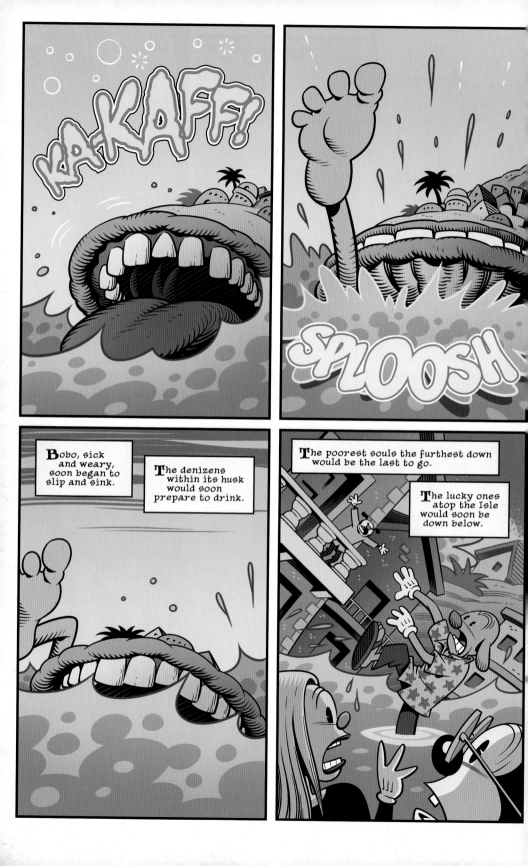

KA-KAFF!

SPLOOSH

Bobo, sick and weary, soon began to slip and sink.

The denizens within its husk would soon prepare to drink.

The poorest souls the furthest down would be the last to go.

The lucky ones atop the Isle would soon be down below.

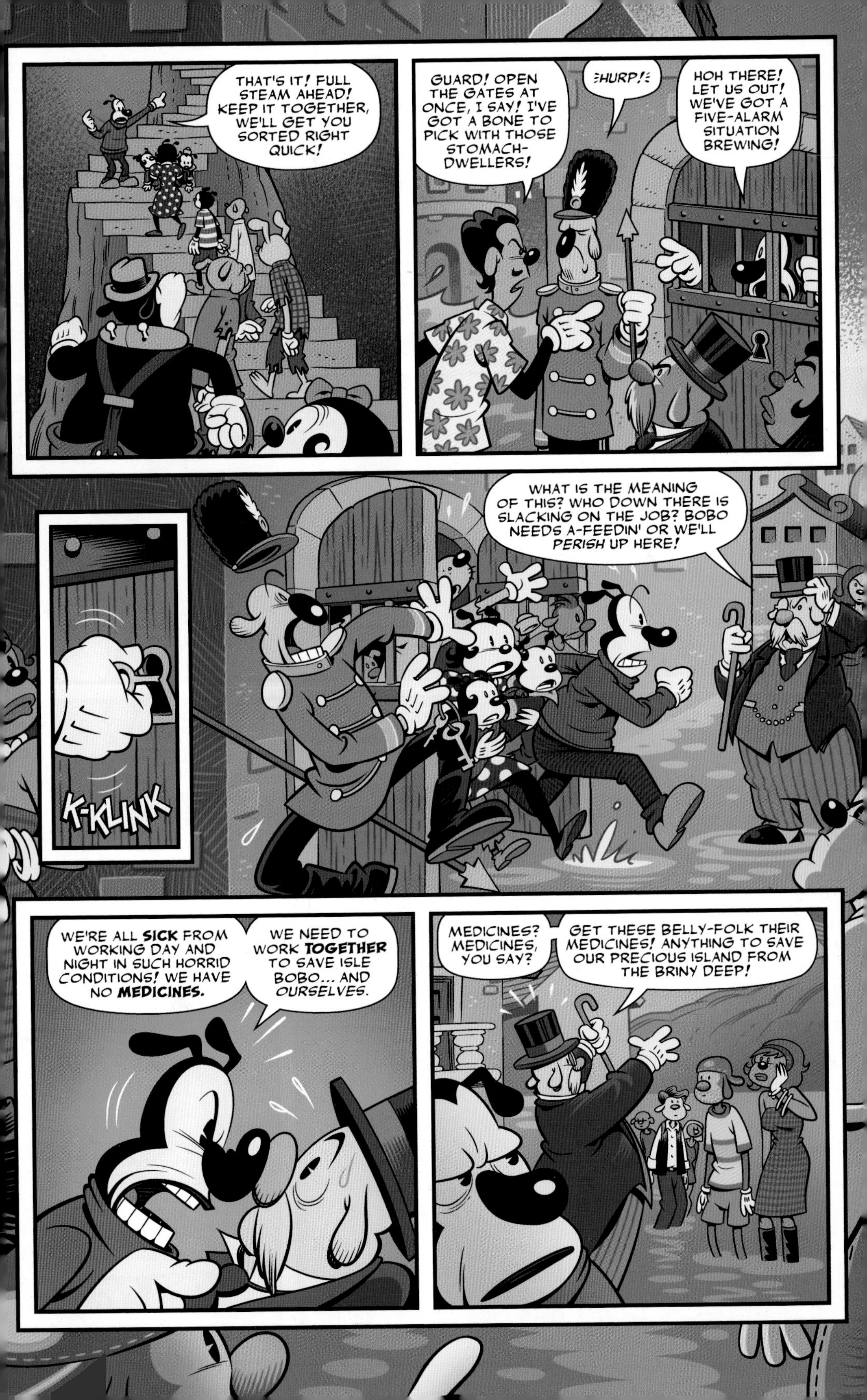
THAT'S IT! FULL STEAM AHEAD! KEEP IT TOGETHER, WE'LL GET YOU SORTED RIGHT QUICK!
GUARD! OPEN THE GATES AT ONCE, I SAY! I'VE GOT A BONE TO PICK WITH THOSE STOMACH-DWELLERS!
HURP!
HOH THERE! LET US OUT! WE'VE GOT A FIVE-ALARM SITUATION BREWING!
K-KLINK
WHAT IS THE MEANING OF THIS? WHO DOWN THERE IS SLACKING ON THE JOB? BOBO NEEDS A-FEEDIN' OR WE'LL PERISH UP HERE!
WE'RE ALL SICK FROM WORKING DAY AND NIGHT IN SUCH HORRID CONDITIONS! WE HAVE NO MEDICINES.
WE NEED TO WORK TOGETHER TO SAVE ISLE BOBO... AND OURSELVES.
MEDICINES? MEDICINES, YOU SAY?
GET THESE BELLY-FOLK THEIR MEDICINES! ANYTHING TO SAVE OUR PRECIOUS ISLAND FROM THE BRINY DEEP!

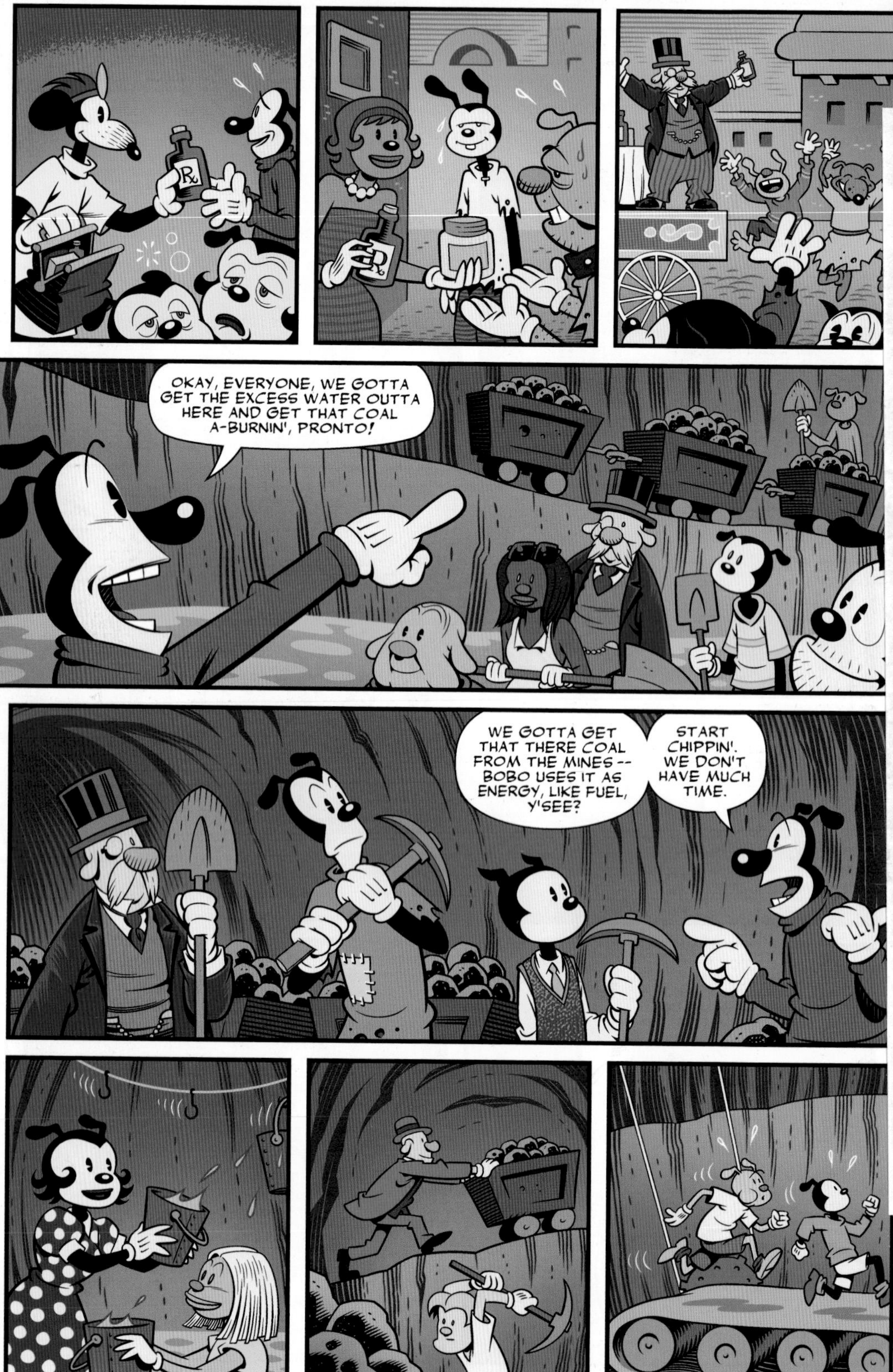
OKAY, EVERYONE, WE GOTTA GET THE EXCESS WATER OUTTA HERE AND GET THAT COAL A-BURNIN', PRONTO!
WE GOTTA GET THAT THERE COAL FROM THE MINES -- BOBO USES IT AS ENERGY, LIKE FUEL, Y'SEE?
START CHIPPIN'. WE DON'T HAVE MUCH TIME.

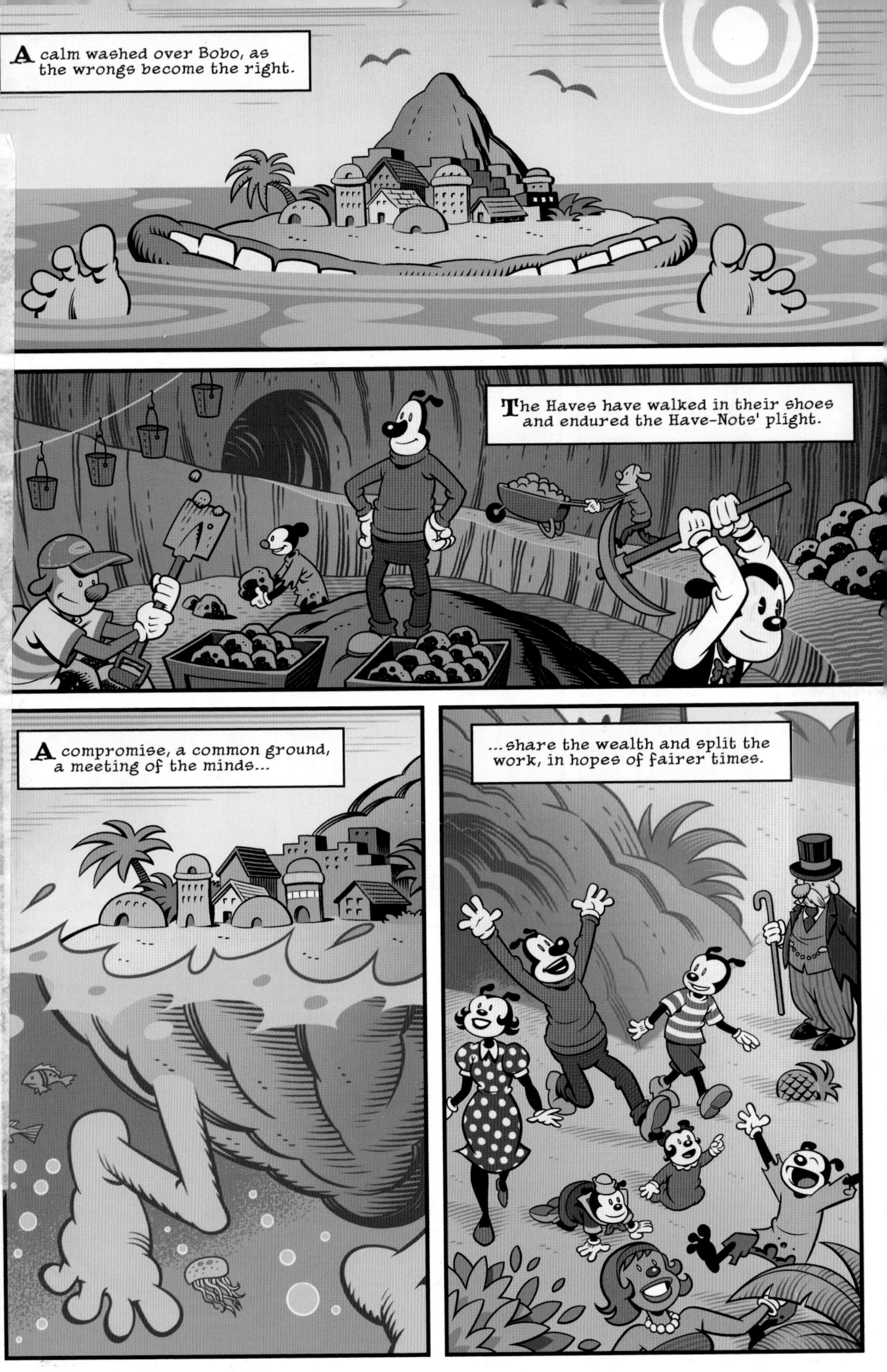
A calm washed over Bobo, as the wrongs become the right.
The Haves have walked in their shoes and endured the Have-Nots' plight.
A compromise, a common ground, a meeting of the minds...
...share the wealth and split the work, in hopes of fairer times.

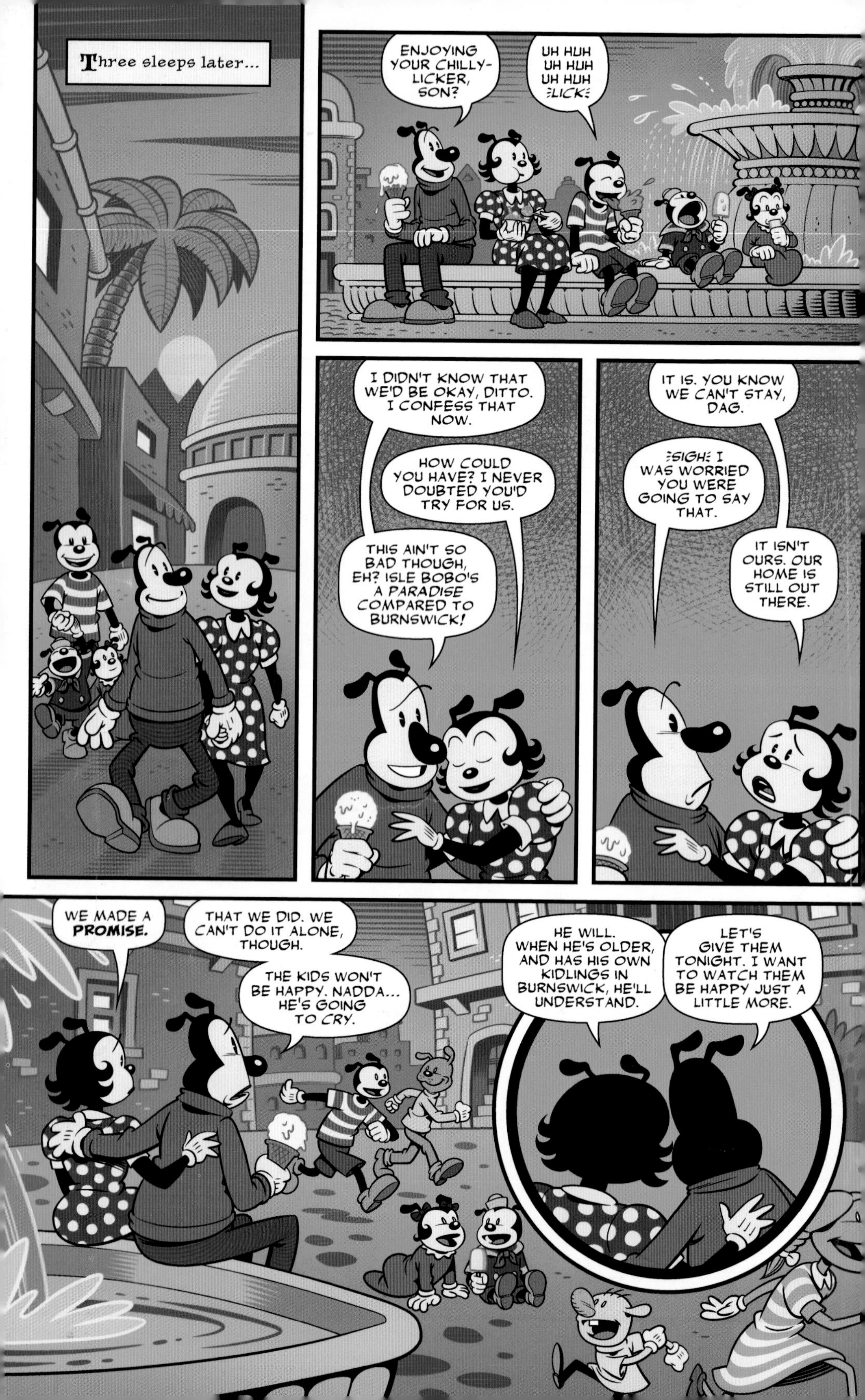
Three sleeps later...
ENJOYING YOUR CHILLY-LICKER, SON?
UH HUH UH HUH UH HUH ⸗LICK⸗
I DIDN'T KNOW THAT WE'D BE OKAY, DITTO. I CONFESS THAT NOW.
HOW COULD YOU HAVE? I NEVER DOUBTED YOU'D TRY FOR US.
THIS AIN'T SO BAD THOUGH, EH? ISLE BOBO'S A PARADISE COMPARED TO BURNSWICK!
IT IS. YOU KNOW WE CAN'T STAY, DAG.
⸗SIGH⸗ I WAS WORRIED YOU WERE GOING TO SAY THAT.
IT ISN'T OURS. OUR HOME IS STILL OUT THERE.
WE MADE A PROMISE.
THAT WE DID. WE CAN'T DO IT ALONE, THOUGH.
THE KIDS WON'T BE HAPPY. NADDA... HE'S GOING TO CRY.
HE WILL. WHEN HE'S OLDER, AND HAS HIS OWN KIDLINGS IN BURNSWICK, HE'LL UNDERSTAND.
LET'S GIVE THEM TONIGHT. I WANT TO WATCH THEM BE HAPPY JUST A LITTLE MORE.

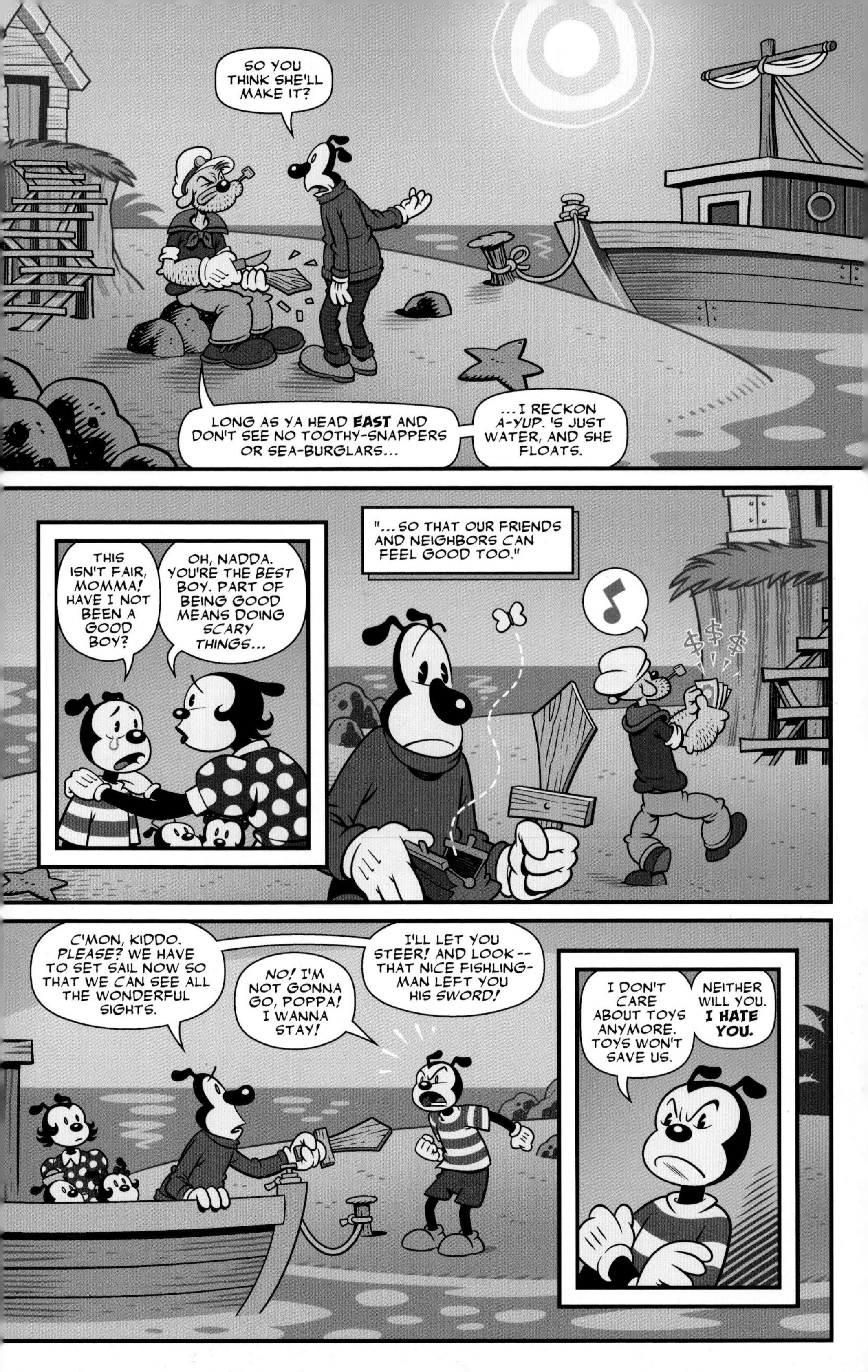

SO YOU THINK SHE'LL MAKE IT?
LONG AS YA HEAD **EAST** AND DON'T SEE NO TOOTHY-SNAPPERS OR SEA-BURGLARS...
...I RECKON *A-YUP*. 'S JUST WATER, AND SHE FLOATS.
"...SO THAT OUR FRIENDS AND NEIGHBORS CAN FEEL GOOD TOO."
THIS ISN'T FAIR, MOMMA! HAVE I NOT BEEN A GOOD BOY?
OH, NADDA. YOU'RE THE *BEST* BOY. PART OF BEING GOOD MEANS DOING *SCARY* THINGS...
C'MON, KIDDO. *PLEASE?* WE HAVE TO SET SAIL NOW SO THAT WE CAN SEE ALL THE WONDERFUL SIGHTS.
NO! I'M NOT GONNA GO, POPPA! I WANNA STAY!
I'LL LET YOU STEER! AND LOOK--THAT NICE FISHLING-MAN LEFT YOU HIS *SWORD!*
I DON'T CARE ABOUT TOYS ANYMORE. TOYS WON'T SAVE US.
NEITHER WILL YOU. **I HATE YOU.**

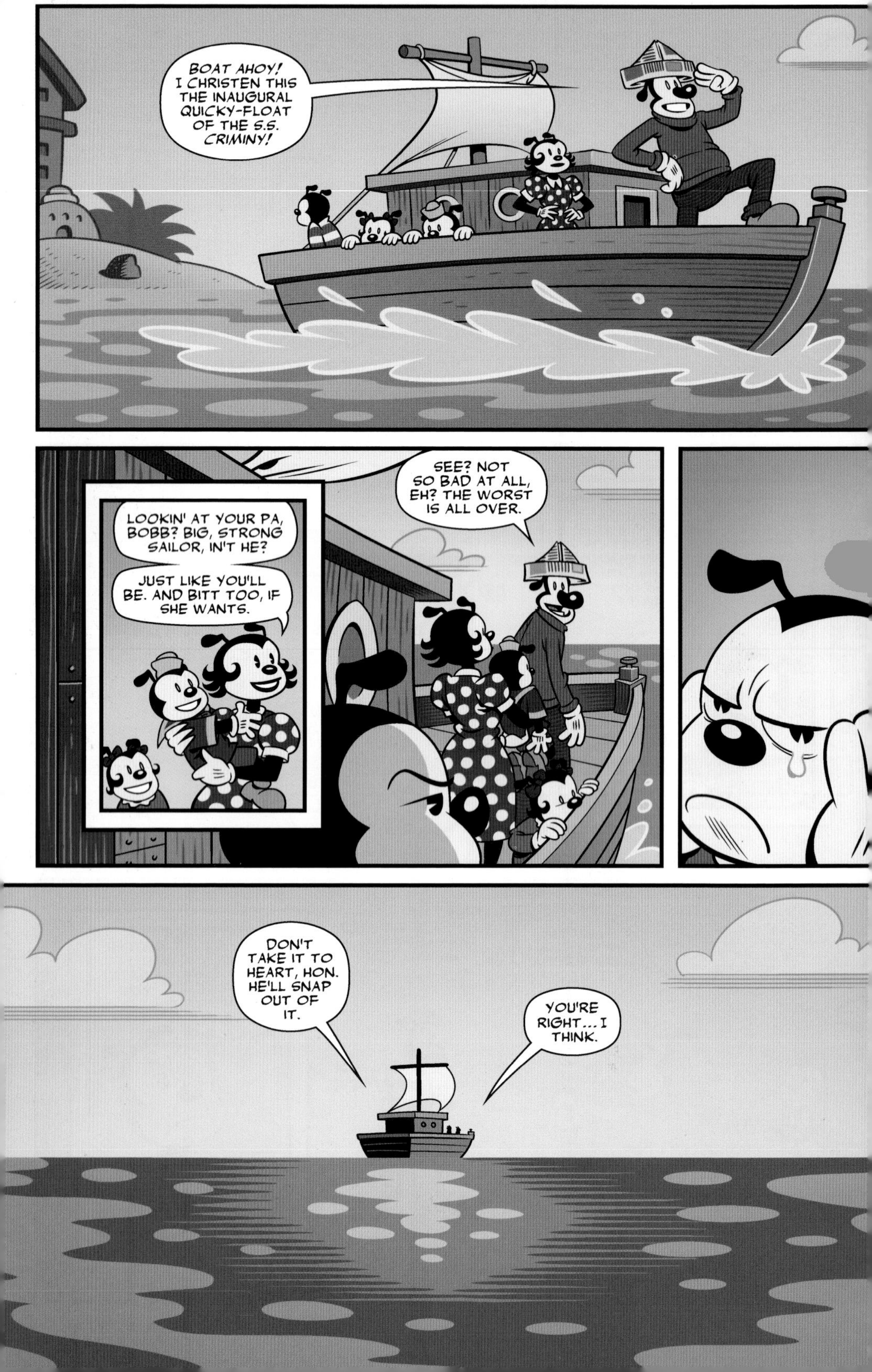
BOAT AHOY! I CHRISTEN THIS THE INAUGURAL QUICKY-FLOAT OF THE S.S. CRIMINY!
LOOKIN' AT YOUR PA, BOBB? BIG, STRONG SAILOR, IN'T HE?
JUST LIKE YOU'LL BE. AND BITT TOO, IF SHE WANTS.
SEE? NOT SO BAD AT ALL, EH? THE WORST IS ALL OVER.
DON'T TAKE IT TO HEART, HON. HE'LL SNAP OUT OF IT.
YOU'RE RIGHT... I THINK.

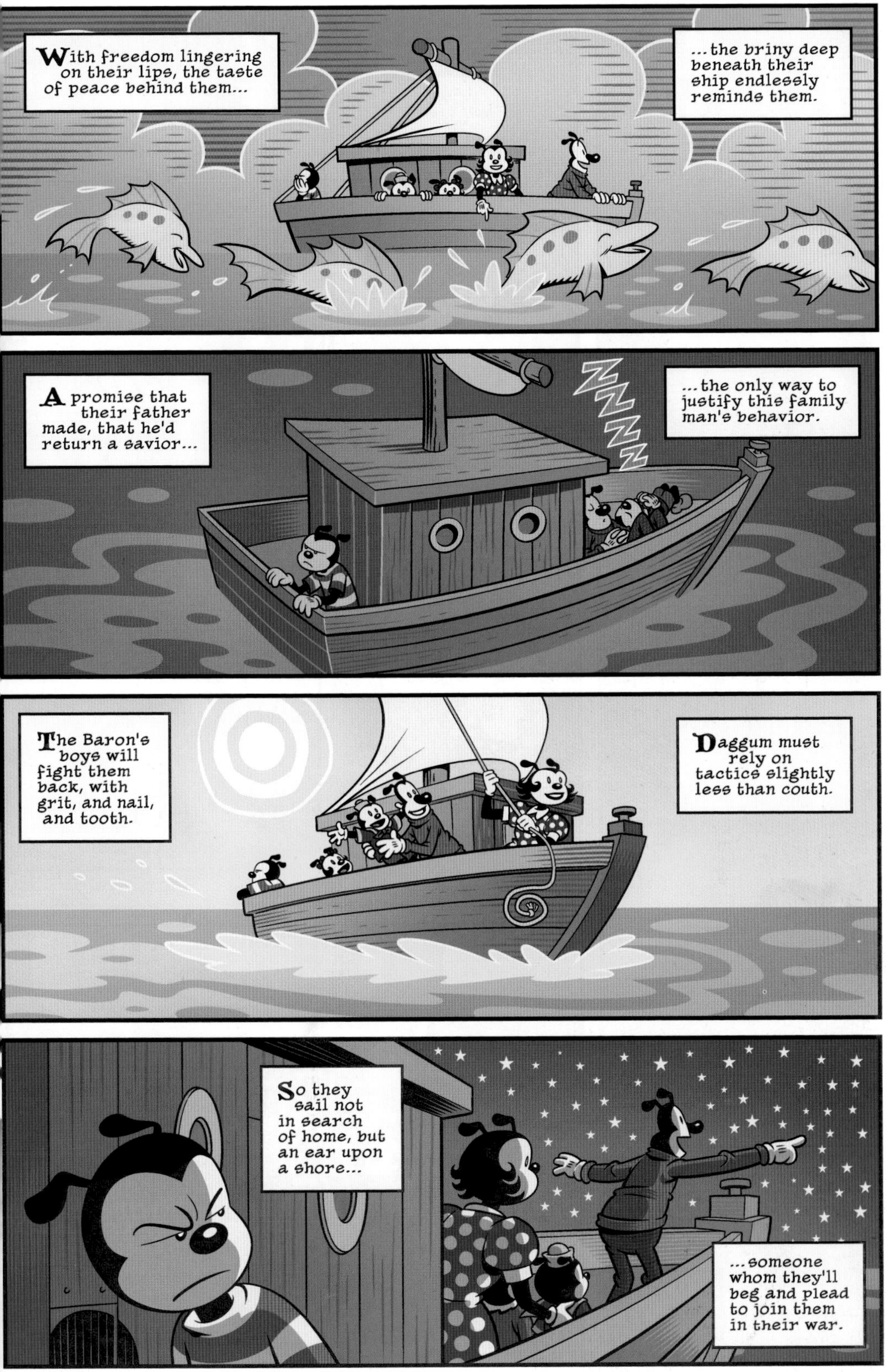
With freedom lingering on their lips, the taste of peace behind them...
...the briny deep beneath their ship endlessly reminds them.
A promise that their father made, that he'd return a savior...
...the only way to justify this family man's behavior.
The Baron's boys will fight them back, with grit, and nail, and tooth.
Daggum must rely on tactics slightly less than couth.
So they sail not in search of home, but an ear upon a shore...
...someone whom they'll beg and plead to join them in their war.

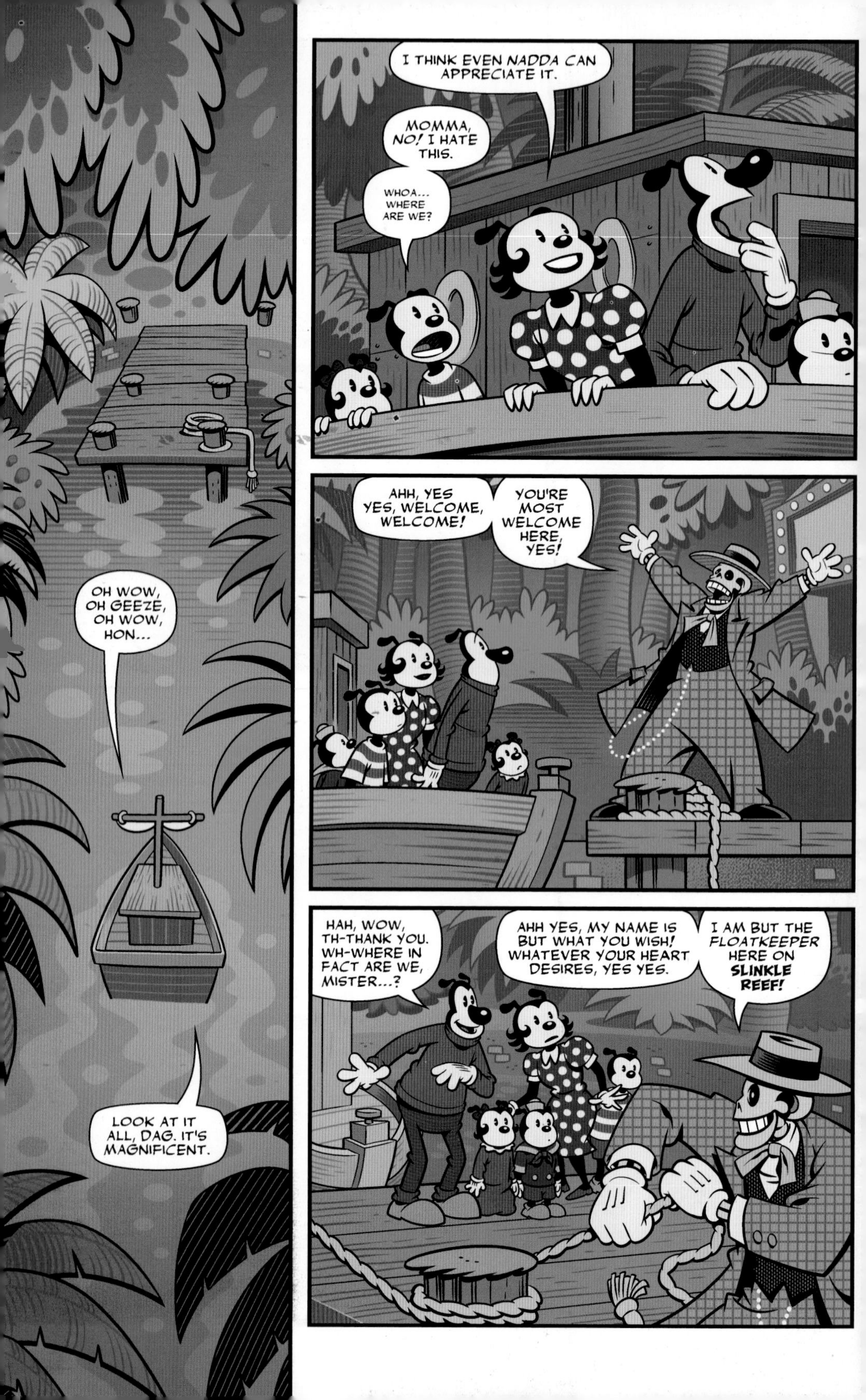
OH WOW, OH GEEZE, OH WOW, HON...
LOOK AT IT ALL, DAG. IT'S MAGNIFICENT.
I THINK EVEN NADDA CAN APPRECIATE IT.
MOMMA, NO! I HATE THIS.
WHOA... WHERE ARE WE?
AHH, YES YES, WELCOME, WELCOME!
YOU'RE MOST WELCOME HERE, YES!
HAH, WOW, TH-THANK YOU. WH-WHERE IN FACT ARE WE, MISTER...?
AHH YES, MY NAME IS BUT WHAT YOU WISH! WHATEVER YOUR HEART DESIRES, YES YES.
I AM BUT THE FLOATKEEPER HERE ON SLINKLE REEF!

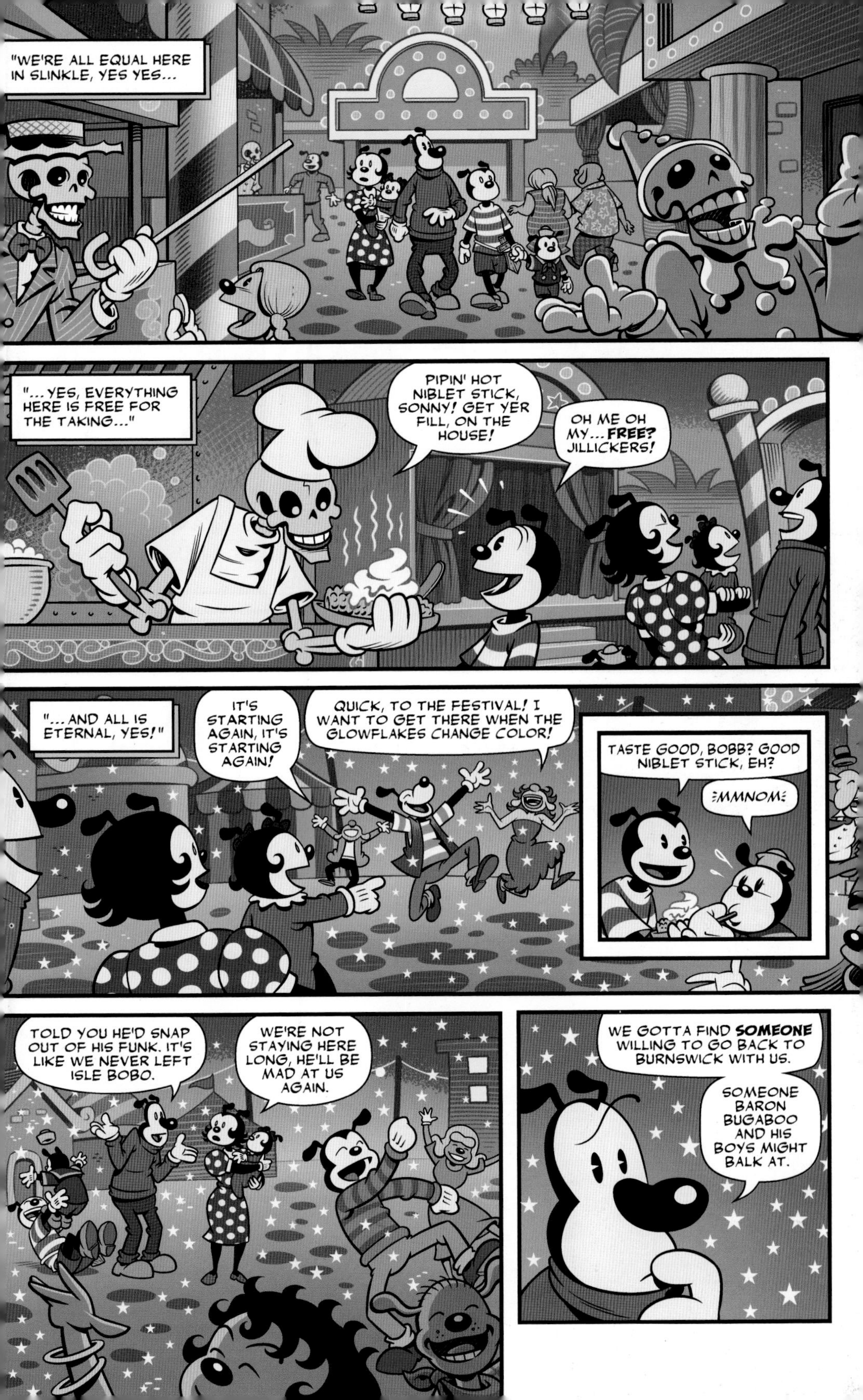
"WE'RE ALL EQUAL HERE IN SLINKLE, YES YES...
"...YES, EVERYTHING HERE IS FREE FOR THE TAKING..."
PIPIN' HOT NIBLET STICK, SONNY! GET YER FILL, ON THE HOUSE!
OH ME OH MY... **FREE?** JILLICKERS!
"...AND ALL IS ETERNAL, YES!"
IT'S STARTING AGAIN, IT'S STARTING AGAIN!
QUICK, TO THE FESTIVAL! I WANT TO GET THERE WHEN THE GLOWFLAKES CHANGE COLOR!
TASTE GOOD, BOBB? GOOD NIBLET STICK, EH?
MMNOM
TOLD YOU HE'D SNAP OUT OF HIS FUNK. IT'S LIKE WE NEVER LEFT ISLE BOBO.
WE'RE NOT STAYING HERE LONG, HE'LL BE MAD AT US AGAIN.
WE GOTTA FIND **SOMEONE** WILLING TO GO BACK TO BURNSWICK WITH US.
SOMEONE BARON BUGABOO AND HIS BOYS MIGHT BALK AT.

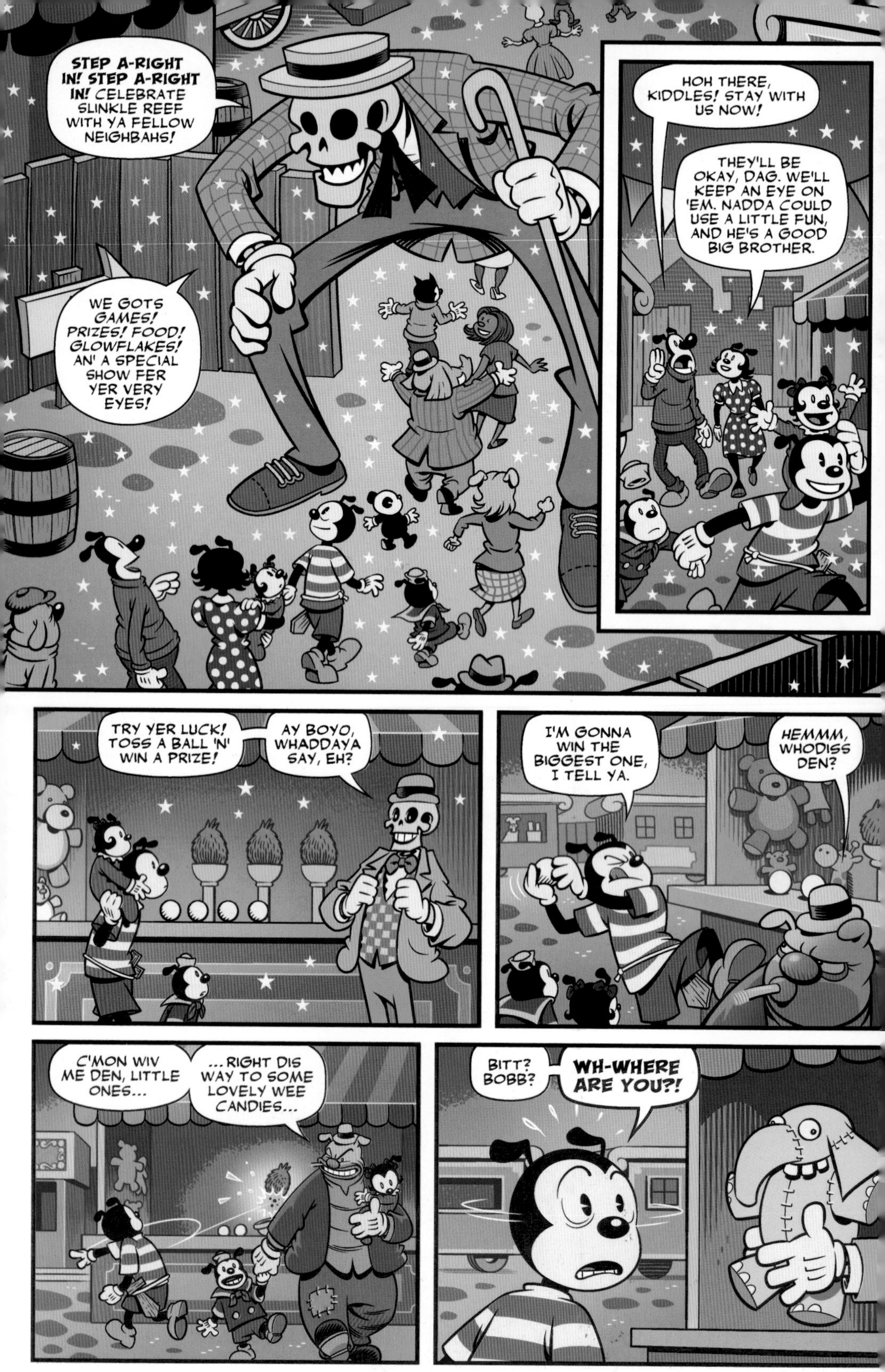
STEP A-RIGHT IN! STEP A-RIGHT IN! CELEBRATE SLINKLE REEF WITH YA FELLOW NEIGHBAHS!
WE GOTS GAMES! PRIZES! FOOD! GLOWFLAKES! AN' A SPECIAL SHOW FER YER VERY EYES!
HOH THERE, KIDDLES! STAY WITH US NOW!
THEY'LL BE OKAY, DAG. WE'LL KEEP AN EYE ON 'EM. NADDA COULD USE A LITTLE FUN, AND HE'S A GOOD BIG BROTHER.
TRY YER LUCK! TOSS A BALL 'N' WIN A PRIZE!
AY BOYO, WHADDAYA SAY, EH?
I'M GONNA WIN THE BIGGEST ONE, I TELL YA.
HEMMM, WHODISS DEN?
C'MON WIV ME DEN, LITTLE ONES...
...RIGHT DIS WAY TO SOME LOVELY WEE CANDIES...
BITT? BOBB?
WH-WHERE ARE YOU?!

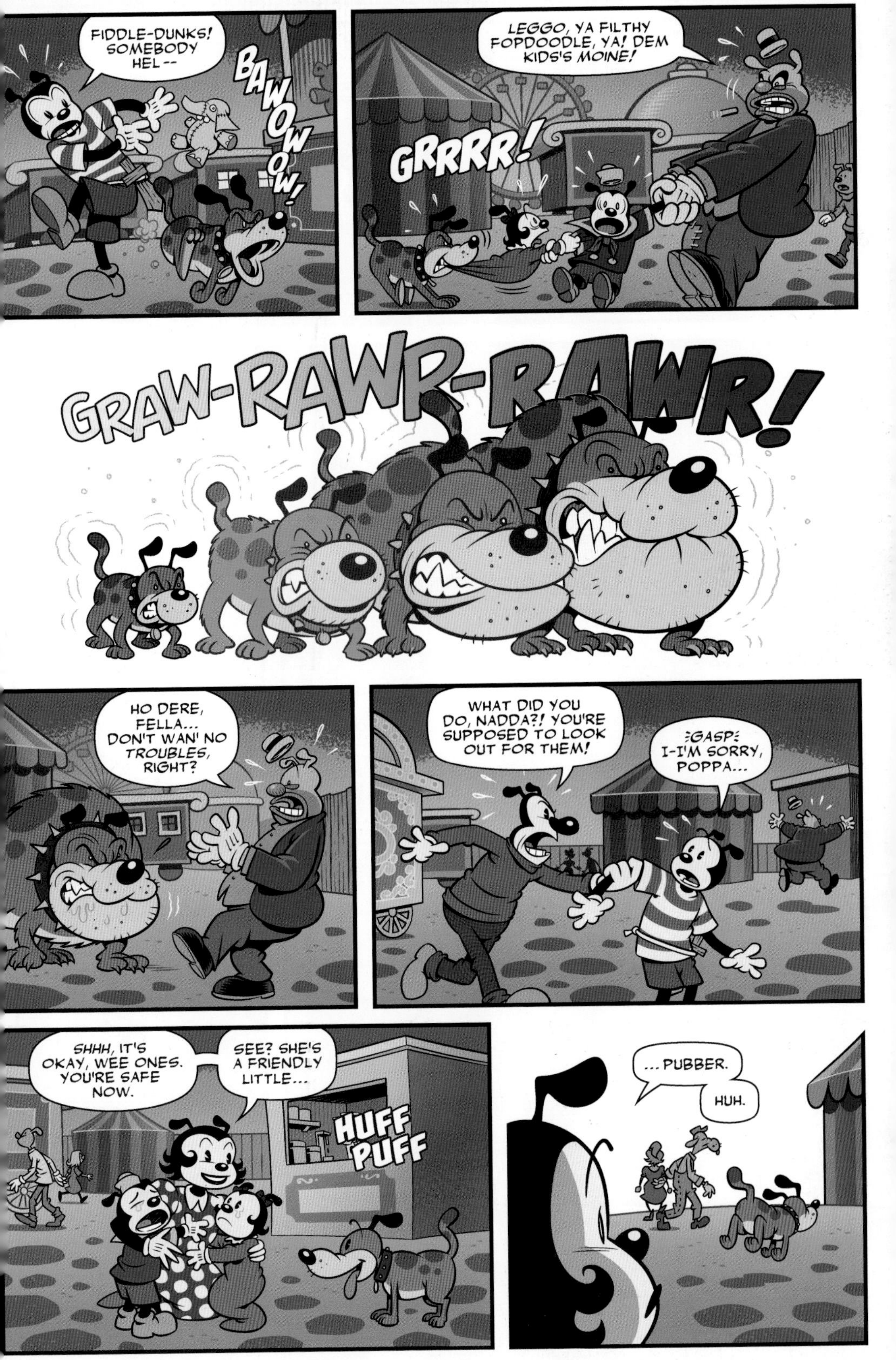
FIDDLE-DUNKS! SOMEBODY HEL--
BAWOWOWOW!
LEGGO, YA FILTHY FOPDOODLE, YA! DEM KIDS'S MOINE!
GRRRRR!
GRAW-RAWR-RAWR!
HO DERE, FELLA... DON'T WAN' NO TROUBLES, RIGHT?
WHAT DID YOU DO, NADDA?! YOU'RE SUPPOSED TO LOOK OUT FOR THEM!
:GASP: I-I'M SORRY, POPPA...
SHHH, IT'S OKAY, WEE ONES. YOU'RE SAFE NOW.
SEE? SHE'S A FRIENDLY LITTLE...
HUFF PUFF
...PUBBER.
HUH.

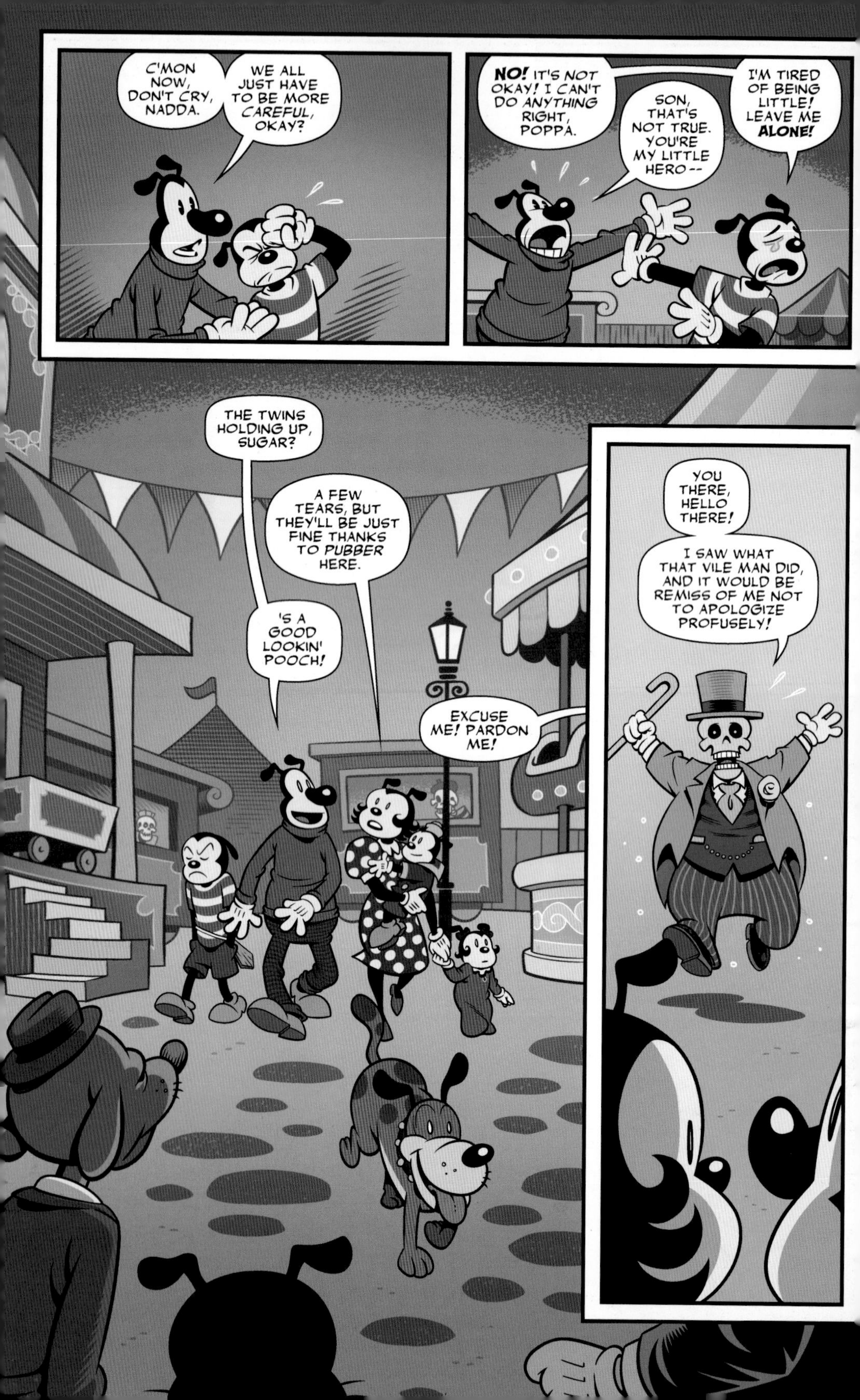

C'MON NOW, DON'T CRY, NADDA.
WE ALL JUST HAVE TO BE MORE *CAREFUL*, OKAY?
NO! IT'S NOT OKAY! I CAN'T DO *ANYTHING* RIGHT, POPPA.
SON, THAT'S NOT TRUE. YOU'RE MY LITTLE HERO --
I'M TIRED OF BEING LITTLE! LEAVE ME **ALONE!**
THE TWINS HOLDING UP, SUGAR?
A FEW TEARS, BUT THEY'LL BE JUST FINE THANKS TO *PUBBER* HERE.
'S A GOOD LOOKIN' POOCH!
EXCUSE ME! PARDON ME!
YOU THERE, HELLO THERE!
I SAW WHAT THAT VILE MAN DID, AND IT WOULD BE REMISS OF ME NOT TO APOLOGIZE PROFUSELY!

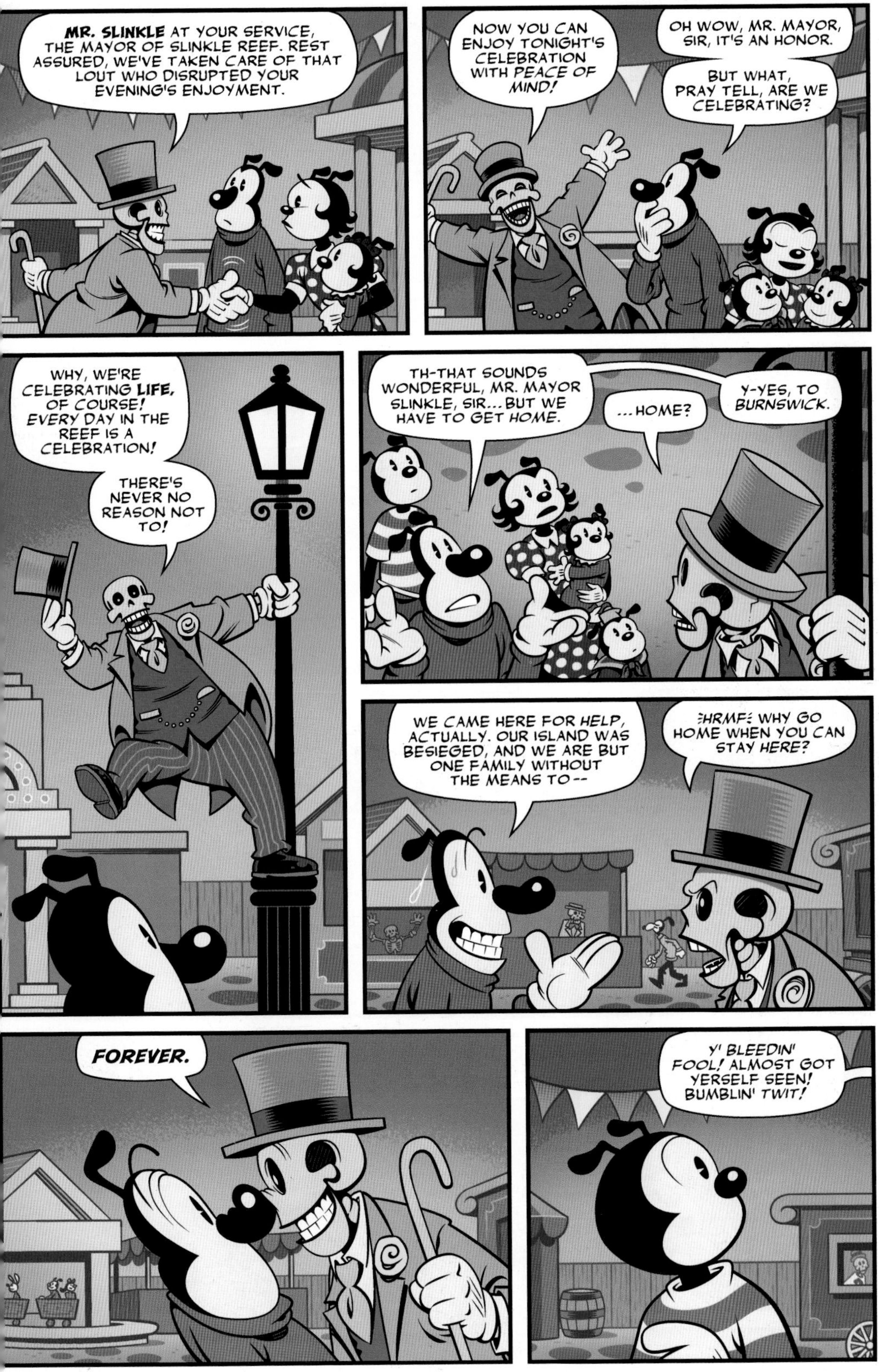
MR. SLINKLE AT YOUR SERVICE, THE MAYOR OF SLINKLE REEF. REST ASSURED, WE'VE TAKEN CARE OF THAT LOUT WHO DISRUPTED YOUR EVENING'S ENJOYMENT.
NOW YOU CAN ENJOY TONIGHT'S CELEBRATION WITH PEACE OF MIND!
OH WOW, MR. MAYOR, SIR, IT'S AN HONOR.
BUT WHAT, PRAY TELL, ARE WE CELEBRATING?
WHY, WE'RE CELEBRATING LIFE, OF COURSE! EVERY DAY IN THE REEF IS A CELEBRATION!
THERE'S NEVER NO REASON NOT TO!
TH-THAT SOUNDS WONDERFUL, MR. MAYOR SLINKLE, SIR... BUT WE HAVE TO GET HOME.
...HOME?
Y-YES, TO BURNSWICK.
WE CAME HERE FOR HELP, ACTUALLY. OUR ISLAND WAS BESIEGED, AND WE ARE BUT ONE FAMILY WITHOUT THE MEANS TO--
HRMF! WHY GO HOME WHEN YOU CAN STAY HERE?
FOREVER.
Y' BLEEDIN' FOOL! ALMOST GOT YERSELF SEEN! BUMBLIN' TWIT!

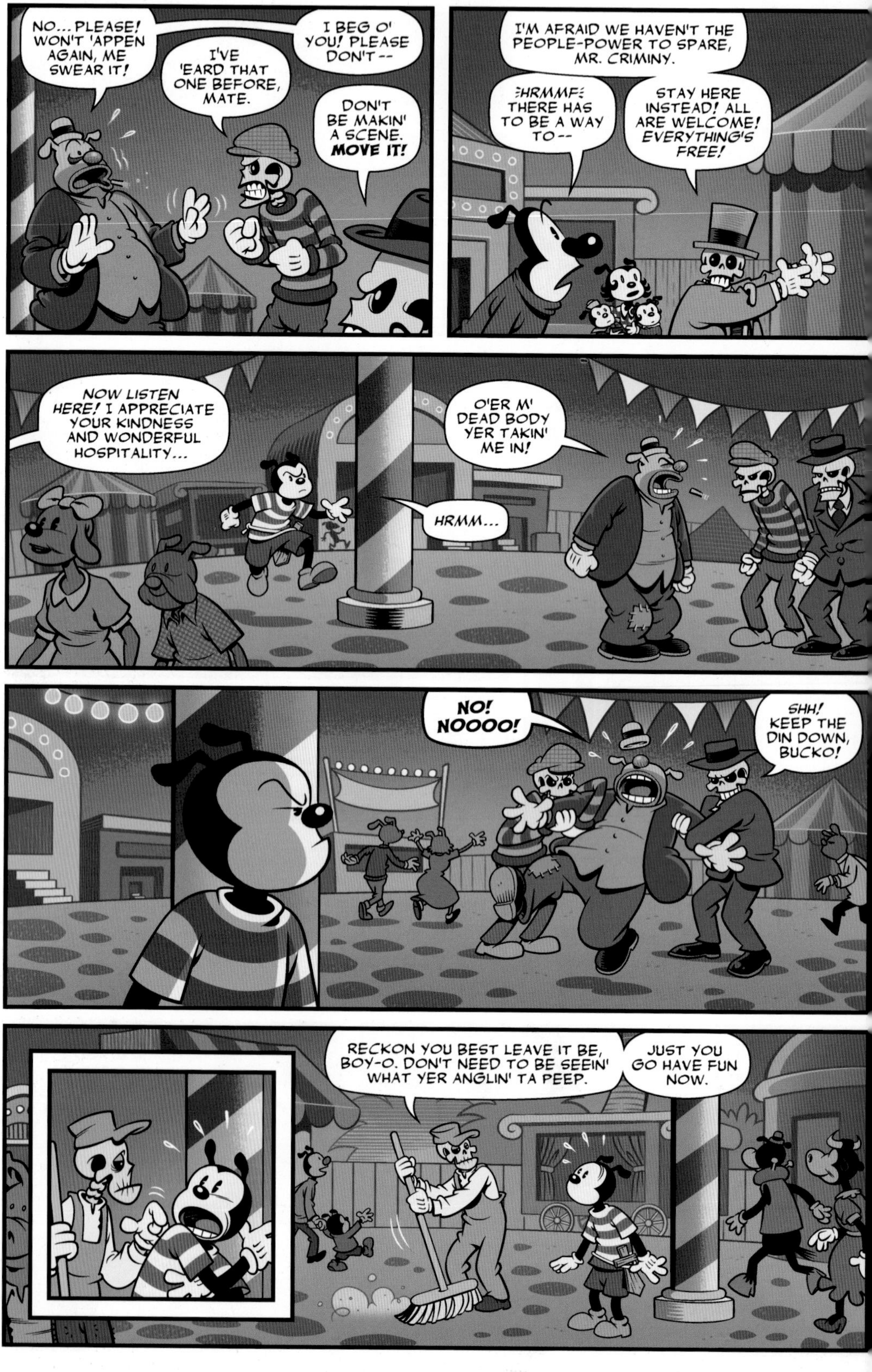
NO... PLEASE! WON'T 'APPEN AGAIN, ME SWEAR IT!
I'VE 'EARD THAT ONE BEFORE, MATE.
I BEG O' YOU! PLEASE DON'T --
DON'T BE MAKIN' A SCENE. MOVE IT!
I'M AFRAID WE HAVEN'T THE PEOPLE-POWER TO SPARE, MR. CRIMINY.
HRMMF! THERE HAS TO BE A WAY TO --
STAY HERE INSTEAD! ALL ARE WELCOME! EVERYTHING'S FREE!
NOW LISTEN HERE! I APPRECIATE YOUR KINDNESS AND WONDERFUL HOSPITALITY...
HRMM...
O'ER M' DEAD BODY YER TAKIN' ME IN!
NO! NOOOO!
SHH! KEEP THE DIN DOWN, BUCKO!
RECKON YOU BEST LEAVE IT BE, BOY-O. DON'T NEED TO BE SEEIN' WHAT YER ANGLIN' TA PEEP.
JUST YOU GO HAVE FUN NOW.

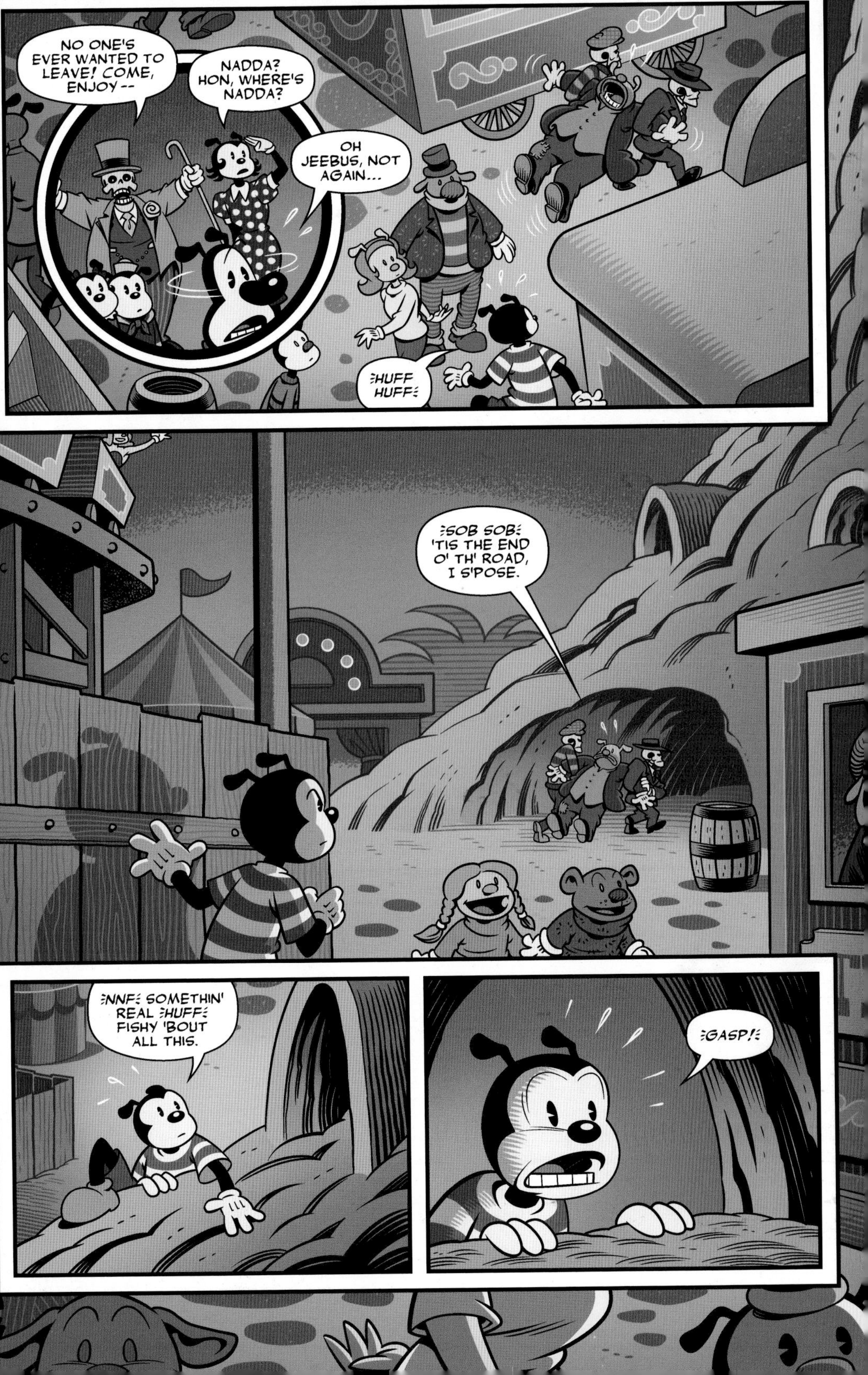
NO ONE'S EVER WANTED TO LEAVE! COME, ENJOY --
NADDA? HON, WHERE'S NADDA?
OH JEEBUS, NOT AGAIN...
HUFF HUFF
SOB SOB 'TIS THE END O' TH' ROAD, I S'POSE.
NNF SOMETHIN' REAL HUFF FISHY 'BOUT ALL THIS.
GASP!

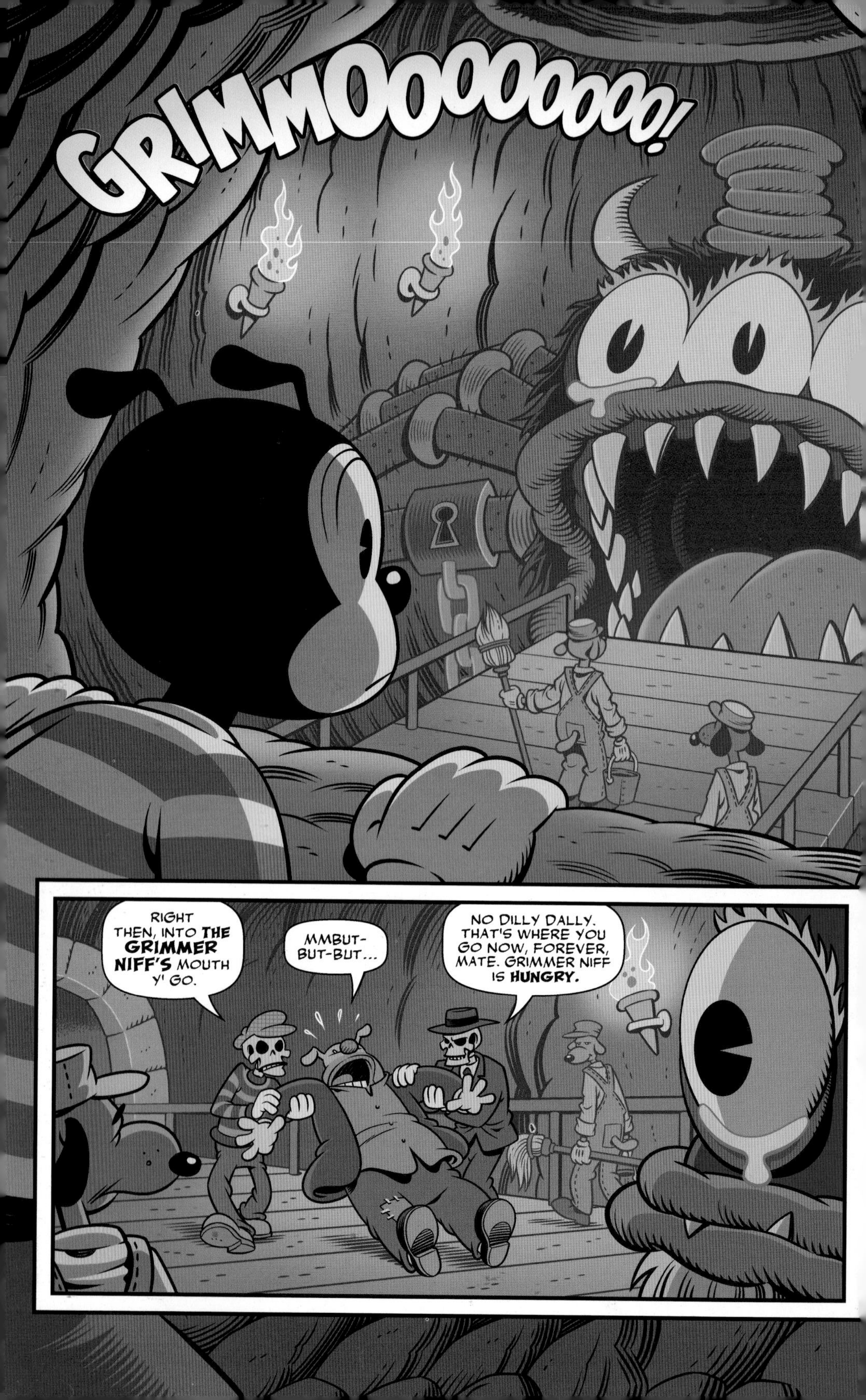
GRIMMOOOOOOOO!
RIGHT THEN, INTO THE GRIMMER NIFF'S MOUTH Y' GO.
MMBUT-BUT-BUT...
NO DILLY DALLY. THAT'S WHERE YOU GO NOW, FOREVER, MATE. GRIMMER NIFF IS HUNGRY.

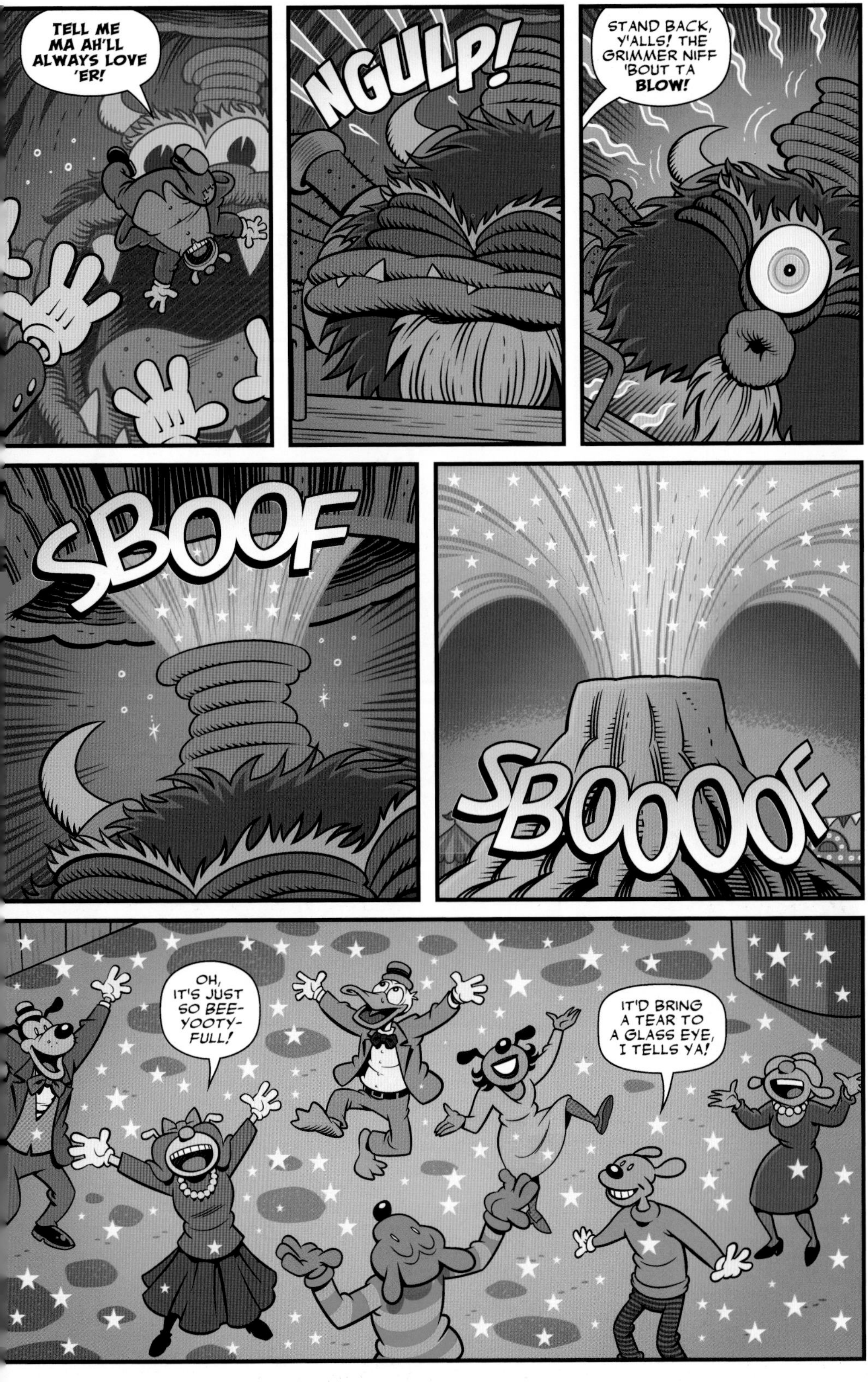
TELL ME MA AH'LL ALWAYS LOVE 'ER!
NGULP!
STAND BACK, Y'ALLS! THE GRIMMER NIFF 'BOUT TA BLOW!
SBOOF
SBOOOOF
OH, IT'S JUST SO BEE-YOOTY-FULL!
IT'D BRING A TEAR TO A GLASS EYE, I TELLS YA!

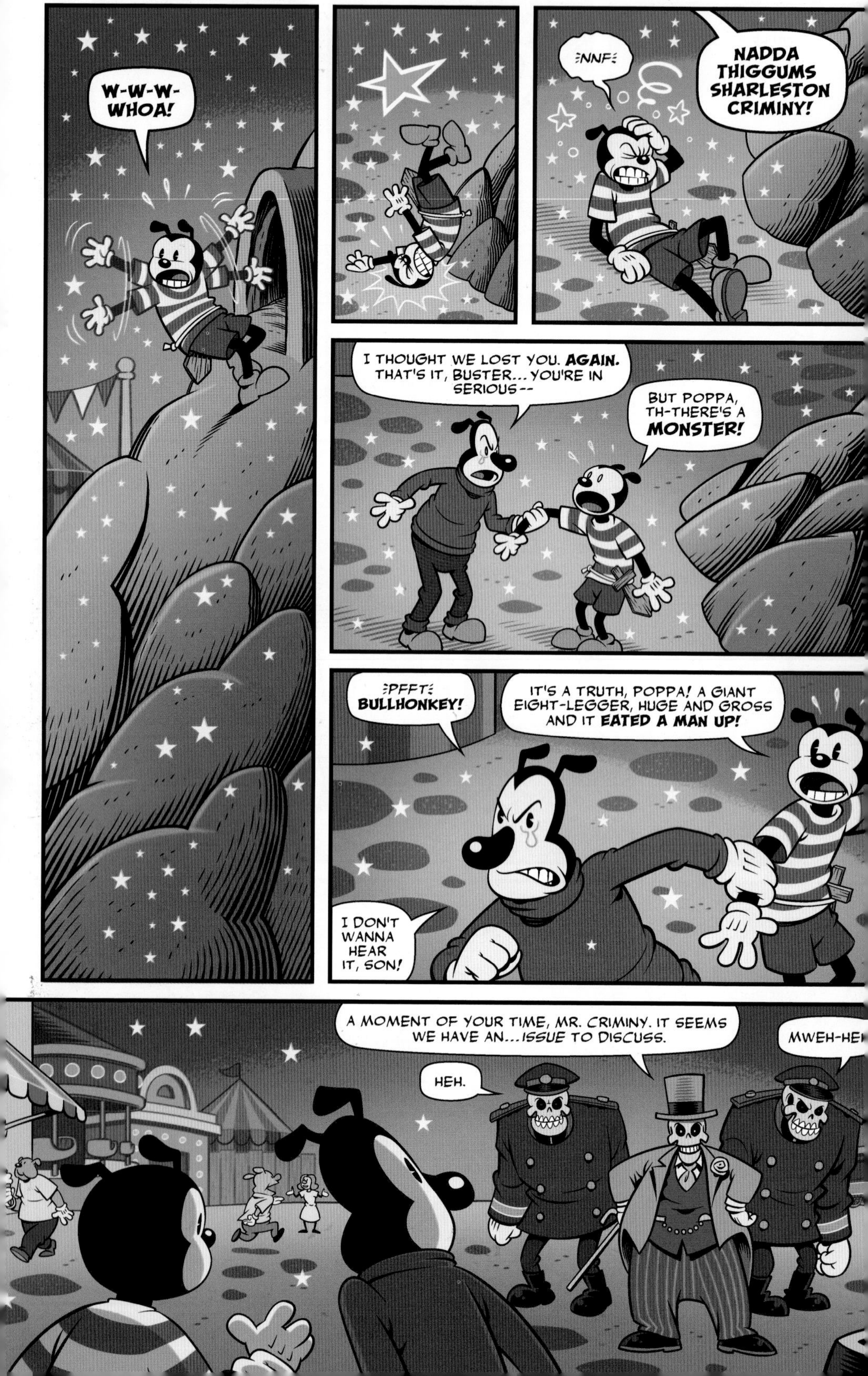
W-W-W-WHOA!
NNF
NADDA THIGGUMS SHARLESTON CRIMINY!
I THOUGHT WE LOST YOU. AGAIN. THAT'S IT, BUSTER... YOU'RE IN SERIOUS--
BUT POPPA, TH-THERE'S A MONSTER!
PFFT BULLHONKEY!
IT'S A TRUTH, POPPA! A GIANT EIGHT-LEGGER, HUGE AND GROSS AND IT EATED A MAN UP!
I DON'T WANNA HEAR IT, SON!
A MOMENT OF YOUR TIME, MR. CRIMINY. IT SEEMS WE HAVE AN... ISSUE TO DISCUSS.
HEH.
MWEH-HE

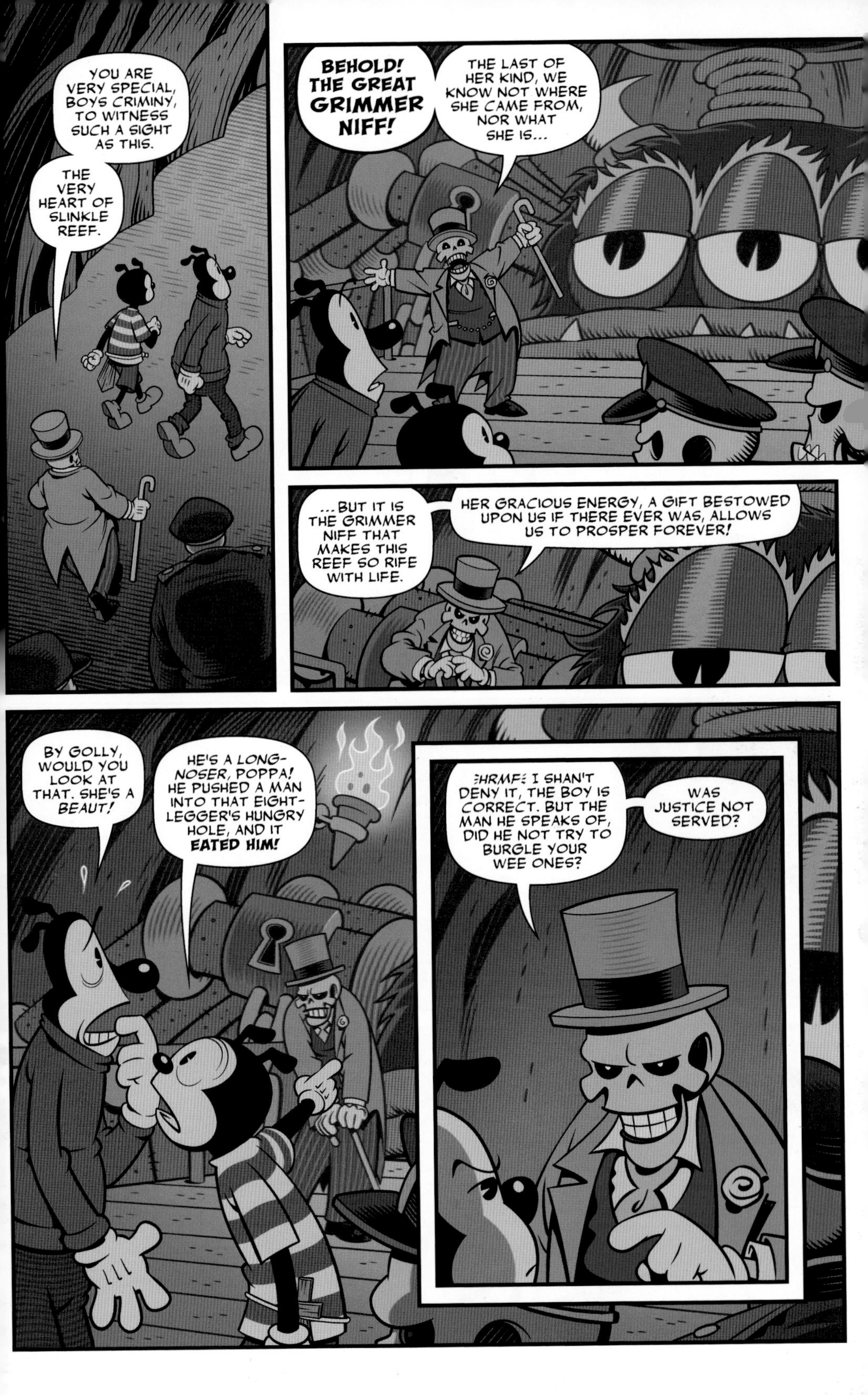
YOU ARE VERY SPECIAL, BOYS CRIMINY, TO WITNESS SUCH A SIGHT AS THIS.
THE VERY HEART OF SLINKLE REEF.
BEHOLD! THE GREAT GRIMMER NIFF!
THE LAST OF HER KIND, WE KNOW NOT WHERE SHE CAME FROM, NOR WHAT SHE IS...
...BUT IT IS THE GRIMMER NIFF THAT MAKES THIS REEF SO RIFE WITH LIFE.
HER GRACIOUS ENERGY, A GIFT BESTOWED UPON US IF THERE EVER WAS, ALLOWS US TO PROSPER FOREVER!
BY GOLLY, WOULD YOU LOOK AT THAT. SHE'S A BEAUT!
HE'S A LONG-NOSER, POPPA! HE PUSHED A MAN INTO THAT EIGHT-LEGGER'S HUNGRY HOLE, AND IT EATED HIM!
HRMF! I SHAN'T DENY IT, THE BOY IS CORRECT. BUT THE MAN HE SPEAKS OF, DID HE NOT TRY TO BURGLE YOUR WEE ONES?
WAS JUSTICE NOT SERVED?

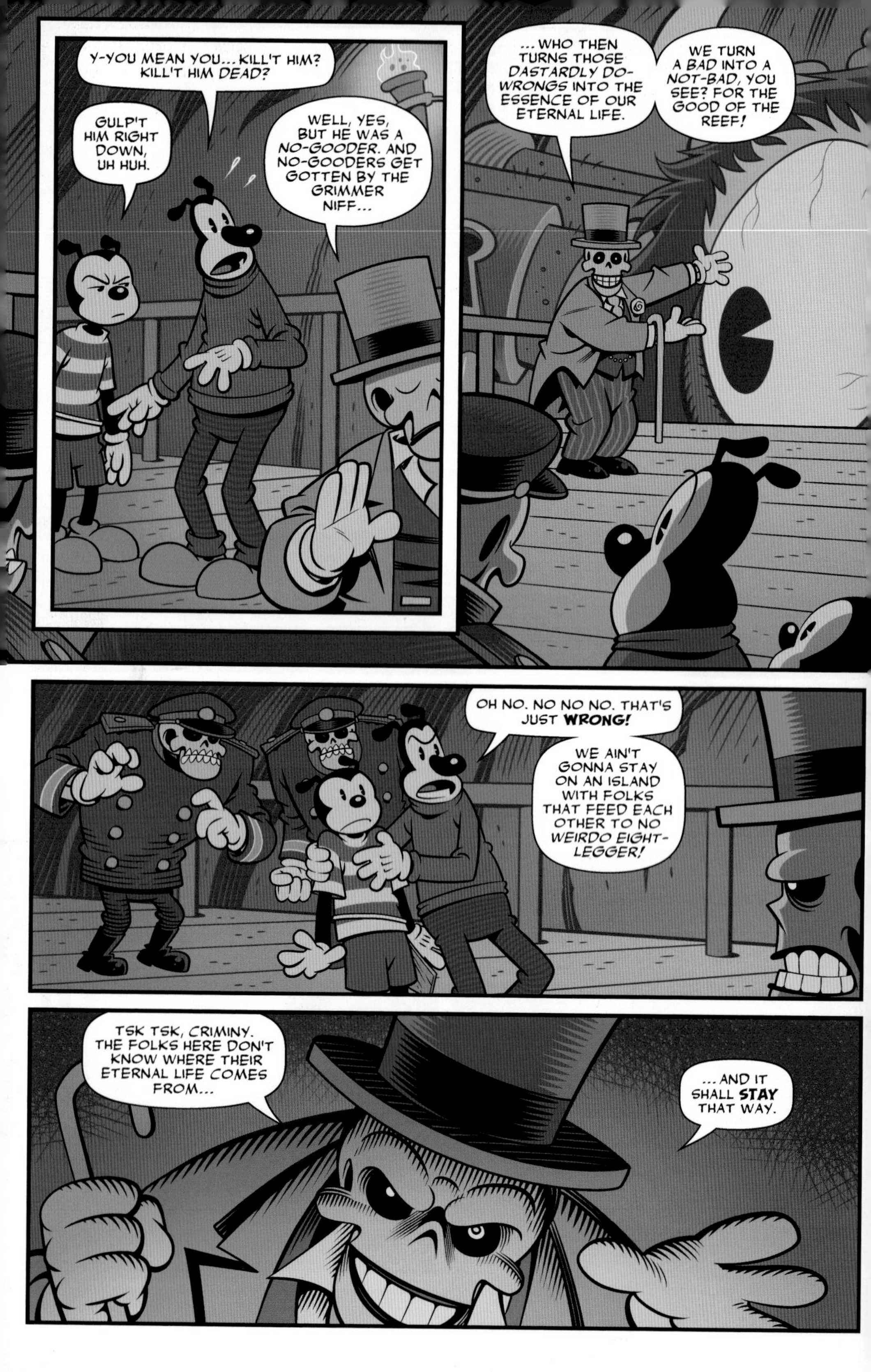
Y-YOU MEAN YOU... KILL'T HIM? KILL'T HIM DEAD?
GULP'T HIM RIGHT DOWN, UH HUH.
WELL, YES, BUT HE WAS A NO-GOODER. AND NO-GOODERS GET GOTTEN BY THE GRIMMER NIFF...
...WHO THEN TURNS THOSE DASTARDLY DO-WRONGS INTO THE ESSENCE OF OUR ETERNAL LIFE.
WE TURN A BAD INTO A NOT-BAD, YOU SEE? FOR THE GOOD OF THE REEF!
OH NO. NO NO NO. THAT'S JUST WRONG!
WE AIN'T GONNA STAY ON AN ISLAND WITH FOLKS THAT FEED EACH OTHER TO NO WEIRDO EIGHT-LEGGER!
TSK TSK, CRIMINY. THE FOLKS HERE DON'T KNOW WHERE THEIR ETERNAL LIFE COMES FROM...
...AND IT SHALL STAY THAT WAY.

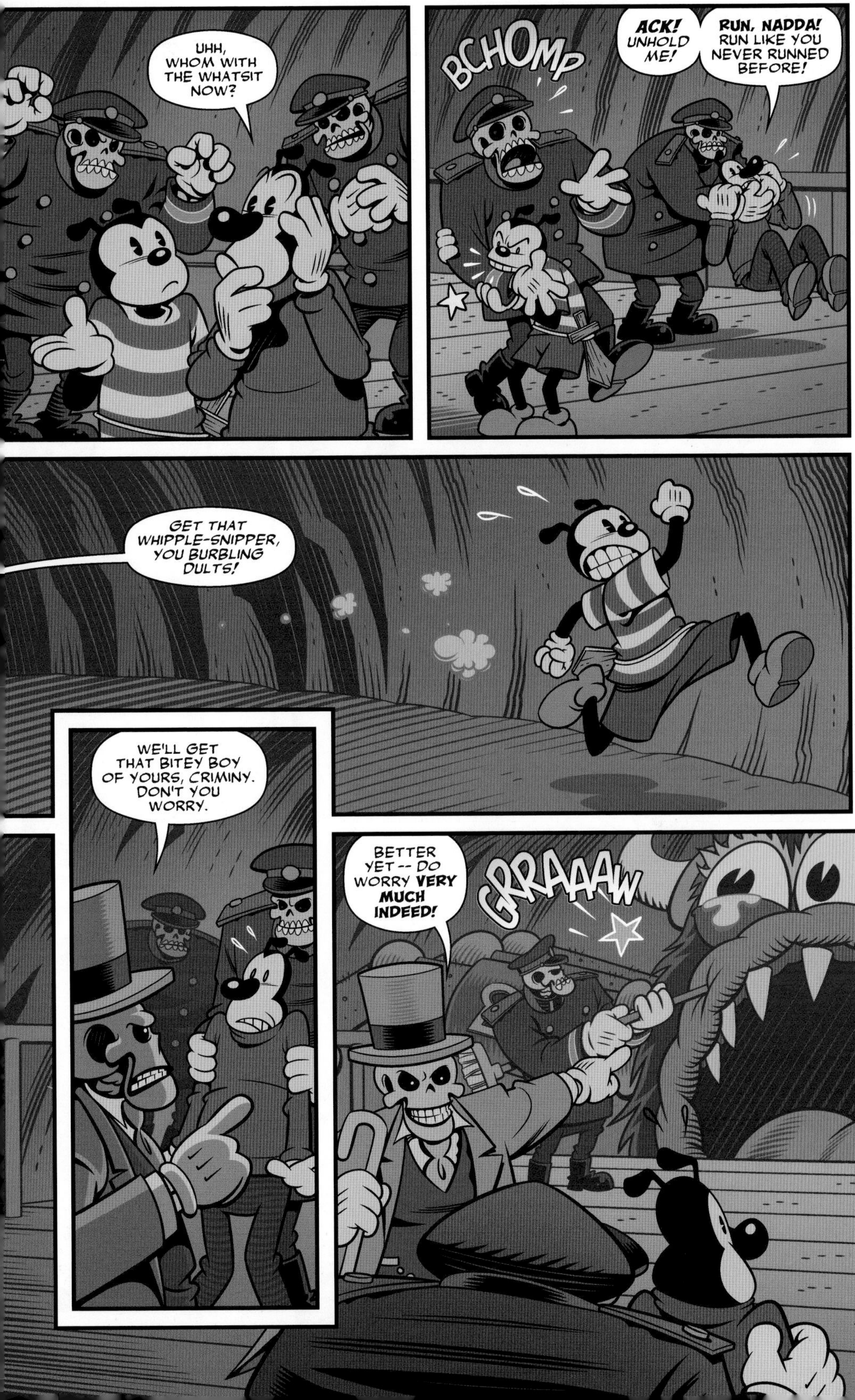
UHH, WHOM WITH THE WHATSIT NOW?
BCHOMP
ACK! UNHOLD ME!
RUN, NADDA! RUN LIKE YOU NEVER RUNNED BEFORE!
GET THAT WHIPPLE-SNIPPER, YOU BURBLING DULTS!
WE'LL GET THAT BITEY BOY OF YOURS, CRIMINY. DON'T YOU WORRY.
BETTER YET -- DO WORRY VERY MUCH INDEED!
GRRAAAW

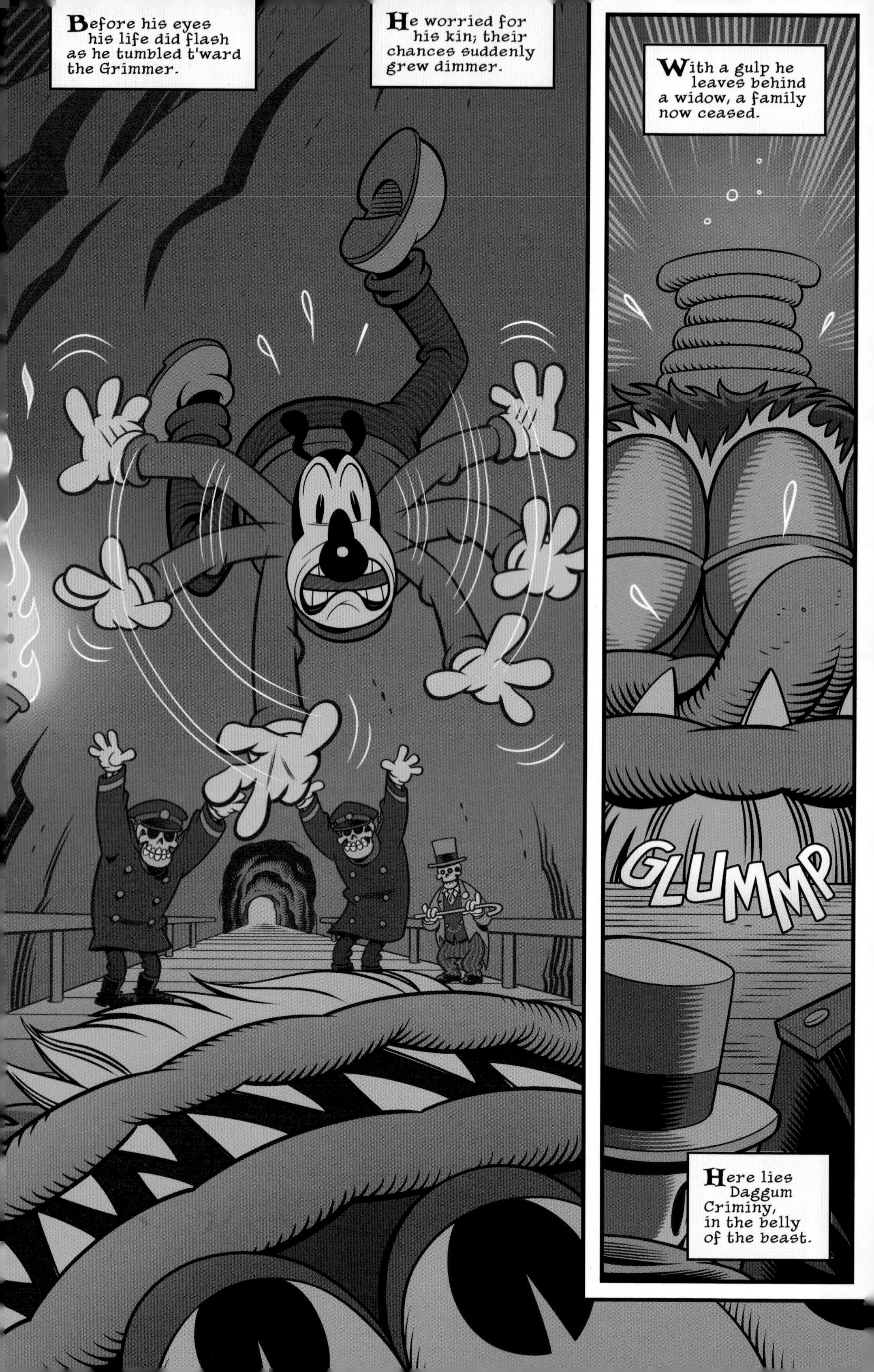
Before his eyes his life did flash as he tumbled t'ward the Grimmer.
He worried for his kin; their chances suddenly grew dimmer.
With a gulp he leaves behind a widow, a family now ceased.
GLUMMP
Here lies Daggum Criminy, in the belly of the beast.

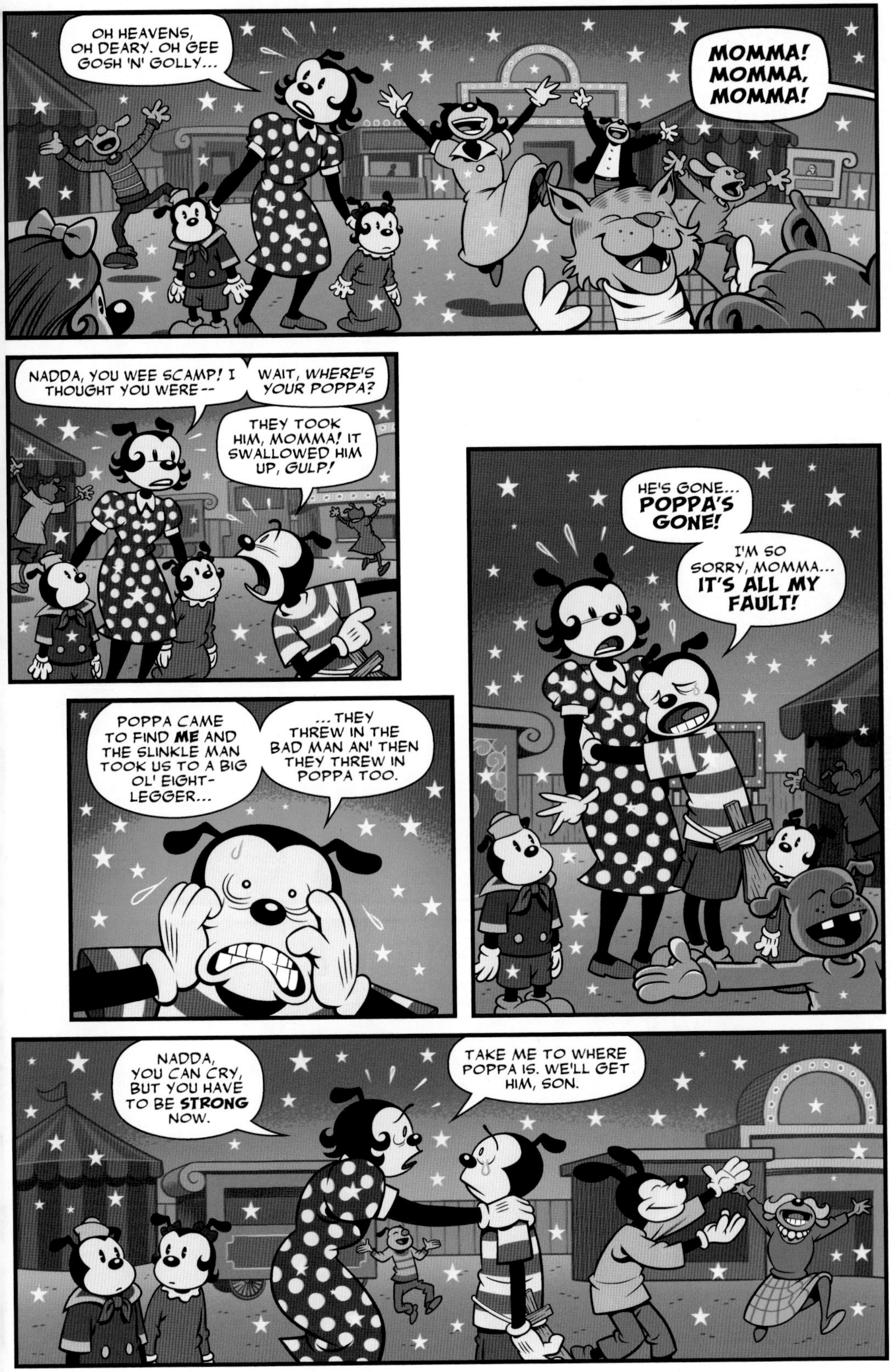
OH HEAVENS, OH DEARY. OH GEE GOSH 'N' GOLLY...
MOMMA! MOMMA, MOMMA!
NADDA, YOU WEE SCAMP! I THOUGHT YOU WERE--
WAIT, WHERE'S YOUR POPPA?
THEY TOOK HIM, MOMMA! IT SWALLOWED HIM UP, GULP!
HE'S GONE... POPPA'S GONE!
I'M SO SORRY, MOMMA... IT'S ALL MY FAULT!
POPPA CAME TO FIND ME AND THE SLINKLE MAN TOOK US TO A BIG OL' EIGHT-LEGGER...
...THEY THREW IN THE BAD MAN AN' THEN THEY THREW IN POPPA TOO.
NADDA, YOU CAN CRY, BUT YOU HAVE TO BE STRONG NOW.
TAKE ME TO WHERE POPPA IS. WE'LL GET HIM, SON.

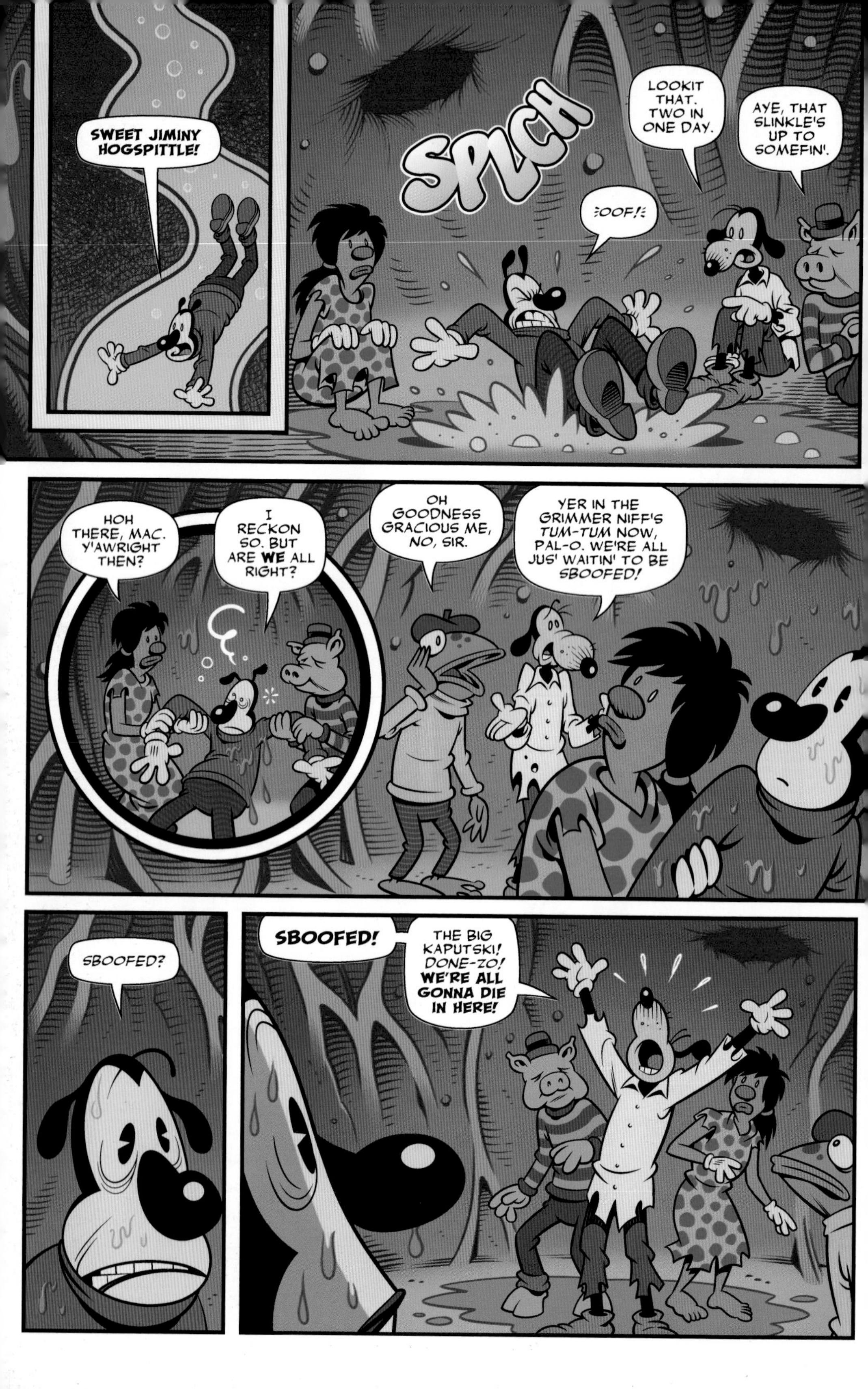
SWEET JIMINY HOGSPITTLE!
SPLCH
LOOKIT THAT. TWO IN ONE DAY.
AYE, THAT SLINKLE'S UP TO SOMEFIN'.
OOF!
HOH THERE, MAC. Y'AWRIGHT THEN?
I RECKON SO. BUT ARE WE ALL RIGHT?
OH GOODNESS GRACIOUS ME, NO, SIR.
YER IN THE GRIMMER NIFF'S TUM-TUM NOW, PAL-O. WE'RE ALL JUS' WAITIN' TO BE SBOOFED!
SBOOFED?
SBOOFED!
THE BIG KAPUTSKI! DONE-ZO! WE'RE ALL GONNA DIE IN HERE!

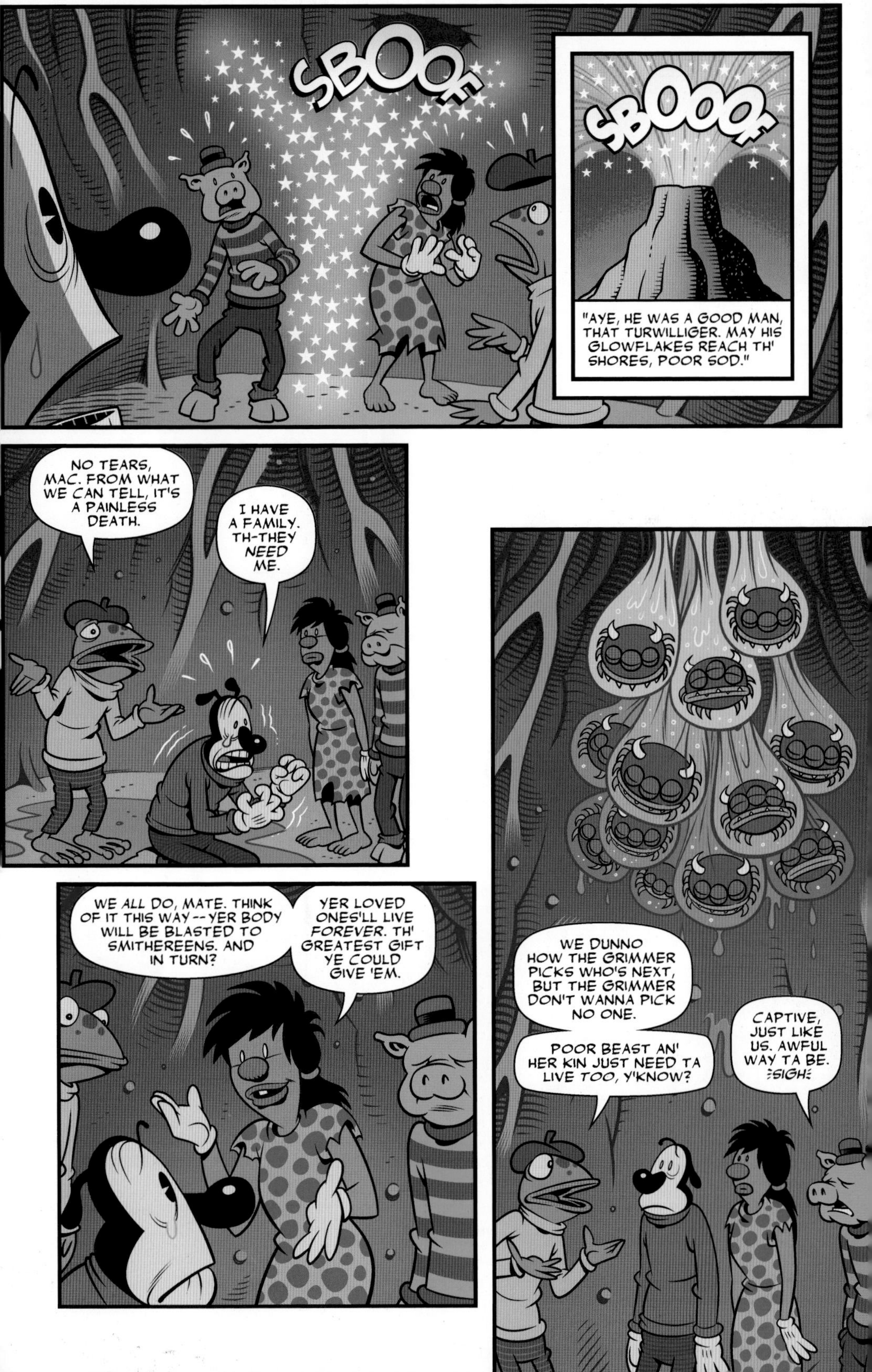
SBOOF
SBOOOF
"AYE, HE WAS A GOOD MAN, THAT TURWILLIGER. MAY HIS GLOWFLAKES REACH TH' SHORES, POOR SOD."
NO TEARS, MAC. FROM WHAT WE CAN TELL, IT'S A PAINLESS DEATH.
I HAVE A FAMILY. TH-THEY NEED ME.
WE ALL DO, MATE. THINK OF IT THIS WAY--YER BODY WILL BE BLASTED TO SMITHEREENS. AND IN TURN?
YER LOVED ONES'LL LIVE FOREVER. TH' GREATEST GIFT YE COULD GIVE 'EM.
WE DUNNO HOW THE GRIMMER PICKS WHO'S NEXT, BUT THE GRIMMER DON'T WANNA PICK NO ONE.
POOR BEAST AN' HER KIN JUST NEED TA LIVE TOO, Y'KNOW?
CAPTIVE, JUST LIKE US. AWFUL WAY TA BE. SIGH

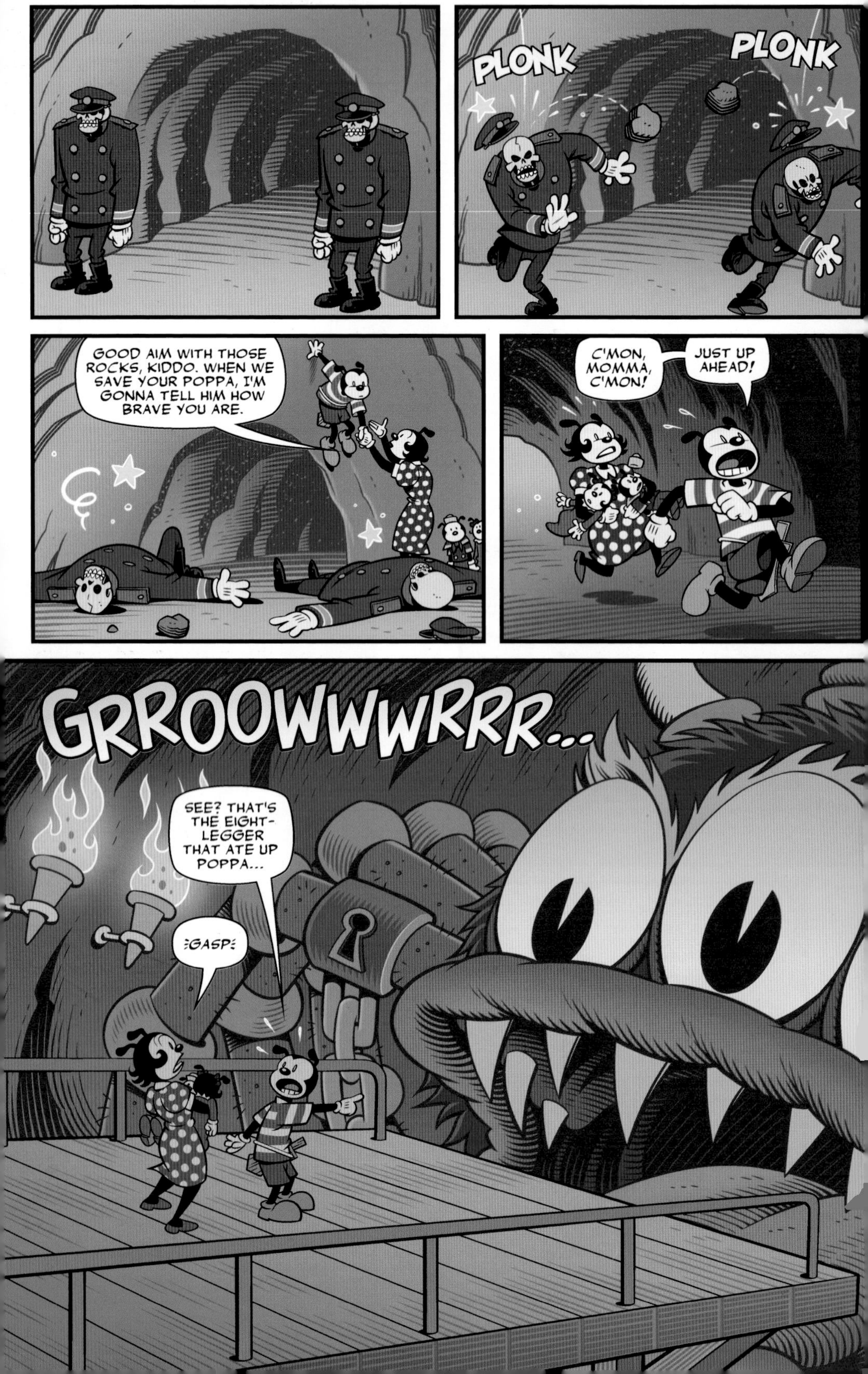
PLONK
PLONK
GOOD AIM WITH THOSE ROCKS, KIDDO. WHEN WE SAVE YOUR POPPA, I'M GONNA TELL HIM HOW BRAVE YOU ARE.
C'MON, MOMMA, C'MON!
JUST UP AHEAD!
GRROOWWWRRR...
SEE? THAT'S THE EIGHT-LEGGER THAT ATE UP POPPA...
GASP

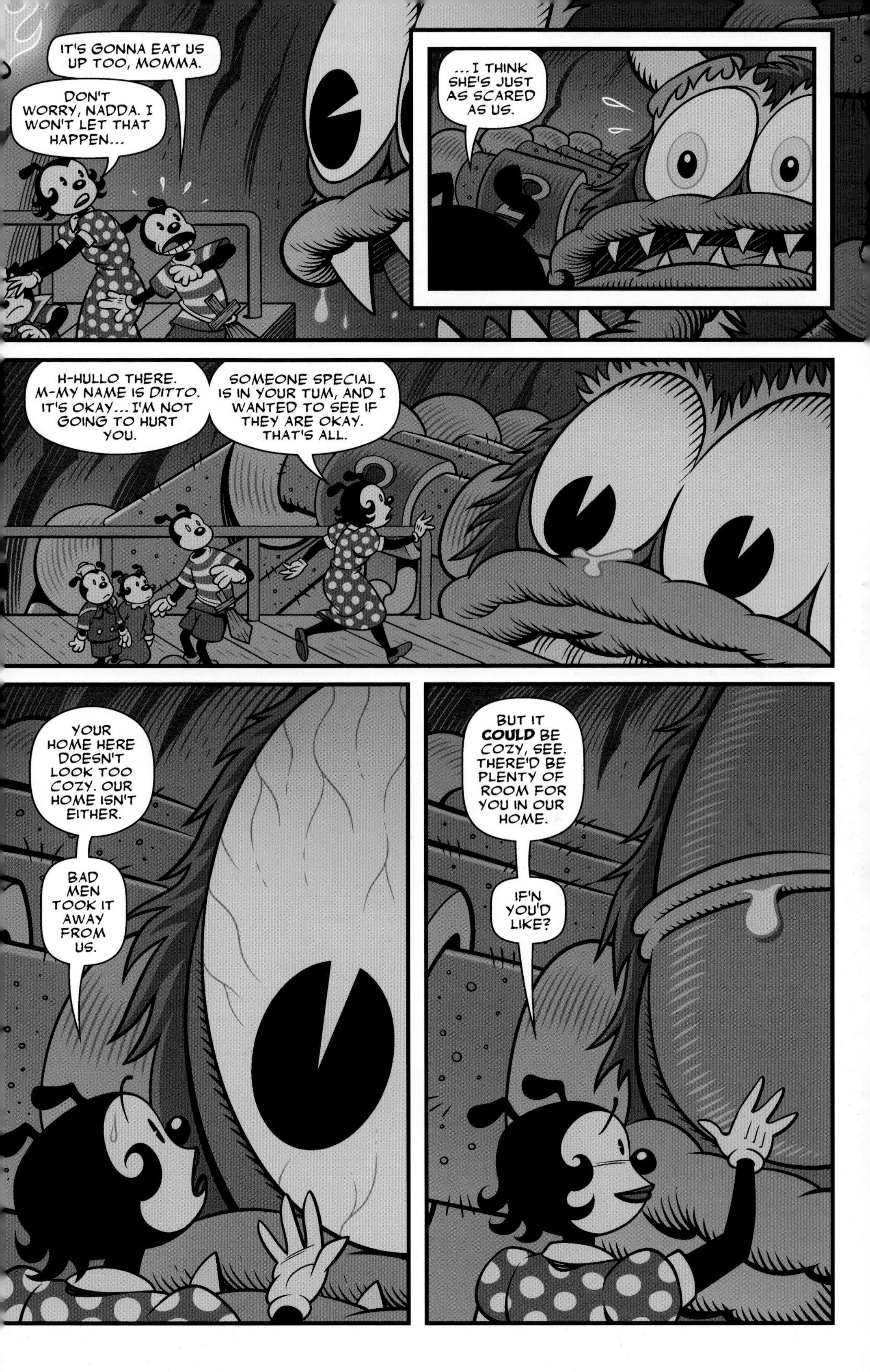
IT'S GONNA EAT US UP TOO, MOMMA.
DON'T WORRY, NADDA. I WON'T LET THAT HAPPEN...
...I THINK SHE'S JUST AS SCARED AS US.
H-HULLO THERE. M-MY NAME IS DITTO. IT'S OKAY... I'M NOT GOING TO HURT YOU.
SOMEONE SPECIAL IS IN YOUR TUM, AND I WANTED TO SEE IF THEY ARE OKAY. THAT'S ALL.
YOUR HOME HERE DOESN'T LOOK TOO COZY. OUR HOME ISN'T EITHER.
BAD MEN TOOK IT AWAY FROM US.
BUT IT COULD BE COZY, SEE. THERE'D BE PLENTY OF ROOM FOR YOU IN OUR HOME.
IF'N YOU'D LIKE?

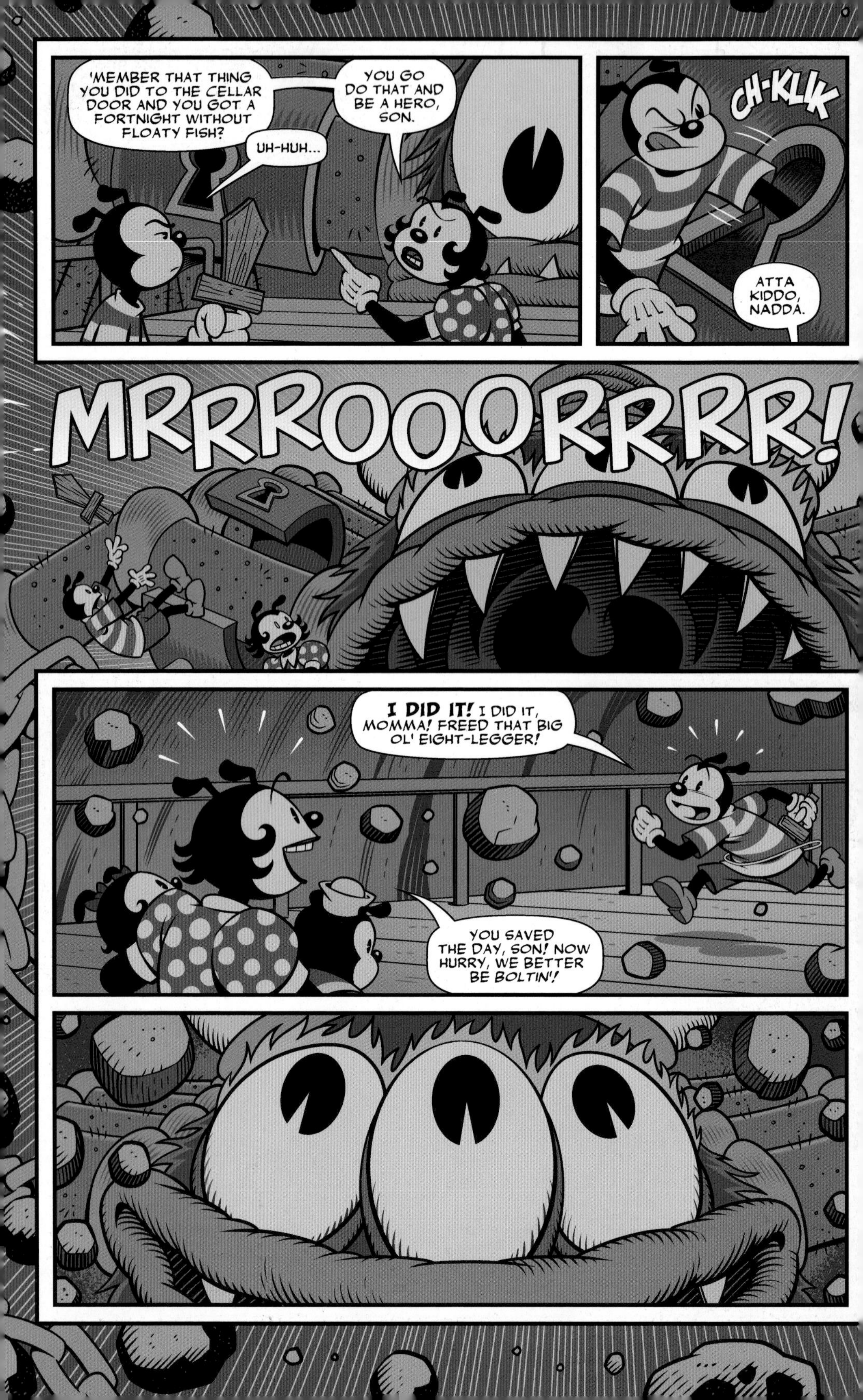
'MEMBER THAT THING YOU DID TO THE CELLAR DOOR AND YOU GOT A FORTNIGHT WITHOUT FLOATY FISH?
UH-HUH...
YOU GO DO THAT AND BE A HERO, SON.
CH-KLIK
ATTA KIDDO, NADDA.
MRRROOORRRR!
I DID IT! I DID IT, MOMMA! FREED THAT BIG OL' EIGHT-LEGGER!
YOU SAVED THE DAY, SON! NOW HURRY, WE BETTER BE BOLTIN'!

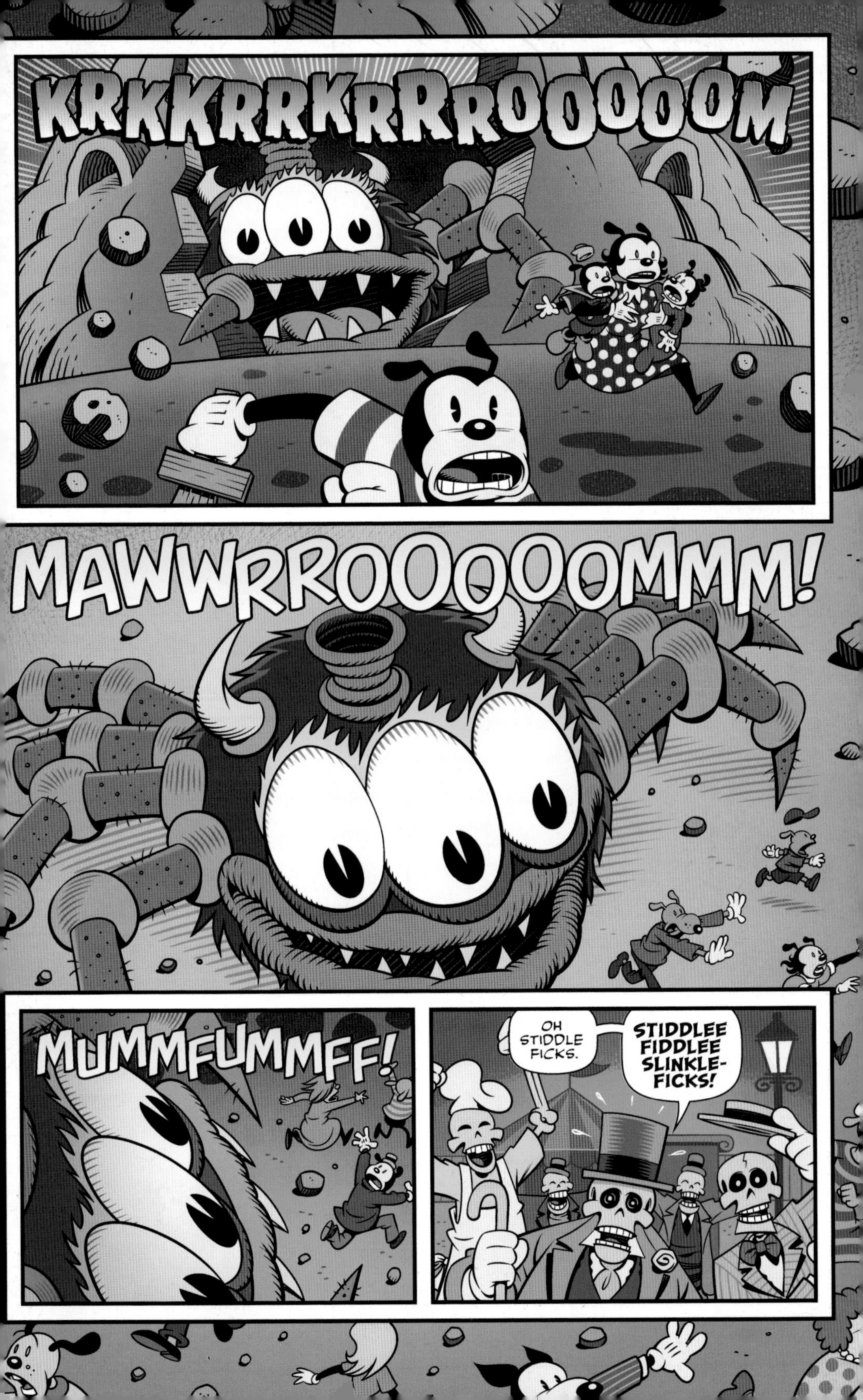
KRKKRRKRRROOOOOOM
MAWWRROOOOOOMMM!
MUMMFUMMFF!
OH STIDDLE FICKS.
STIDDLEE FIDDLEE SLINKLE-FICKS!

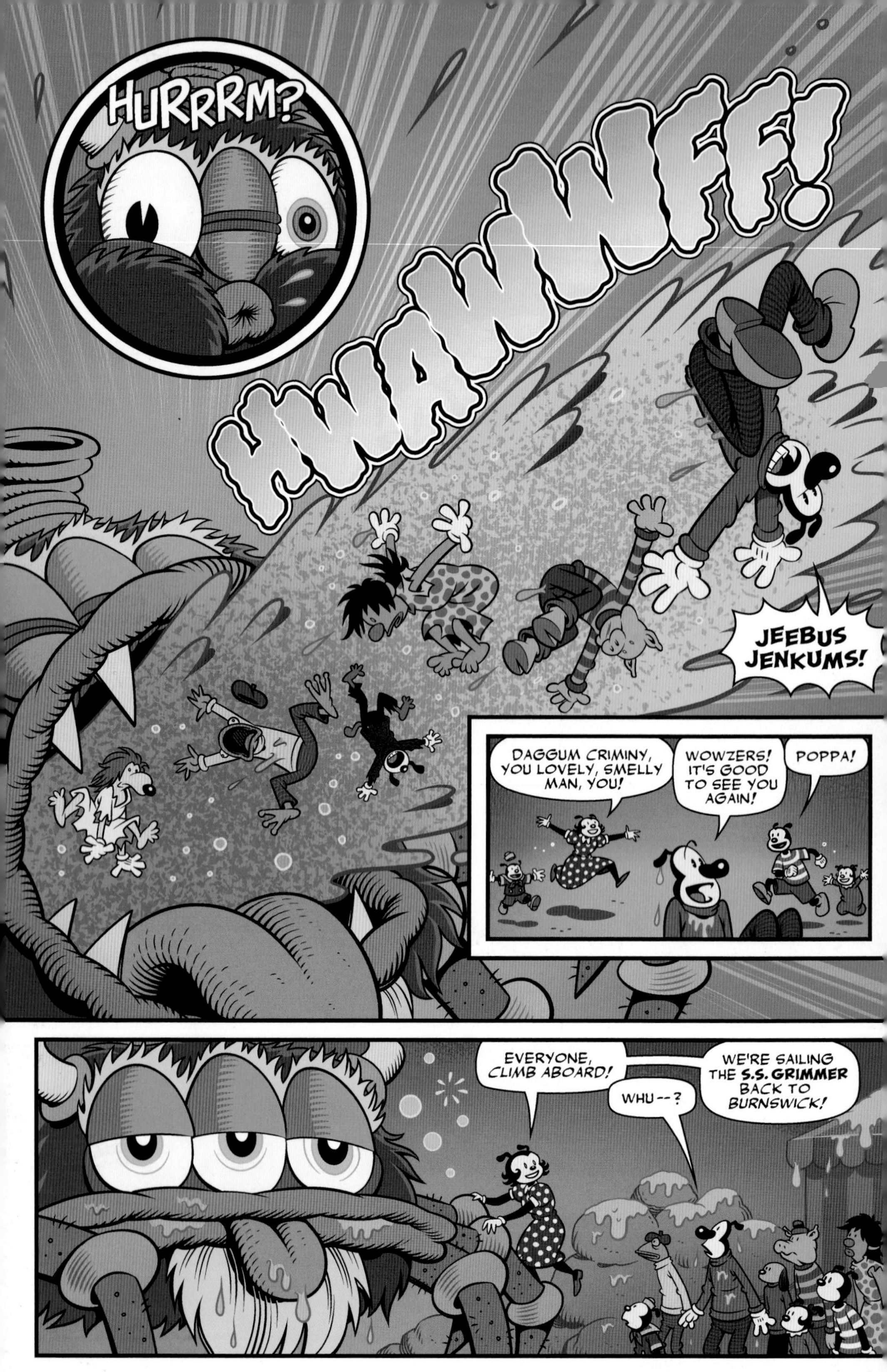
HURRRM?
HWAWWFF!
JEEBUS JENKUMS!
DAGGUM CRIMINY, YOU LOVELY, SMELLY MAN, YOU!
WOWZERS! IT'S GOOD TO SEE YOU AGAIN!
POPPA!
EVERYONE, CLIMB ABOARD!
WHU--?
WE'RE SAILING THE S.S. GRIMMER BACK TO BURNSWICK!

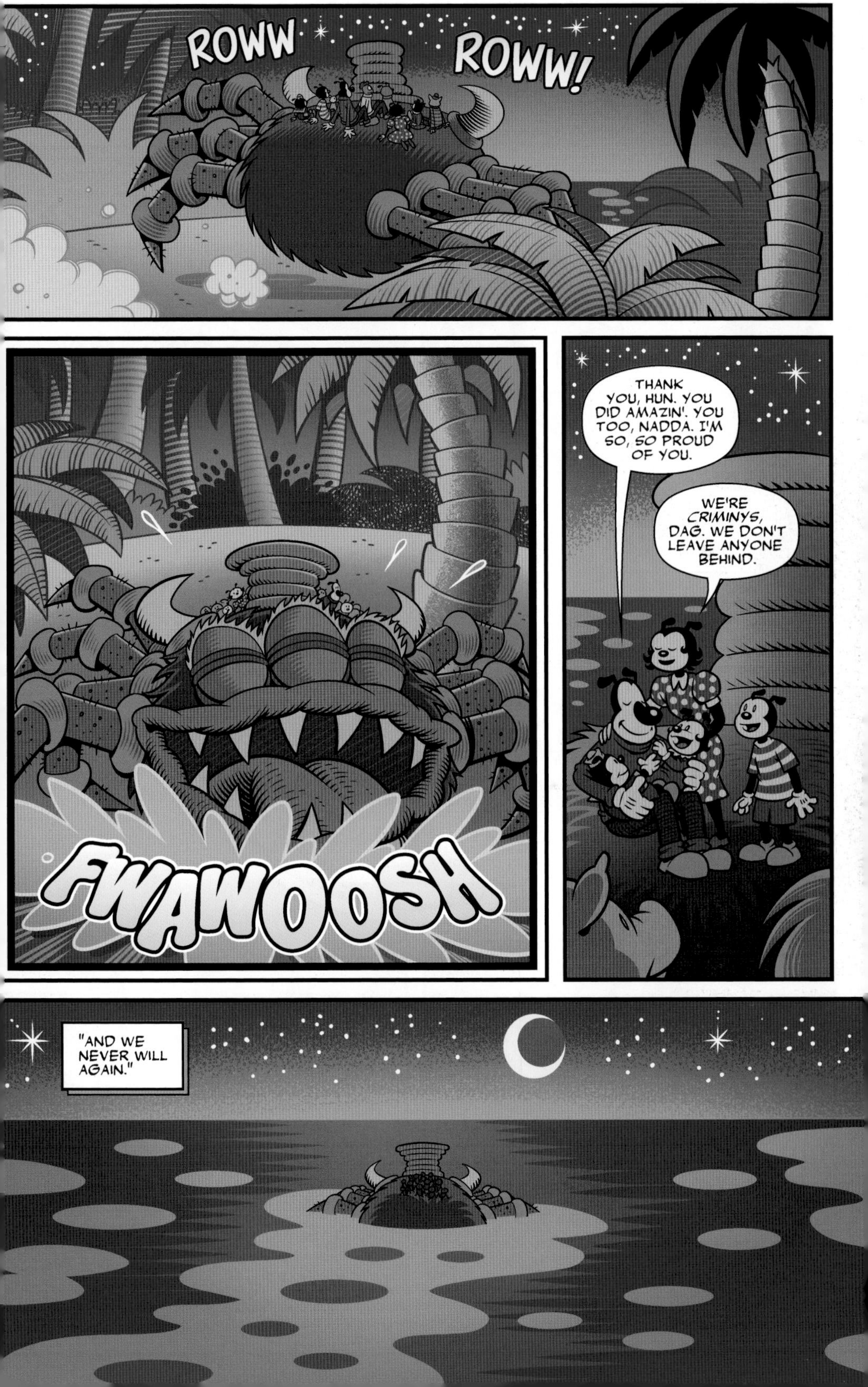
ROWW
ROWW!
FWAWOOSH
THANK YOU, HUN. YOU DID AMAZIN'. YOU TOO, NADDA. I'M SO, SO PROUD OF YOU.
WE'RE CRIMINYS, DAG. WE DON'T LEAVE ANYONE BEHIND.
"AND WE NEVER WILL AGAIN."

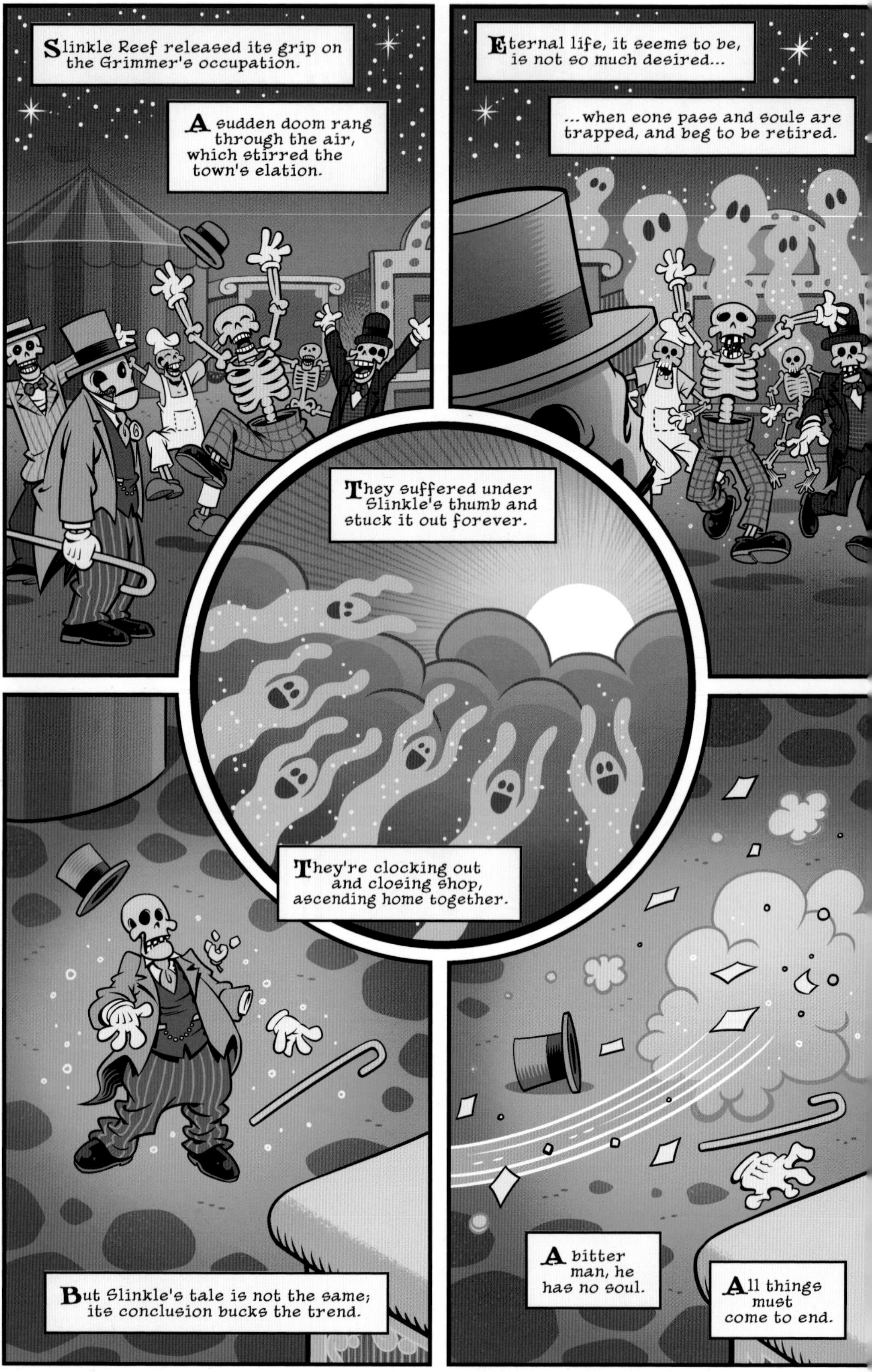
Slinkle Reef released its grip on the Grimmer's occupation.
A sudden doom rang through the air, which stirred the town's elation.
Eternal life, it seems to be, is not so much desired...
...when eons pass and souls are trapped, and beg to be retired.
They suffered under Slinkle's thumb and stuck it out forever.
They're clocking out and closing shop, ascending home together.
But Slinkle's tale is not the same; its conclusion bucks the trend.
A bitter man, he has no soul.
All things must come to end.

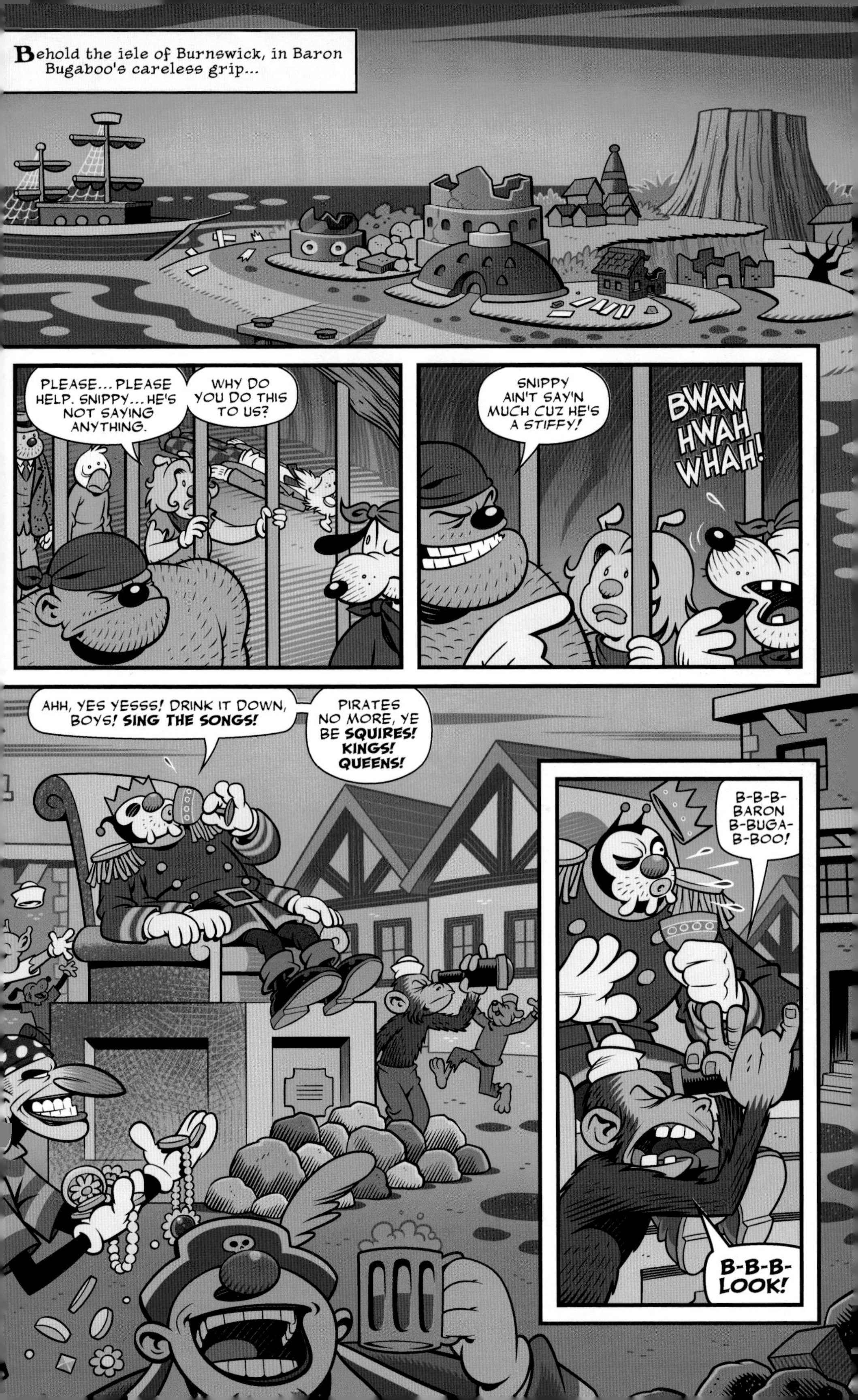
Behold the isle of Burnswick, in Baron Bugaboo's careless grip...
PLEASE... PLEASE HELP. SNIPPY... HE'S NOT SAYING ANYTHING.
WHY DO YOU DO THIS TO US?
SNIPPY AIN'T SAY'N MUCH CUZ HE'S A STIFFY!
BWAW HWAH WHAH!
AHH, YES YESSS! DRINK IT DOWN, BOYS! SING THE SONGS!
PIRATES NO MORE, YE BE SQUIRES! KINGS! QUEENS!
B-B-B-BARON B-BUGA-B-BOO!
B-B-B-LOOK!

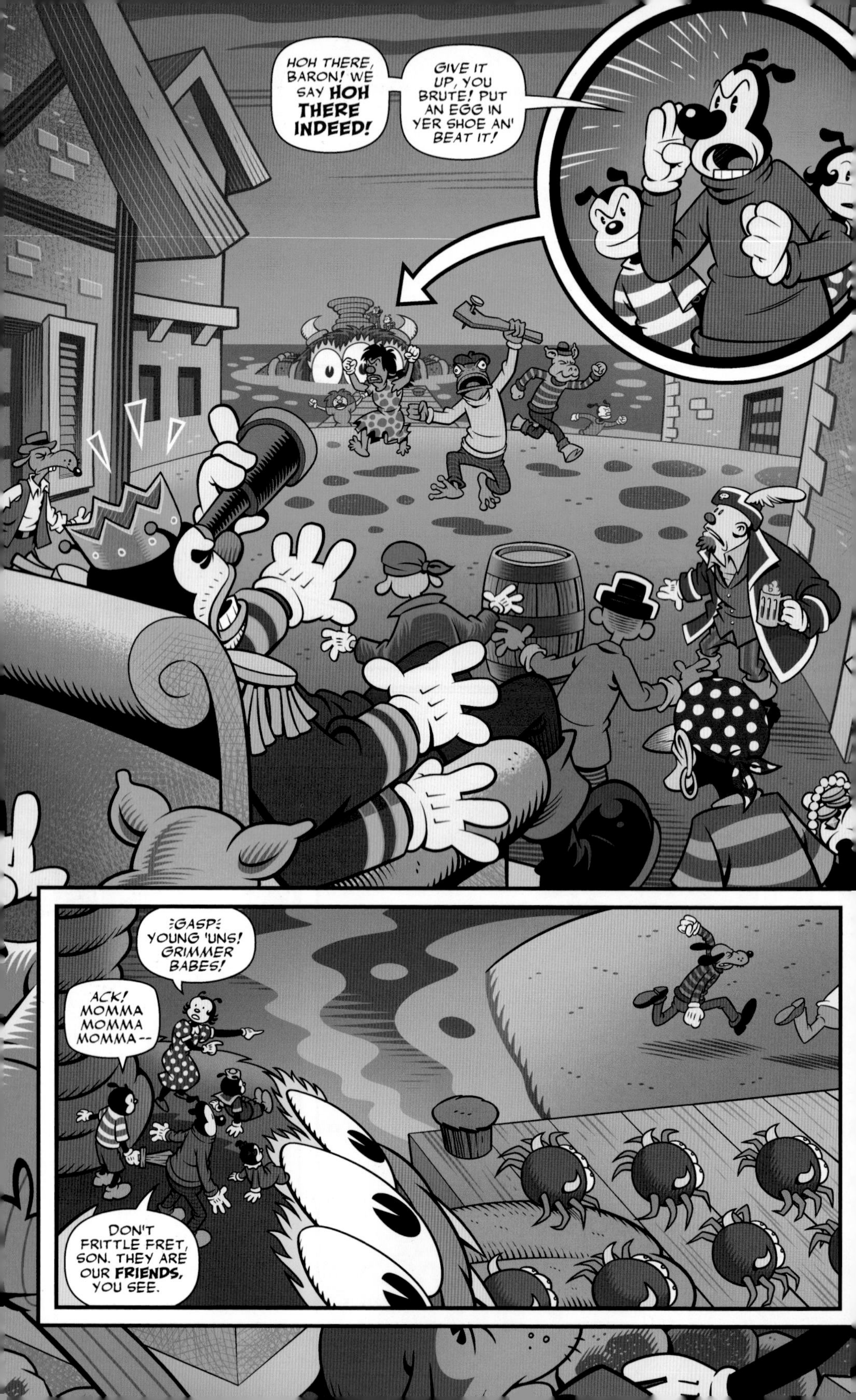
HOH THERE, BARON! WE SAY HOH THERE INDEED!
GIVE IT UP, YOU BRUTE! PUT AN EGG IN YER SHOE AN' BEAT IT!
:GASP: YOUNG 'UNS! GRIMMER BABES!
ACK! MOMMA MOMMA MOMMA--
DON'T FRITTLE FRET, SON. THEY ARE OUR FRIENDS, YOU SEE.

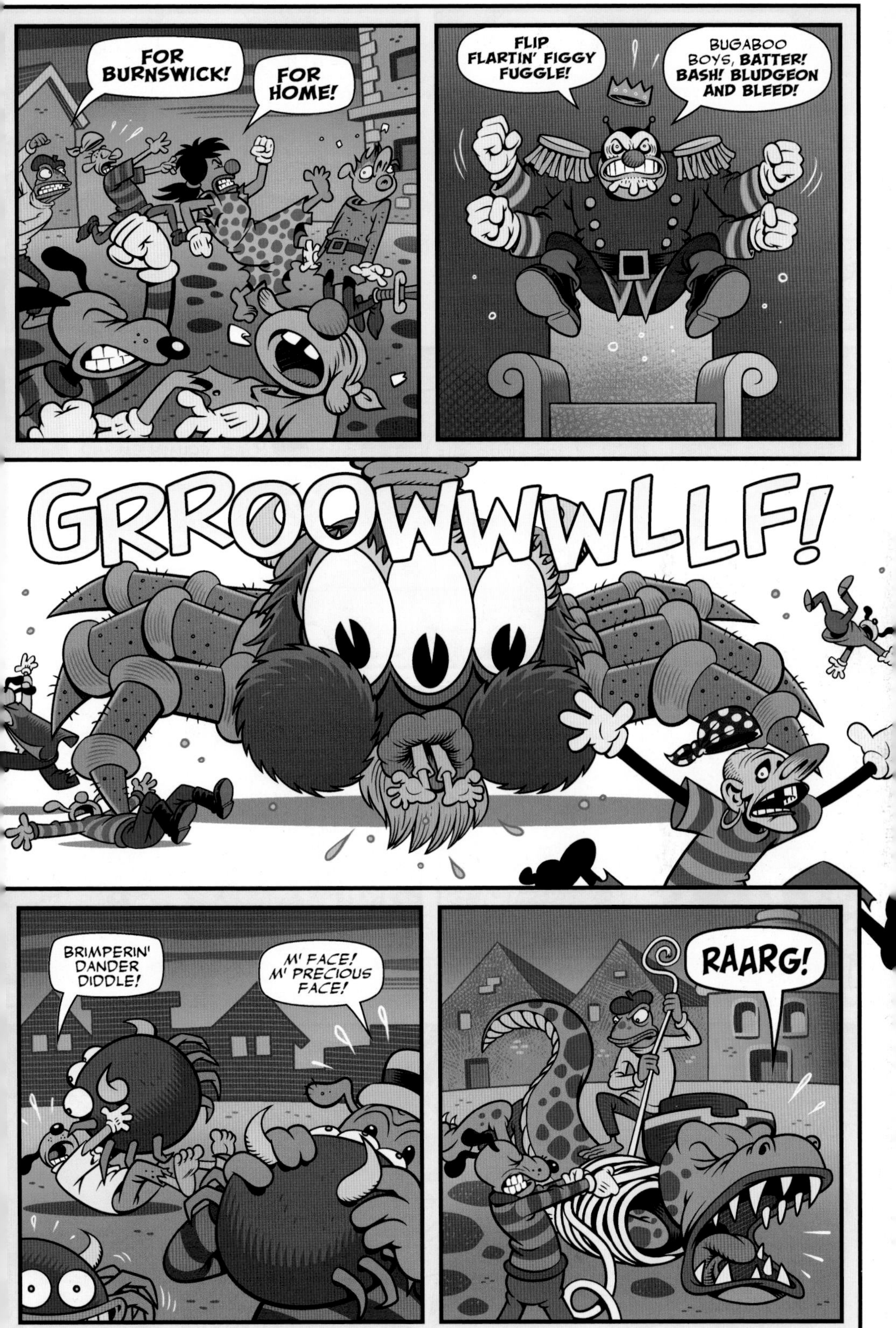
FOR BURNSWICK!
FOR HOME!
FLIP FLARTIN' FIGGY FUGGLE!
BUGABOO BOYS, BATTER! BASH! BLUDGEON AND BLEED!
GRROOWWWLLF!
BRIMPERIN' DANDER DIDDLE!
M' FACE! M' PRECIOUS FACE!
RAARG!

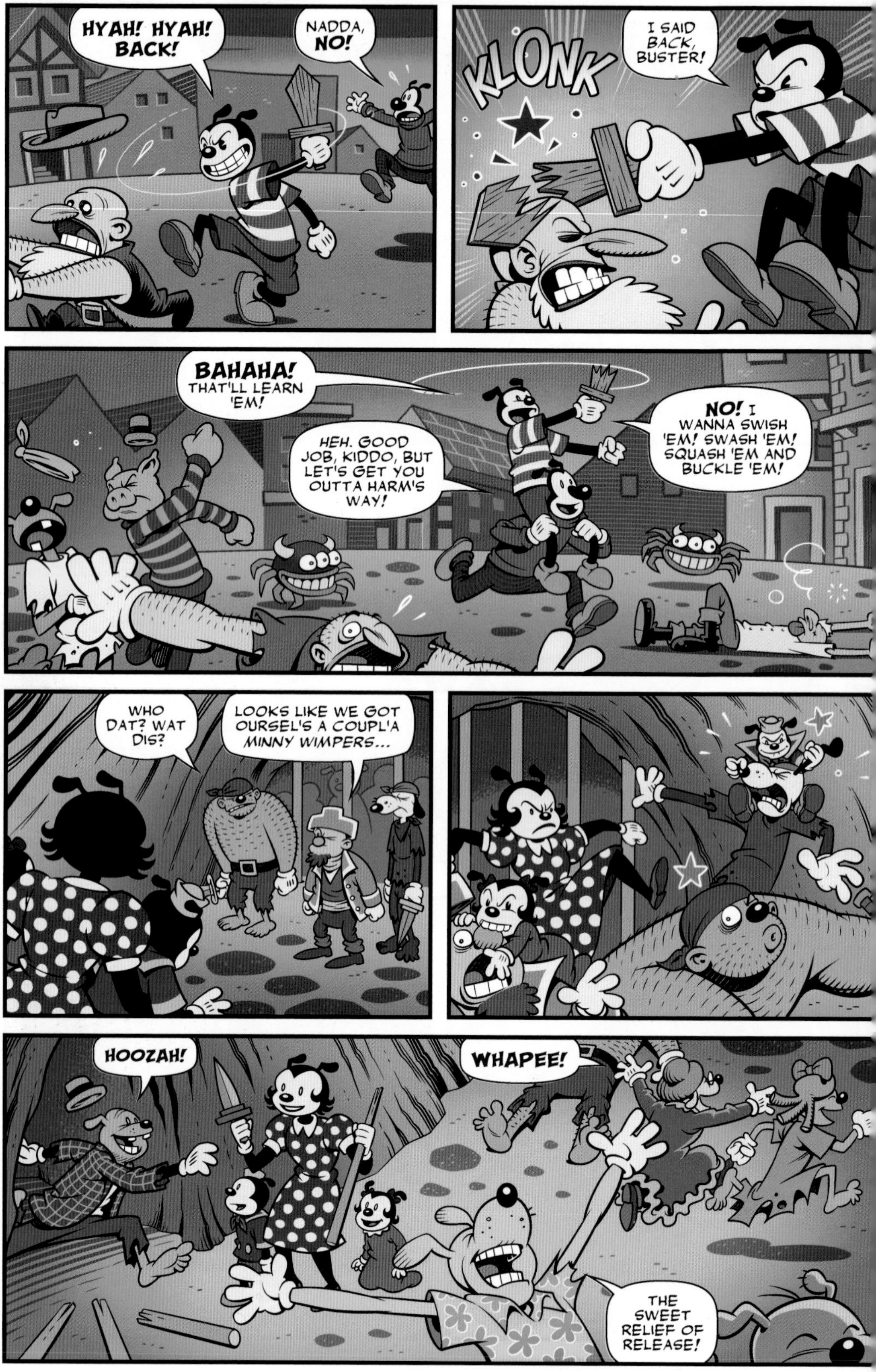

HYAH! HYAH! BACK!
NADDA, NO!
KLONK
I SAID BACK, BUSTER!
BAHAHA! THAT'LL LEARN 'EM!
HEH. GOOD JOB, KIDDO, BUT LET'S GET YOU OUTTA HARM'S WAY!
NO! I WANNA SWISH 'EM! SWASH 'EM! SQUASH 'EM AND BUCKLE 'EM!
WHO DAT? WAT DIS?
LOOKS LIKE WE GOT OURSEL'S A COUPL'A MINNY WIMPERS...
HOOZAH!
WHAPEE!
THE SWEET RELIEF OF RELEASE!

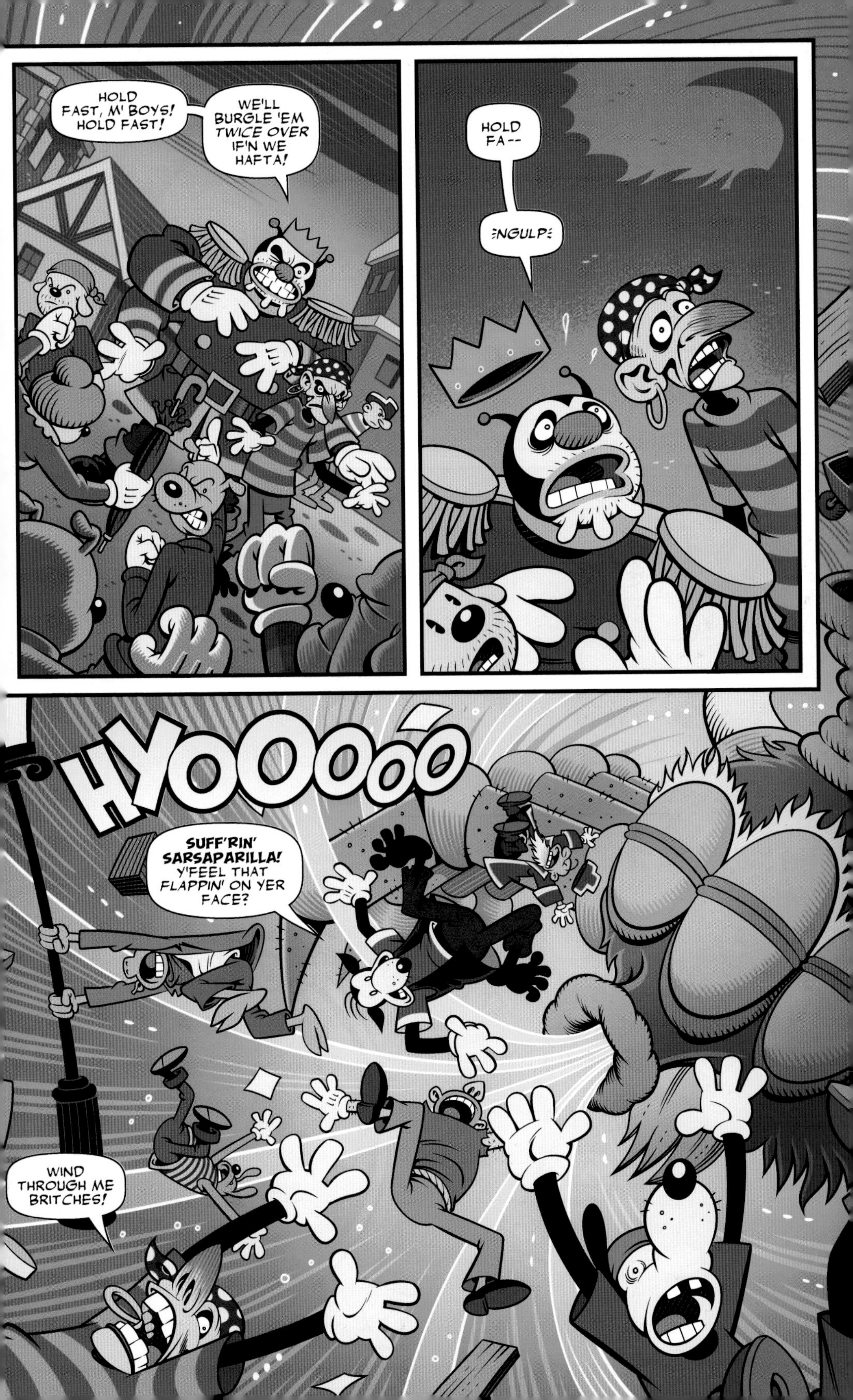
HOLD FAST, M' BOYS! HOLD FAST!
WE'LL BURGLE 'EM TWICE OVER IF'N WE HAFTA!
HOLD FA--
NGULP
HYOOOOO
SUFF'RIN' SARSAPARILLA! Y'FEEL THAT FLAPPIN' ON YER FACE?
WIND THROUGH ME BRITCHES!

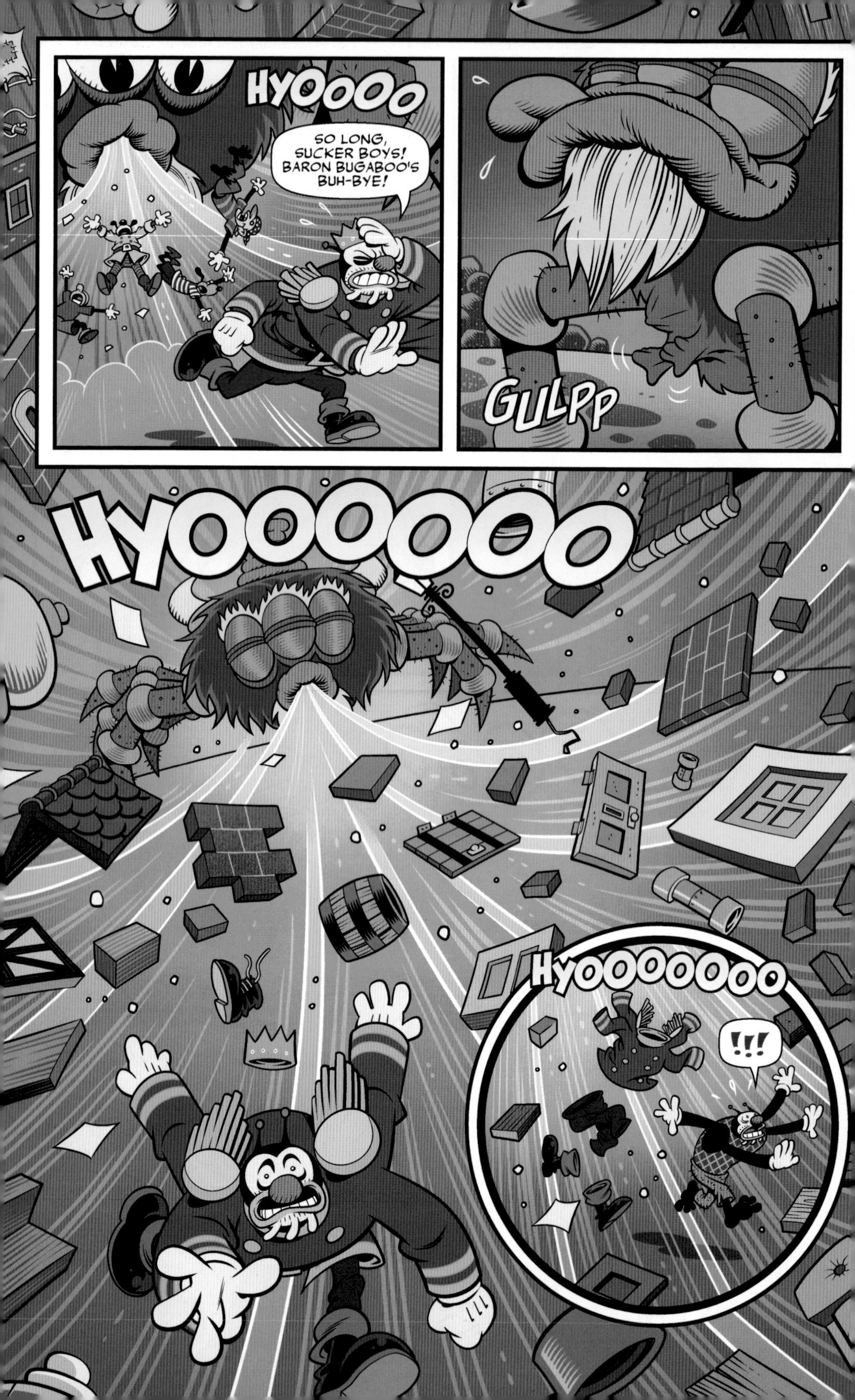
HYOOOO
SO LONG, SUCKER BOYS! BARON BUGABOO'S BUH-BYE!
GULPP
HYOOOOOO
HyOOOOOOO
!?!

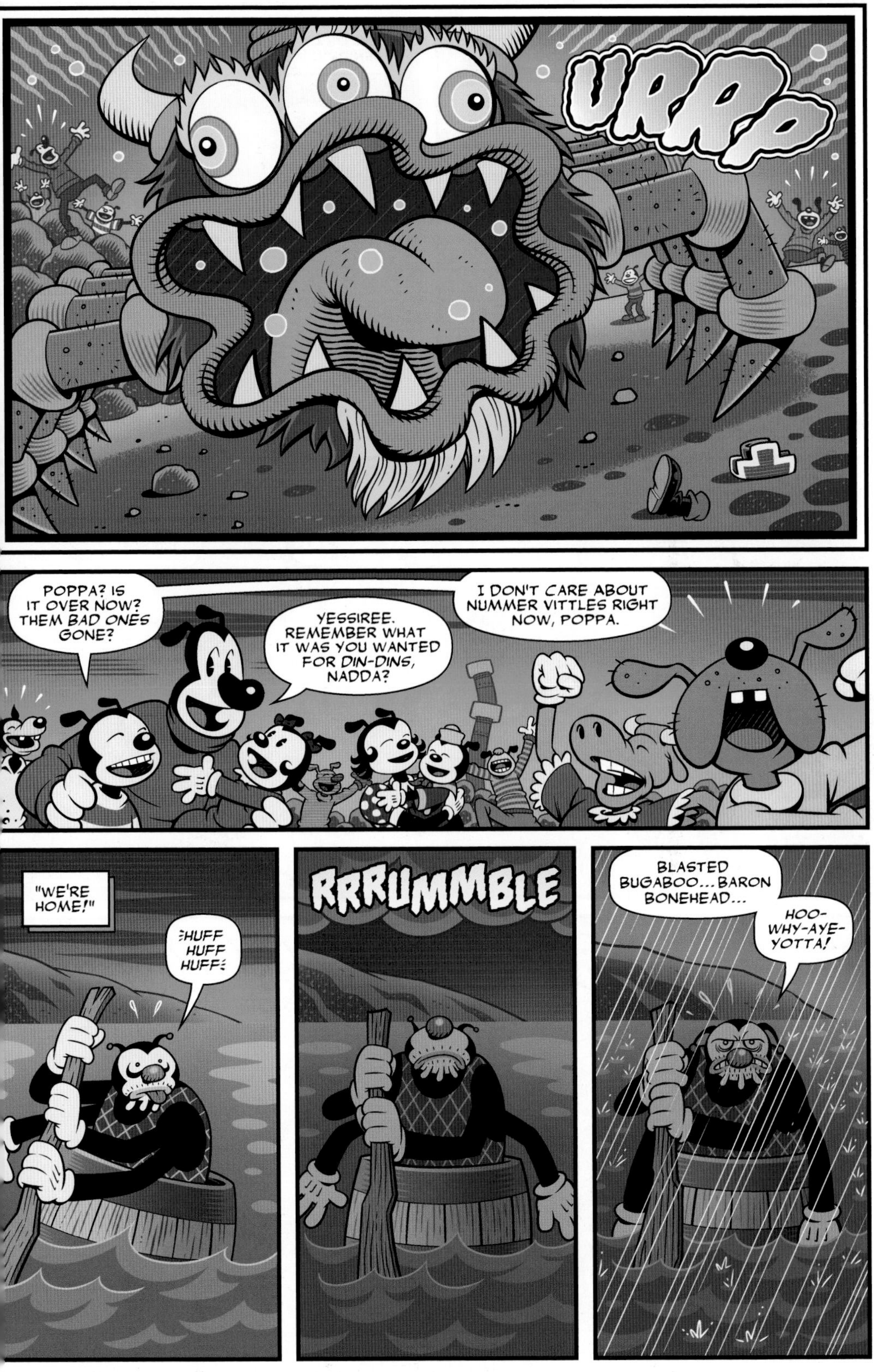
URRP
POPPA? IS IT OVER NOW? THEM BAD ONES GONE?
YESSIREE. REMEMBER WHAT IT WAS YOU WANTED FOR DIN-DINS, NADDA?
I DON'T CARE ABOUT NUMMER VITTLES RIGHT NOW, POPPA.
"WE'RE HOME!"
HUFF HUFF HUFF
RRRUMMBLE
BLASTED BUGABOO... BARON BONEHEAD...
HOO-WHY-AYE-YOTTA!

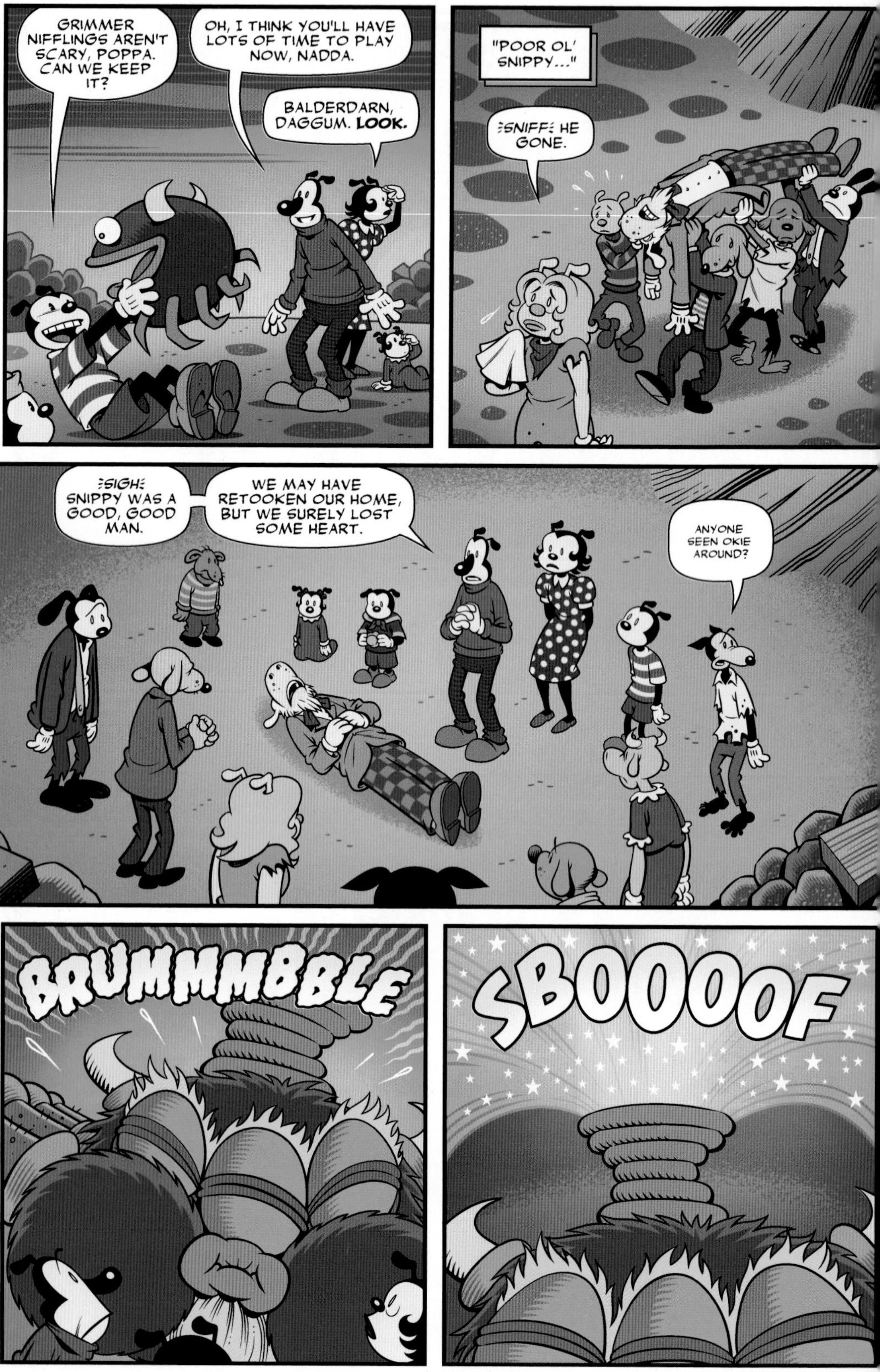
GRIMMER NIFFLINGS AREN'T SCARY, POPPA. CAN WE KEEP IT?
OH, I THINK YOU'LL HAVE LOTS OF TIME TO PLAY NOW, NADDA.
BALDERDARN, DAGGUM. LOOK.
"POOR OL' SNIPPY..."
SNIFF HE GONE.
SIGH SNIPPY WAS A GOOD, GOOD MAN.
WE MAY HAVE RETOOKEN OUR HOME, BUT WE SURELY LOST SOME HEART.
ANYONE SEEN OKIE AROUND?
BRUMMMBBLE
SBOOOOF

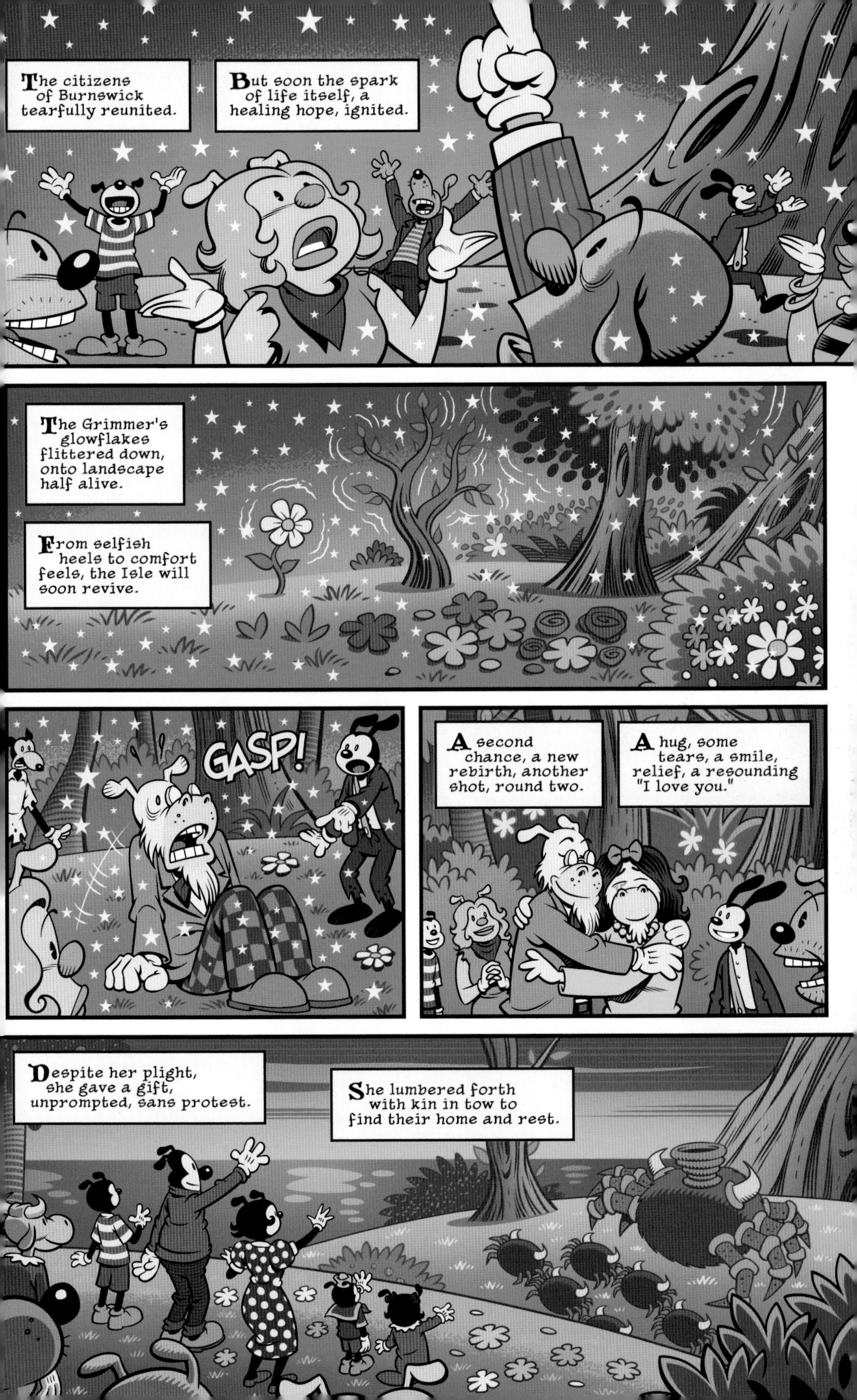
The citizens of Burnswick tearfully reunited.
But soon the spark of life itself, a healing hope, ignited.
The Grimmer's glowflakes flittered down, onto landscape half alive.
From selfish heels to comfort feels, the Isle will soon revive.
GASP!
A second chance, a new rebirth, another shot, round two.
A hug, some tears, a smile, relief, a resounding "I love you."
Despite her plight, she gave a gift, unprompted, sans protest.
She lumbered forth with kin in tow to find their home and rest.

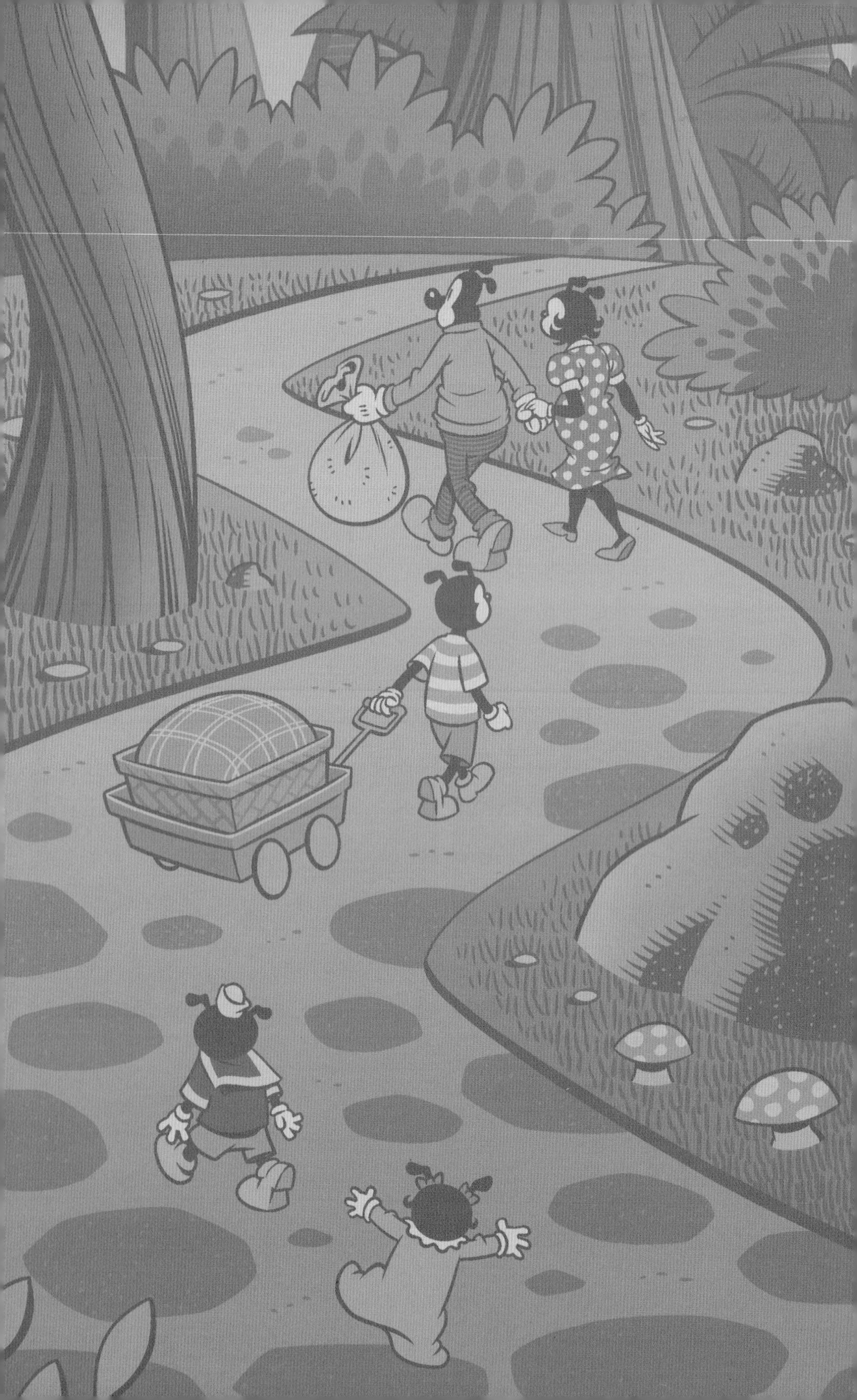

EPILOGUE

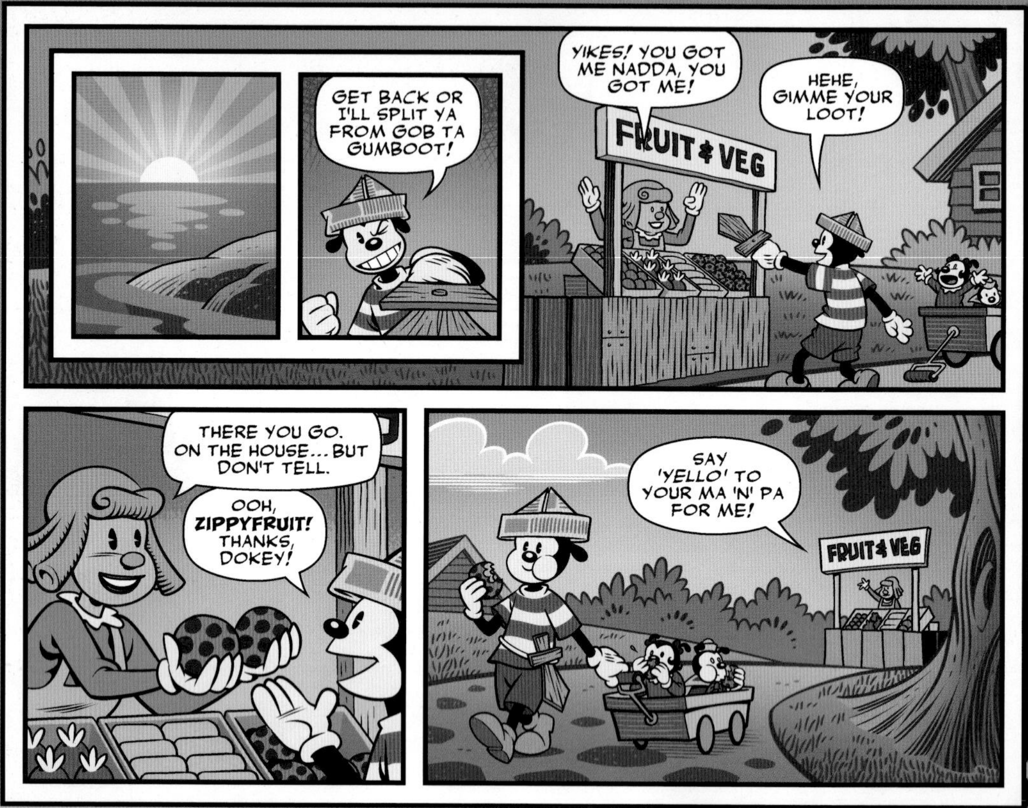
GET BACK OR I'LL SPLIT YA FROM GOB TA GUMBOOT!
YIKES! YOU GOT ME NADDA, YOU GOT ME!
FRUIT & VEG
HEHE, GIMME YOUR LOOT!
THERE YOU GO. ON THE HOUSE... BUT DON'T TELL.
OOH, ZIPPYFRUIT! THANKS, DOKEY!
SAY 'YELLO' TO YOUR MA 'N' PA FOR ME!
FRUIT & VEG

Some time has passed...

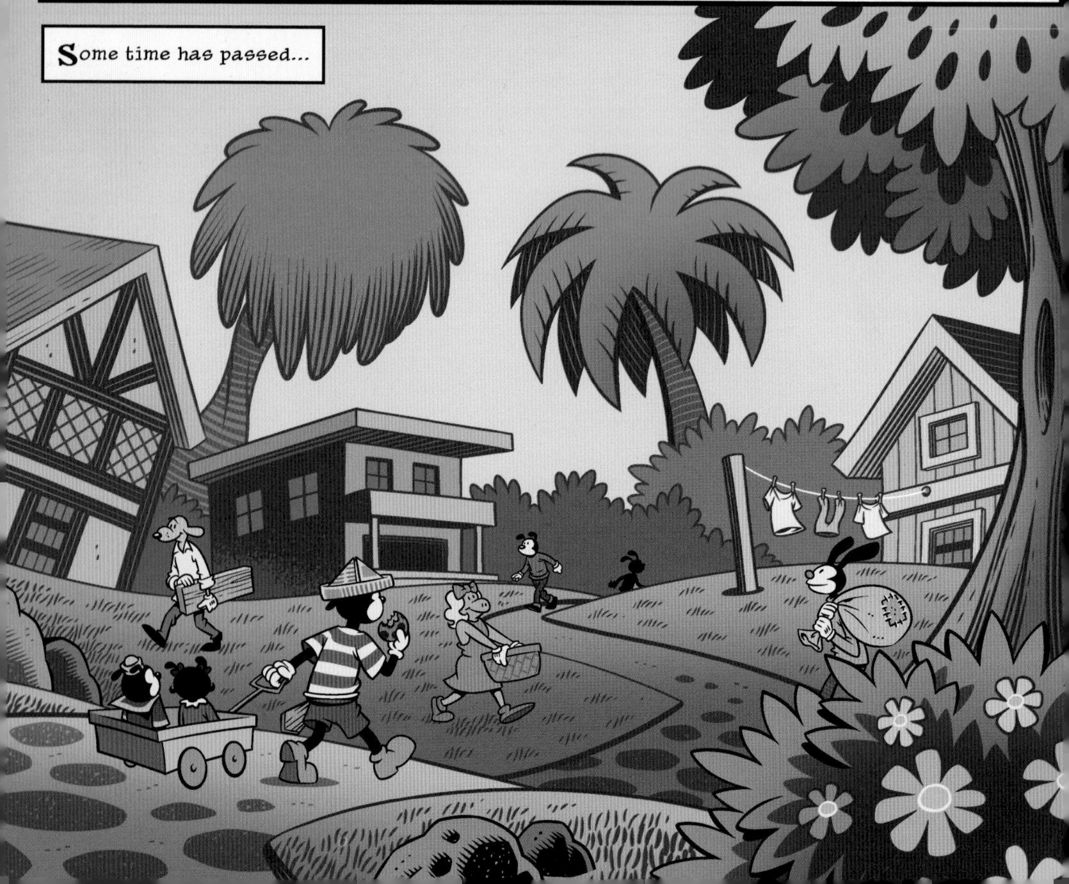

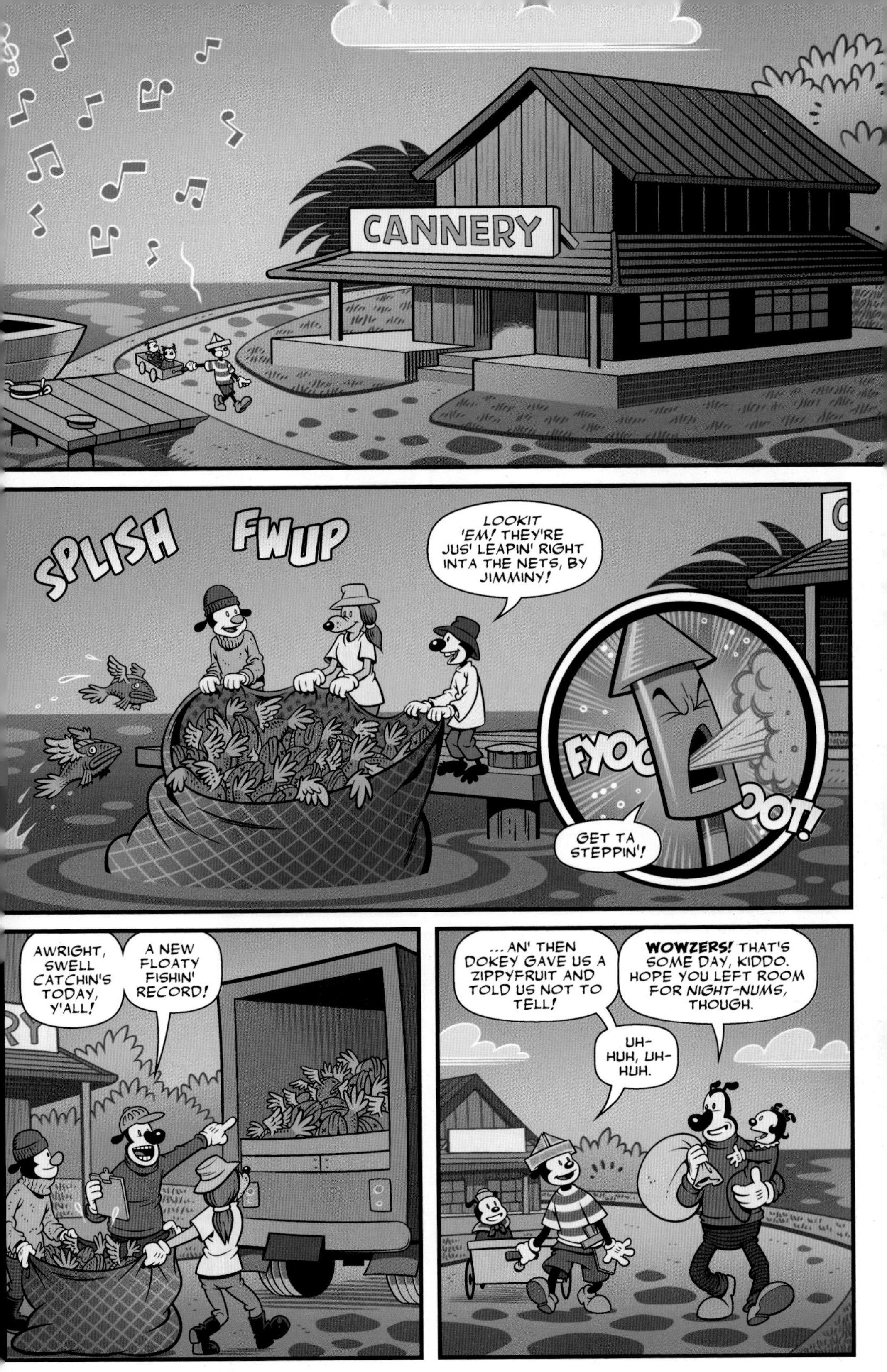
CANNERY
SPLISH
FWUP
LOOKIT 'EM! THEY'RE JUS' LEAPIN' RIGHT INTA THE NETS, BY JIMMINY!
FYOOOOT!
GET TA STEPPIN'!
AWRIGHT, SWELL CATCHIN'S TODAY, Y'ALL!
A NEW FLOATY FISHIN' RECORD!
...AN' THEN DOKEY GAVE US A ZIPPYFRUIT AND TOLD US NOT TO TELL!
UH-HUH, UH-HUH.
WOWZERS! THAT'S SOME DAY, KIDDO. HOPE YOU LEFT ROOM FOR NIGHT-NUMS, THOUGH.

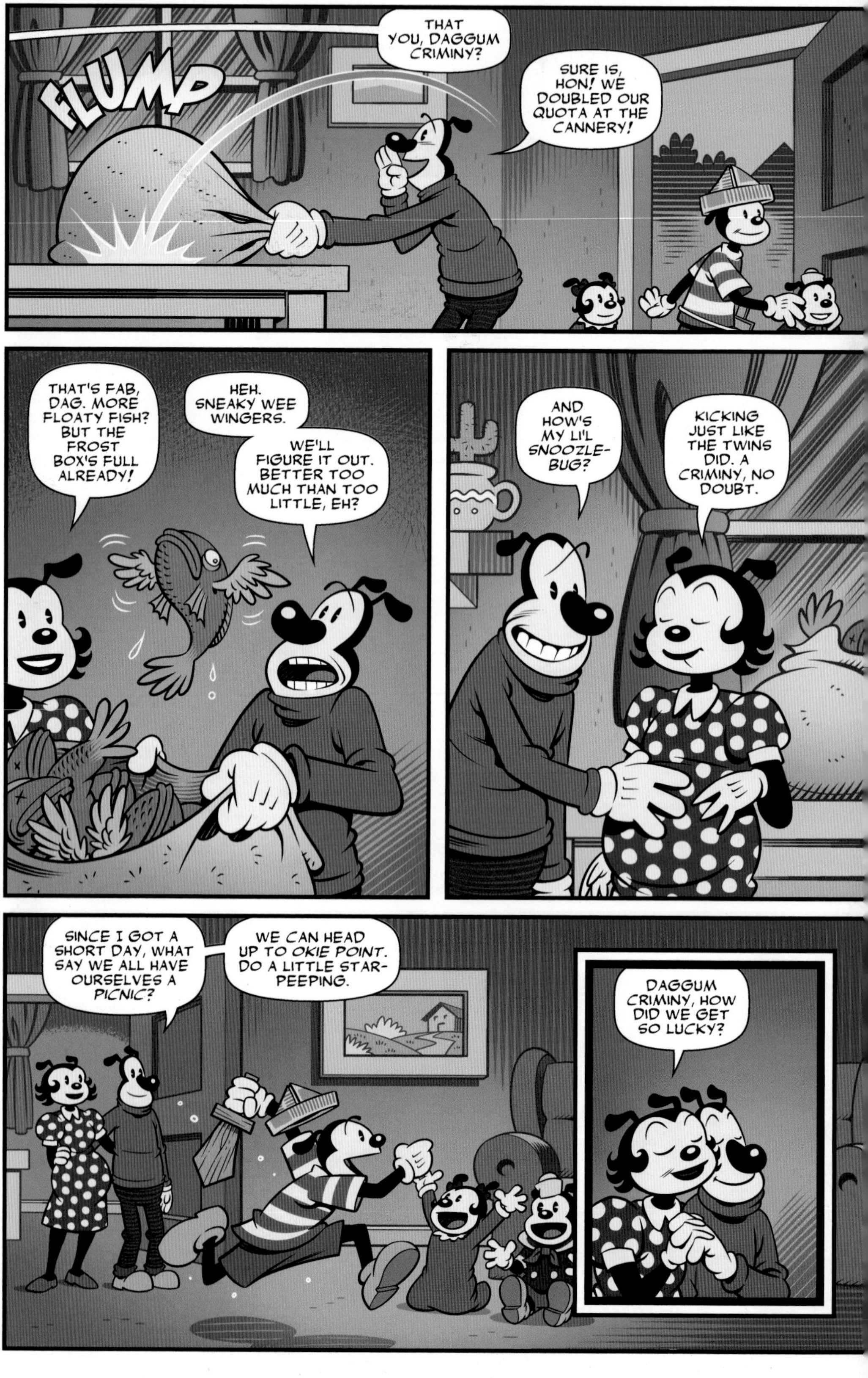
THAT YOU, DAGGUM CRIMINY?
FLUMP
SURE IS, HON! WE DOUBLED OUR QUOTA AT THE CANNERY!
THAT'S FAB, DAG. MORE FLOATY FISH? BUT THE FROST BOX'S FULL ALREADY!
HEH. SNEAKY WEE WINGERS.
WE'LL FIGURE IT OUT. BETTER TOO MUCH THAN TOO LITTLE, EH?
AND HOW'S MY LI'L SNOOZLE-BUG?
KICKING JUST LIKE THE TWINS DID. A CRIMINY, NO DOUBT.
SINCE I GOT A SHORT DAY, WHAT SAY WE ALL HAVE OURSELVES A PICNIC?
WE CAN HEAD UP TO OKIE POINT. DO A LITTLE STAR-PEEPING.
DAGGUM CRIMINY, HOW DID WE GET SO LUCKY?

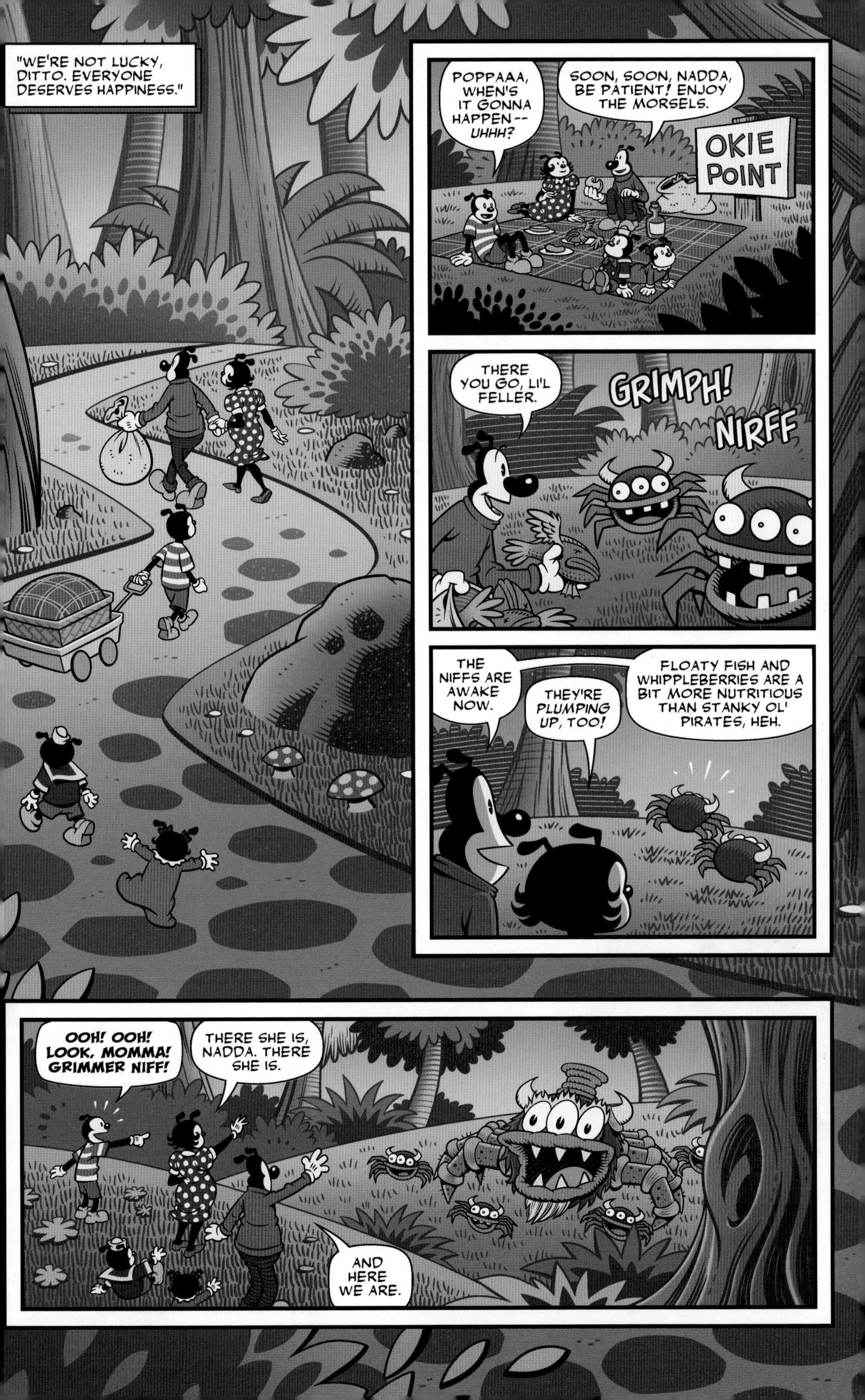
"WE'RE NOT LUCKY, DITTO. EVERYONE DESERVES HAPPINESS."
POPPAAA, WHEN'S IT GONNA HAPPEN-- UHHH?
SOON, SOON, NADDA, BE PATIENT! ENJOY THE MORSELS.
OKIE POINT
THERE YOU GO, LI'L FELLER.
GRIMPH!
NIRFF
THE NIFFS ARE AWAKE NOW.
THEY'RE PLUMPING UP, TOO!
FLOATY FISH AND WHIPPLEBERRIES ARE A BIT MORE NUTRITIOUS THAN STANKY OL' PIRATES, HEH.
OOH! OOH! LOOK, MOMMA! GRIMMER NIFF!
THERE SHE IS, NADDA. THERE SHE IS.
AND HERE WE ARE.

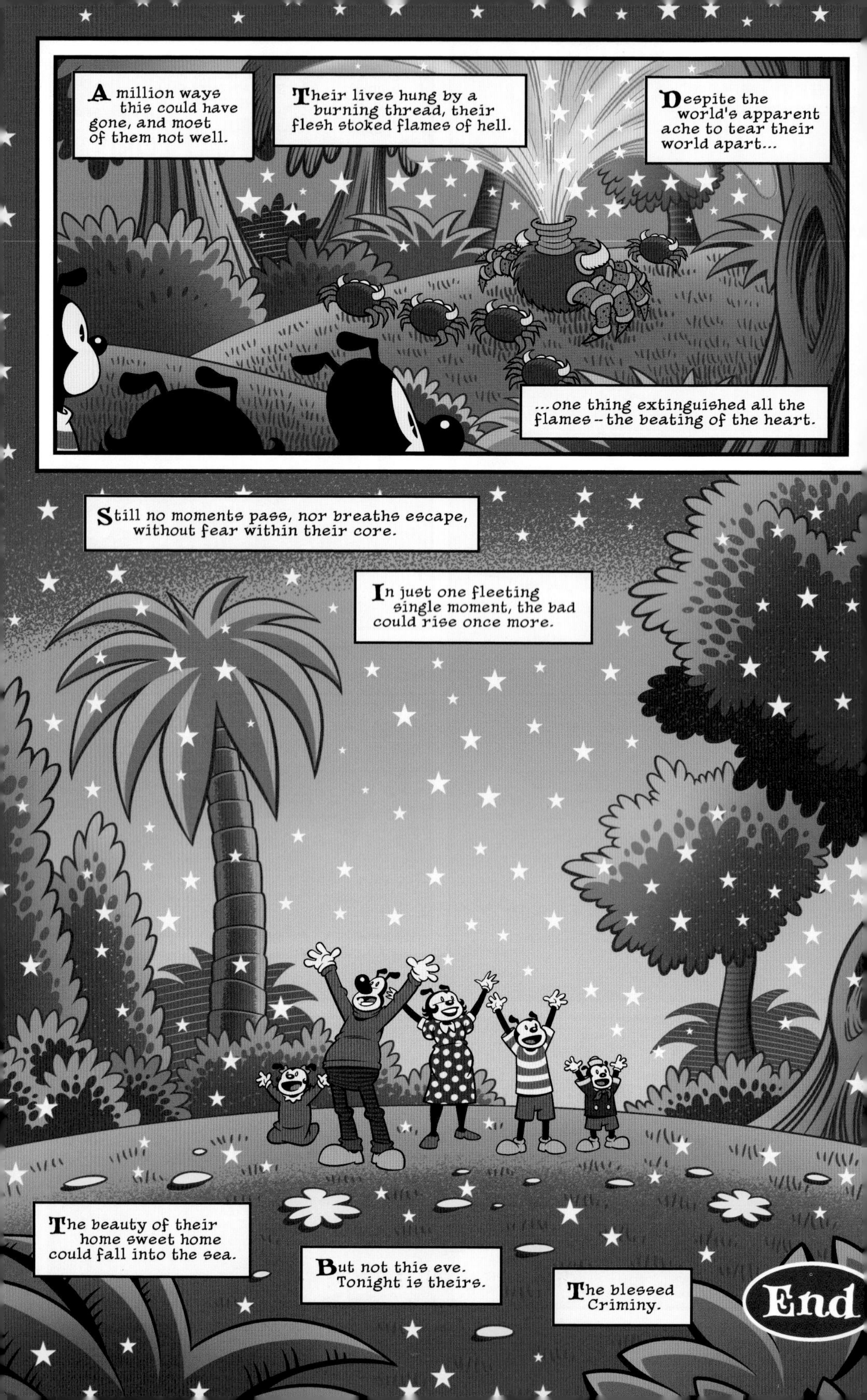
A million ways this could have gone, and most of them not well.
Their lives hung by a burning thread, their flesh stoked flames of hell.
Despite the world's apparent ache to tear their world apart...
...one thing extinguished all the flames – the beating of the heart.
Still no moments pass, nor breaths escape, without fear within their core.
In just one fleeting single moment, the bad could rise once more.
The beauty of their home sweet home could fall into the sea.
But not this eve. Tonight is theirs.
The blessed Criminy.
End

Criminy

SKETCHBOOK

Criminy
GRIMSBY GRAMPSHADE
THE MERETRICIOUS MUSKRAT

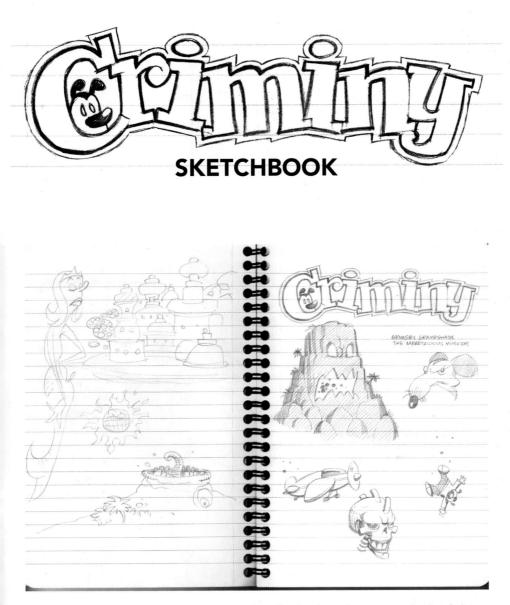

Here's my first pass at a logo design for the book, as well as a few thoughts on how to convey the idea of a living island with a mouth.

At the top left is my first doodle of the Criminys' hometown. I wanted it to have some exotic elements, almost a Dr. Seuss sort of feeling. The final version sticks pretty close to this basic idea.

notes by

ROGER LANGRIDGE
and RYAN FERRIER

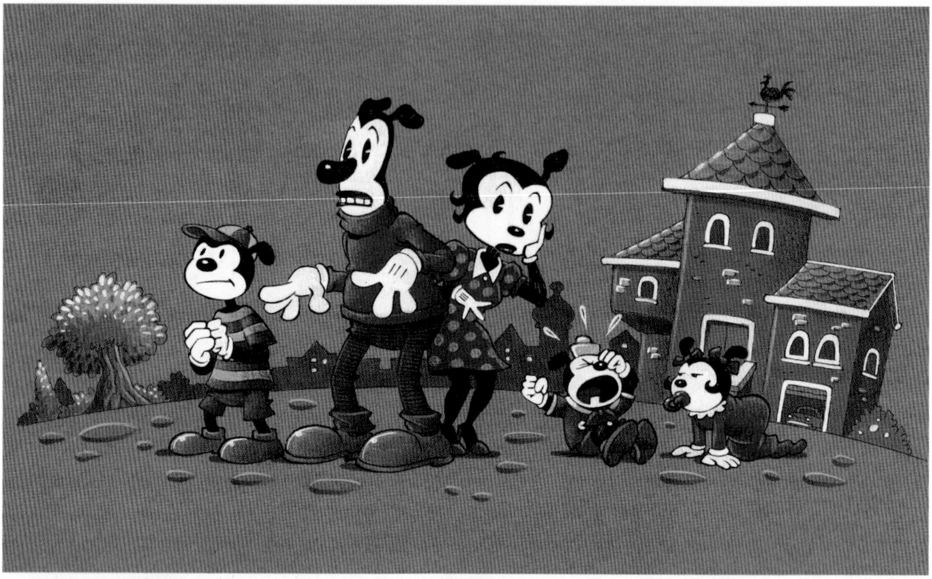

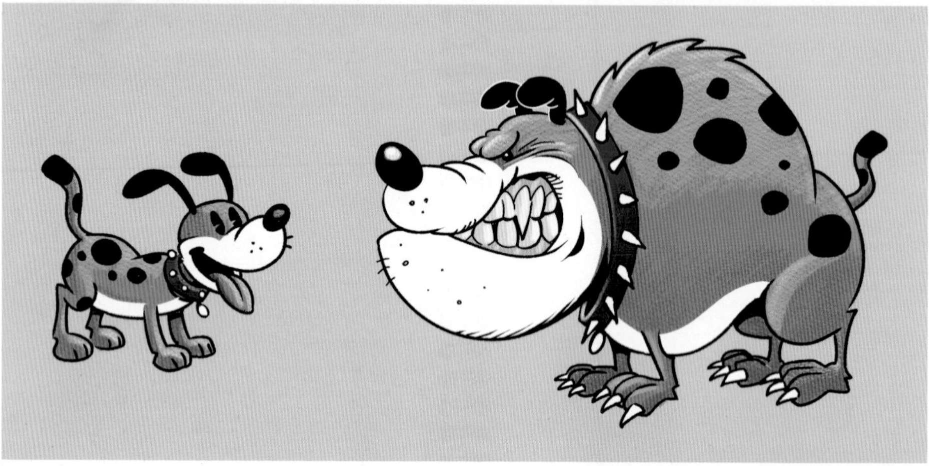

Top: My first crack at the Criminys, taking Max Fleischer cartoons as my primary visual cue. I decided to have them all dress in similar colors to convey the idea that the're a unit.

Middle: Pubber, the Jekyll/Hyde dog. There was a bit of back-and-forth between Ryan and me over his fur color. Ryan pictured him being pink, so this is the revised version. It's an improvement, as its similarity to the Criminys' colors gets across the idea that he's on their side.

Bottom: Lemon Worthy (second version). I'd initially drawn him jollier, less raggedy, and more colorful, but Ryan pushed for more of a hard-up interpretation, so I came back with this one.

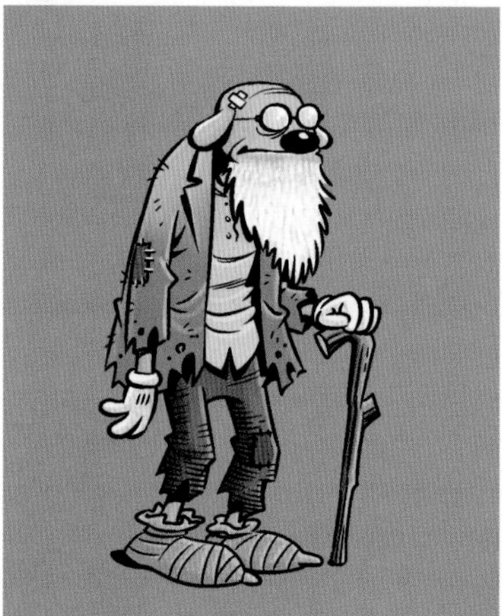

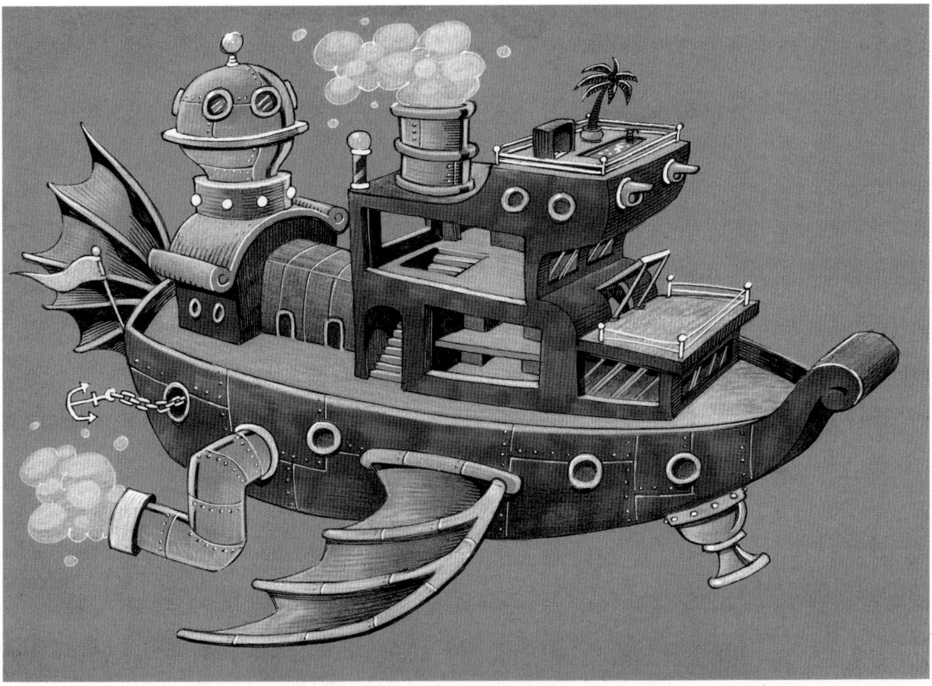

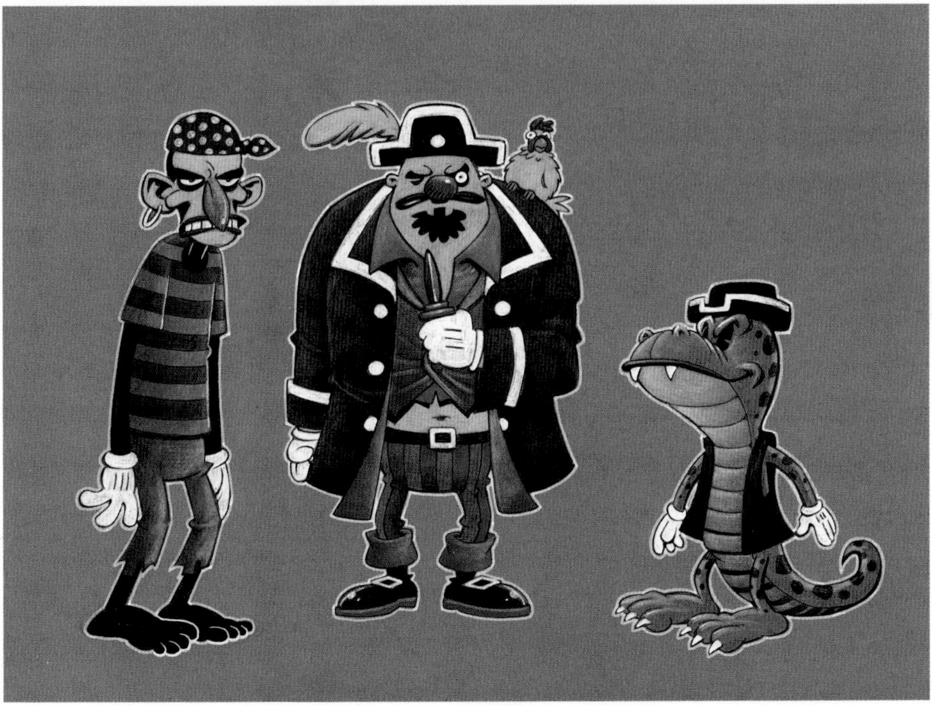

Top: The *S.S. Whalebatross*. The final version warmed up the colors somewhat, giving them a sort of bilious hue. In the script, Ryan asked for a kind of flying city; I didn't quite go that far, but the multiple levels were my attempt to convey the sheer scale of the thing, without making it impossible to draw multiple times.

Bottom: Some random pirates, all of whom made it into the finished book. The lizard guy on the right became much larger, so he could credibly eat people. The colors chosen are deliberately as far away from the Criminys' hot red as possible.

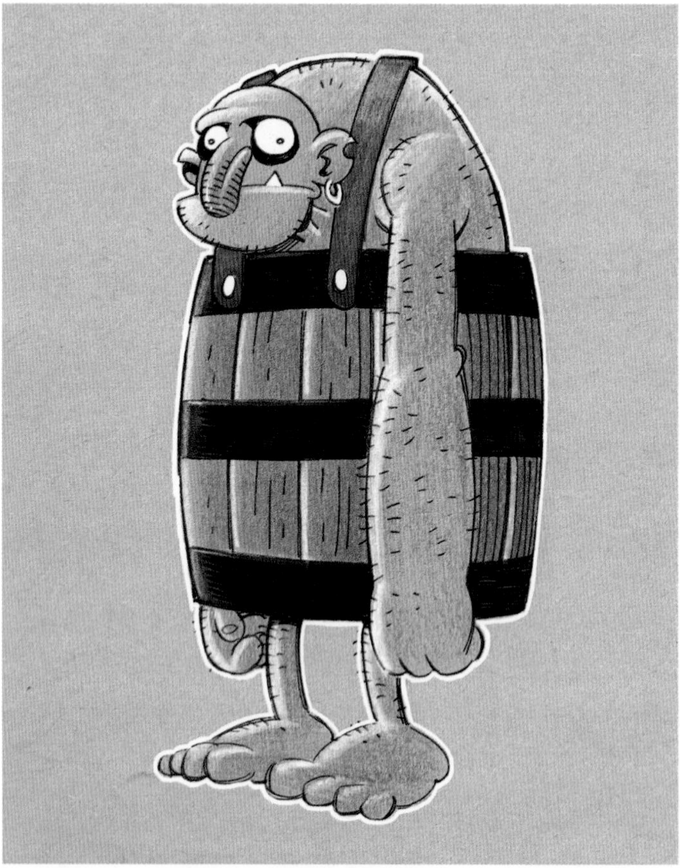

Barrel guy—another pirate? He didn't make the cut, although Baron Bugaboo's final moments had him stripped of his clothes and drifting off in a barrel.

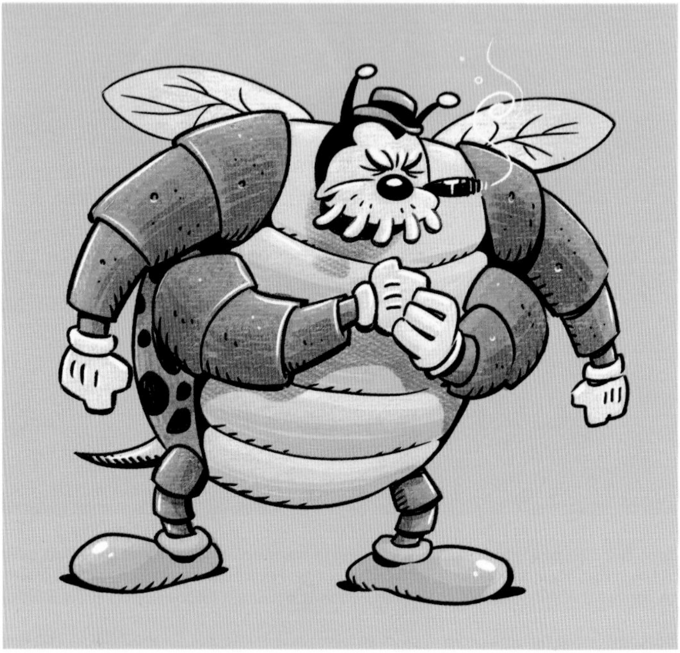

One of the list of names Ryan initially threw at me to visualize was "Big Bug." This guy's visual attributes ended up being split across two characters: our main baddie Baron Bugaboo, and Big Brug, the bullying thug in the *Whalebatross*.

The weird Kapitan. Got him right first time,
I think. The tentacles and bat wings have a
sort of Cthulhu-style thing going on.

I threw an anthropomorphic skeleton into the
first round of sketches because the Max Fleischer
"weird horror" thing was never far from my mind.
Ryan built a whole island around them.

The Sharkark. I imagined its two faces having
a sort of Zaphod Beeblebrox relationship, one
brain steering the body and the other one being
more or less along for the ride.

The Criminys' home, final version. All bright and sunny, colorful utopian towers bumping alongside idyllic suburban homes. I felt like there was enough going on there to credibly be a self-sustaining community without being impossible to draw over and over. The volcano-like mountain in the background became a huge hollow tree in Ryan's final script. I think that was the right call; this place should be all about life and growth. A volcano adds a menacing note, and the threat in our story should all come from the outside.

The guts of Isle Bobo, first pass. We hadn't concocted Isle Bobo when I drew this, I don't think; I just wanted to get down some visual ideas for the kind of grim, threatening places the Criminys might find themselves on their travels. There's a lot of Fleischer-inspired stuff going on here, but the giant spider guy in particular spoke to me as a particularly Fleischeresque detail for some reason.

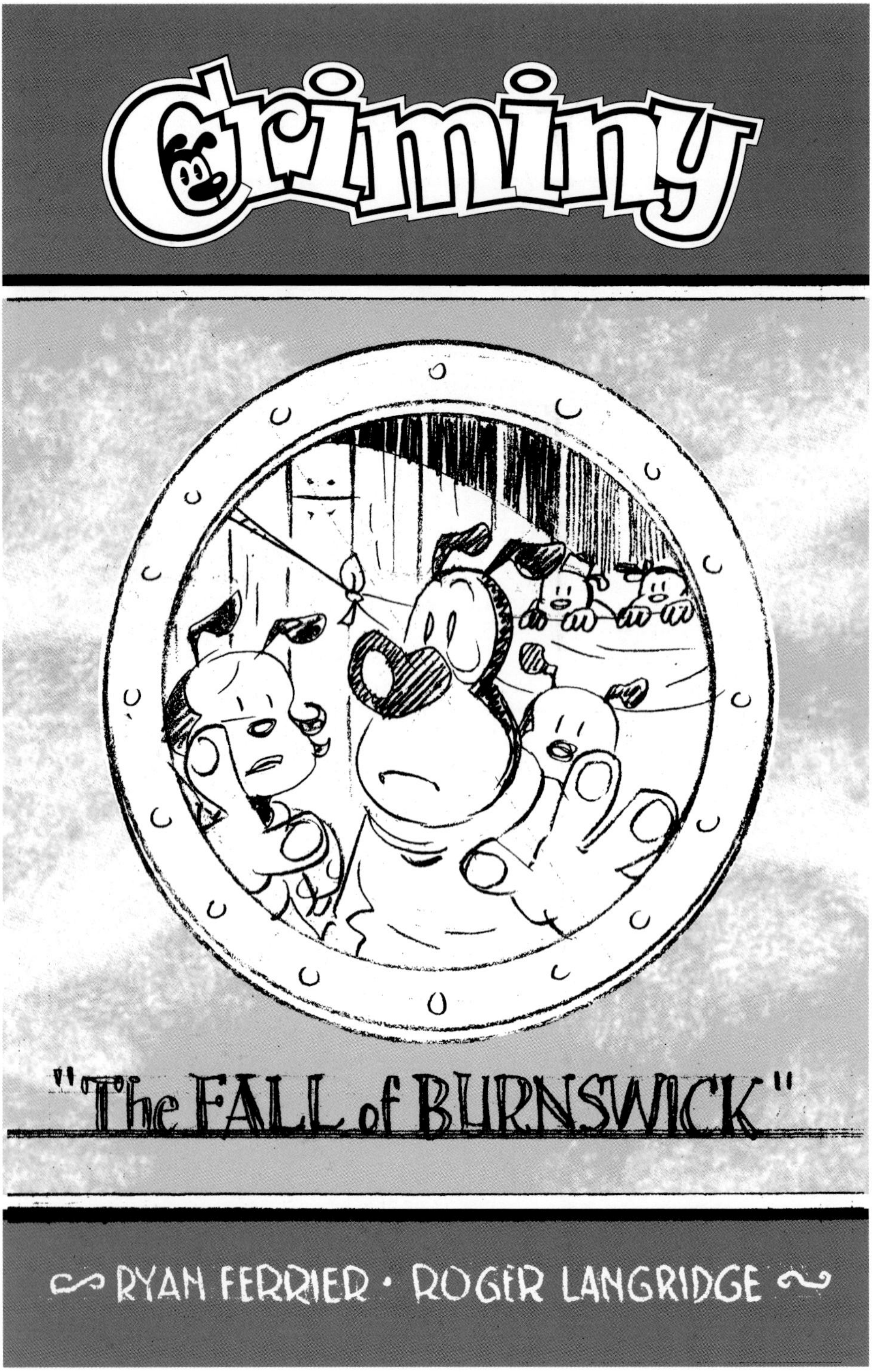
Criminy
"The FALL of BURNSWICK"
RYAN FERRIER • ROGER LANGRIDGE

The remaining pages are various cover concepts. When we were initially pitching *Criminy*, Ryan and I assumed it would be a four-issue series, so I came up with a number of cover ideas that used a circle as a kind of unifying element. In the end, the cover of this book keeps that element in the form of the globe they're all running around.

Criminy

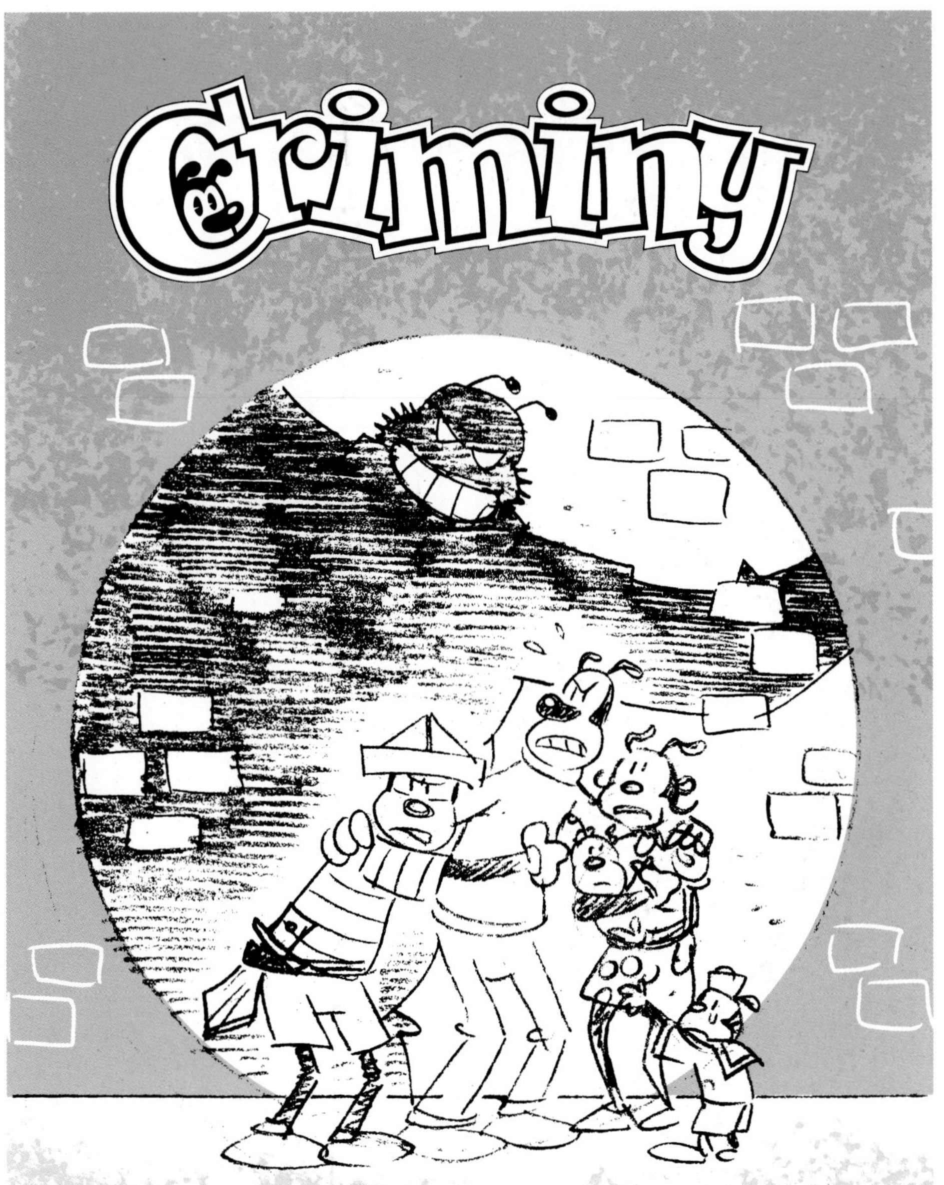

Ryan Ferrier
Roger Langridge

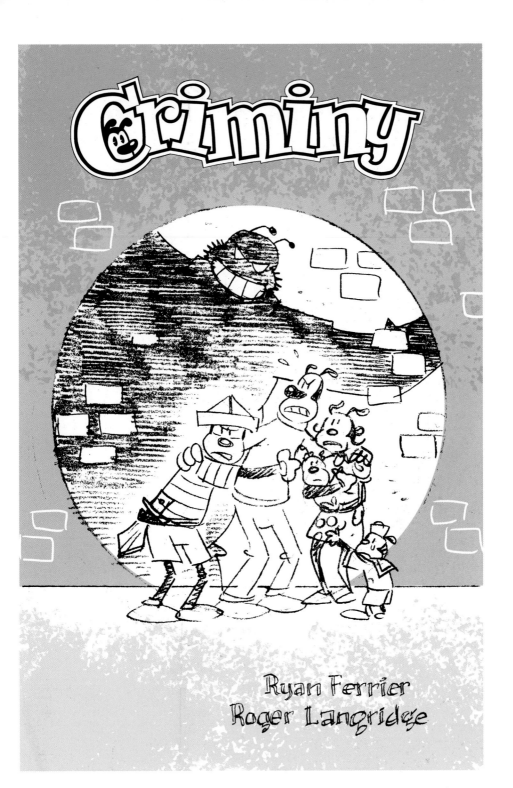

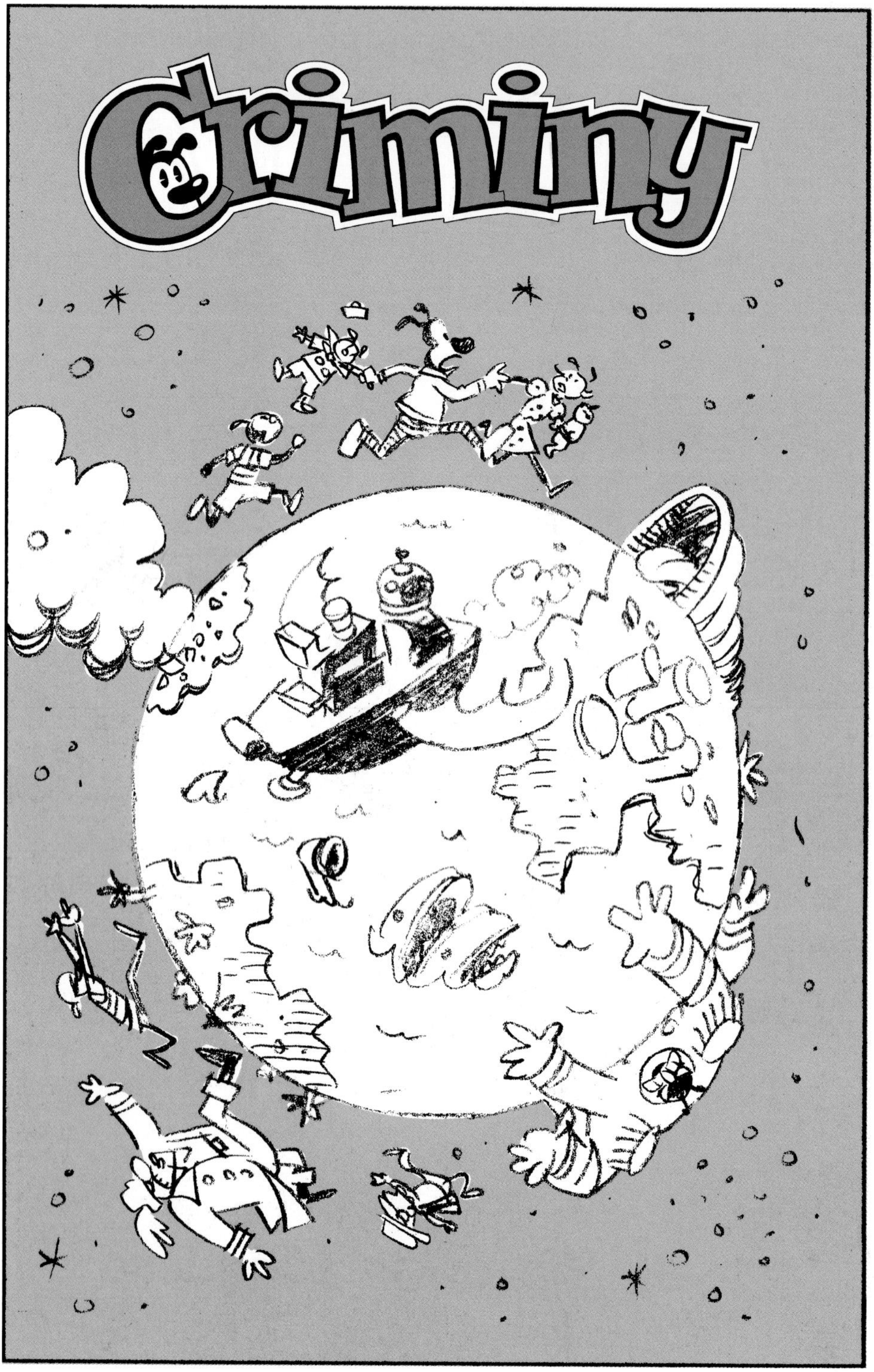
Criminy

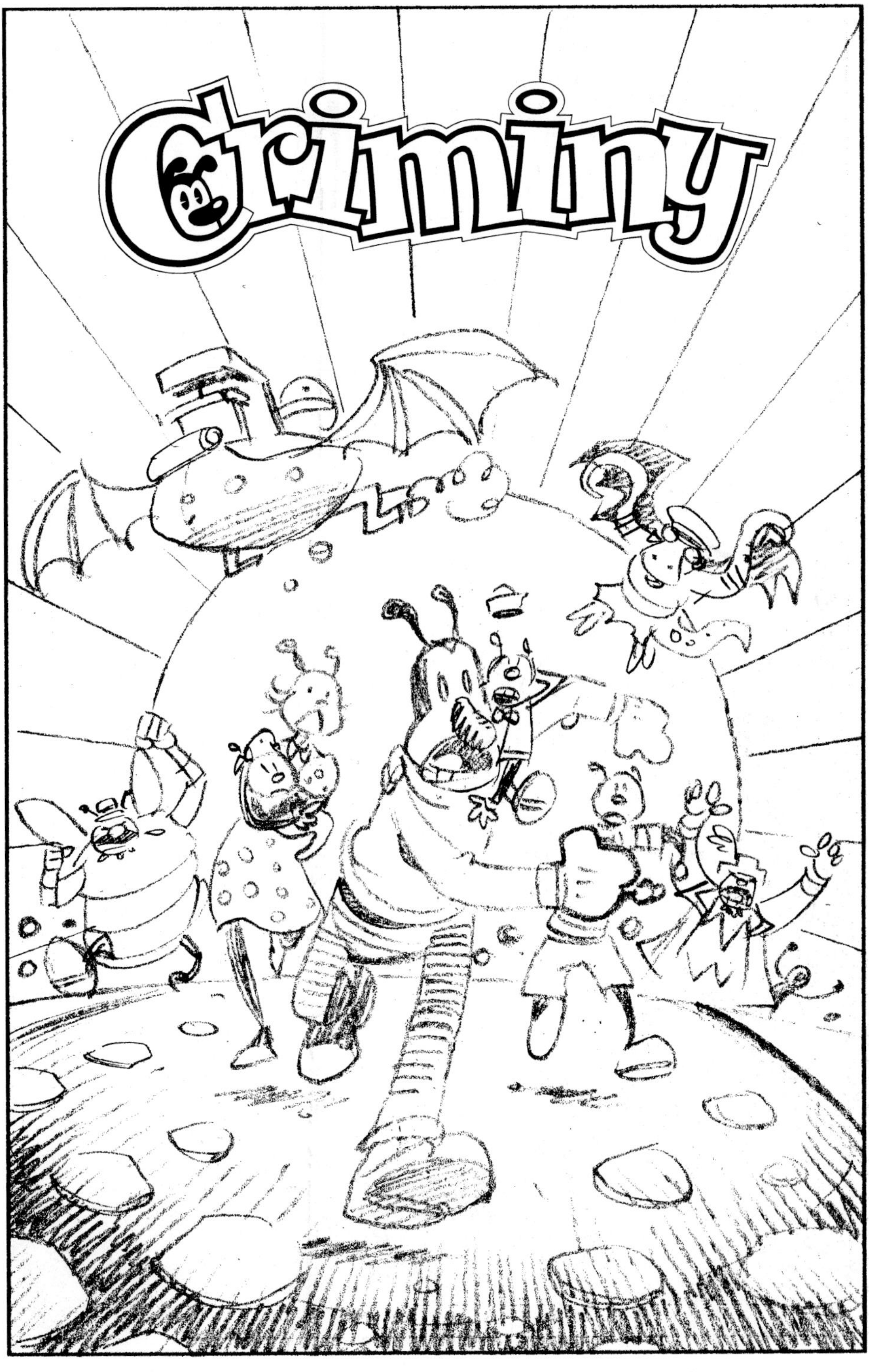
Criminy

REK 6/21

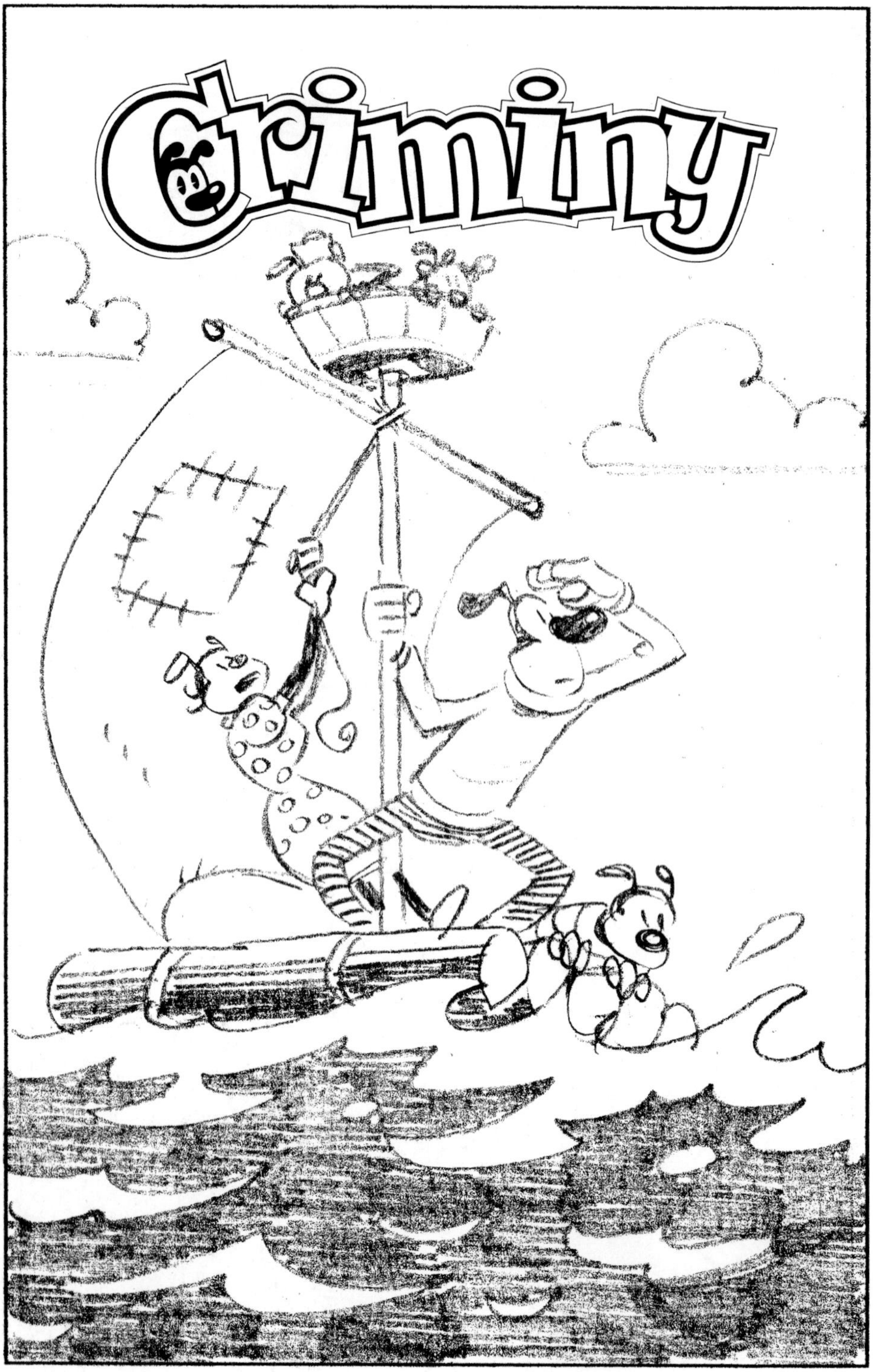
Criminy